The Secret One

The Secret One

RUTH CARDELLO

 Montlake

Published by Montlake, Seattle

www.apub.com

Amazon, the Amazon logo, and Montlake are trademarks of Amazon.com, Inc., or its affiliates.

ISBN-13: 9781542025171
ISBN-10: 1542025176

Cover design by Eileen Carey

Printed in the United States of America

*This book is dedicated to all the men
who understand there is more than one way to be "alpha."
Sometimes the strongest man in the room is the one
who is quietly supporting those around him.*

Don't miss a thing!

www.ruthcardello.com

Sign up for Ruth's newsletter
Yes, let's stay in touch!
https://forms.aweber.com/form/00/819443400.htm

Join Ruth's private fan group:
www.facebook.com/groups/ruthiesroadies

Follow Ruth on Goodreads:
www.goodreads.com/author/show/4820876.Ruth_Cardello

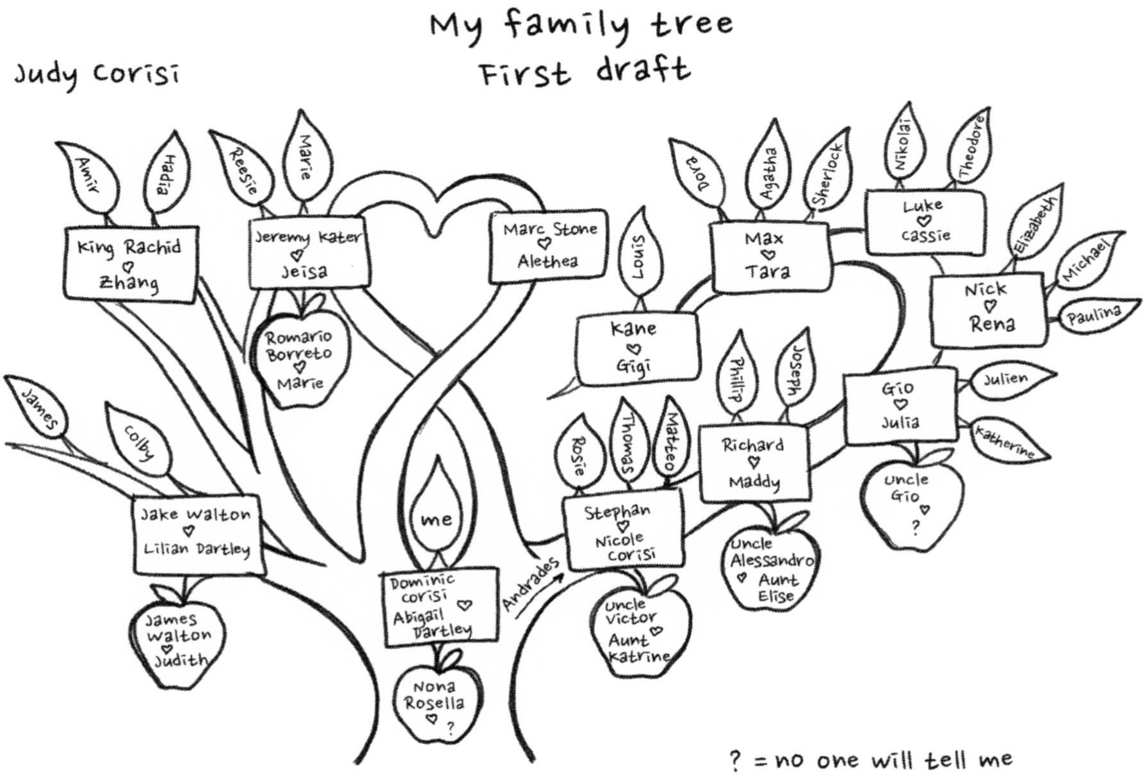
My family tree
First draft
Judy Corisi
Amir
Hadia
King Rachid ♡ Zhang
Reesie
Marie
Jeremy Kater ♡ Jeisa
Romario Borreto ♡ Marie
Marc Stone ♡ Alethea
James
Colby
Jake Walton ♡ Lilian Dartley
James Walton ♡ Judith
me
Dominic Corisi ♡ Abigail Dartley
Nona Rosella ♡ ?
Andrades
Louis
Kane ♡ Gigi
Dora
Agatha
Sherlock
Max ♡ Tara
Nikolai
Theodore
Luke ♡ Cassie
Elizabeth
Michael
Paulina
Nick ♡ Rena
Rosie
Thomas
Matteo
Stephan ♡ Nicole Corisi
Uncle Victor ♡ Aunt Katrine
Phillip
Joseph
Richard ♡ Maddy
Uncle Alessandro ♡ Aunt Elise
Julien
Katherine
Gio ♡ Julia
Uncle Gio ♡ ?
? = no one will tell me

CHAPTER ONE

CHRISTOF

Seven years earlier

Weekends used to be something I looked forward to, but I'd begun to dread them. Funny how one event could turn so many lives upside down.

"Nice to have you stick around for a change, Chris," Bob, my college bud, said as he motioned for the waitress to bring another round of beers. Neither of us were of legal drinking age, but Bob was a regular at this hole-in-the-wall bar and claimed the key to getting served was always leaving a generous tip. Since we hadn't been carded, I couldn't argue the point.

Bob was a good guy, a good friend, but had been a horrible roommate. Thankfully our friendship had rebounded the following year, when we'd each gotten our own dorm rooms.

"Yeah." I downed half the beer in one gulp. *Don't ask about anything. I don't want to think tonight.*

"How's Sebastian?"

Fuck.

It was a fair question. Bob had attended the funeral for my sister-in-law a few months before. He knew my brother wasn't handling her death well. "He's still struggling."

So was I.

Therese was my first experience with losing someone close to me. It had taken a while to wrap my head around how someone could be there one minute, then gone the next. Therese had been the sister I'd never had, and from the moment Sebastian had brought her home to meet us—she'd been one of us.

Her loss had ricocheted through my family. At first we'd all been in shock. My mother cried—a lot. My father remained at her side, quieter than I'd ever seen him.

My brother Sebastian held it together through his wife's funeral and the seemingly endless condolences that followed. I remember thinking he was stronger than I would have been. For him, I kept my emotions locked away as well. Mauricio and Gian, my other brothers, did the same. Right through the first week, we stood in stoic solidarity.

I thought the initial pain would be the hardest part. I was so wrong. The real sadness came after the fanfare had died down. When everyone went home and life tried to return to normal . . . that was when I missed Therese the most. When we gathered and her seat was empty, or when something funny happened and I went to call her, only to remember I couldn't.

I didn't know what to do. Friends only wanted to hear about it so many times, and I didn't want to add the weight of my sorrow to anyone in my family, so I kept my thoughts to myself. For the first time in my life, I felt alone even when I was in a crowd.

That wasn't the hardest part, though.

Sebastian began to unravel. The kind, hardworking brother I'd grown up with, the one who laughed easily and believed family was who mattered most—that brother had died along with his wife.

Sebastian 2.0 was angry, frequently drunk, and prone to lash out at anyone who dared to try to help him. Not physically—I might have preferred that. I could have ducked to avoid those hits.

The problem was Sebastian wanted to be left alone to drink his pain away, but we loved him too much to allow him to.

It wasn't pretty on either side. I'd never lost a wife and unborn child without warning. I tried not to judge him for faltering, but understanding didn't make it easier to hear his alcohol-fueled wish that we were all also gone so there would be no one left to remind him of her.

It didn't make it easier to hear him ramble that he wanted to join her.

I didn't know what to say. None of us did.

Every weekend followed the same routine. I returned home to hear that Dad or my older brother Mauricio had stayed at Sebastian's place with him. I felt guilty that I wasn't doing more, frustrated that nothing we did seemed to be enough.

Mom planned outings with Gian and me as if we were both younger. Because she was trying so hard, I didn't tell her that dragging us to a day at the zoo was too much.

There was no reset button that could bring my family back to how it was before Therese. As that realization set in, none of us knew how to deal with it.

No childhood was perfect, but mine had been good. Better than good. My parents, my brothers, and I had immigrated from Italy. Moving to a new country, learning a new language, and adapting to a new culture had bonded us. For as long as I could remember, it had felt as if we were on the same team. We had common goals and a shared vision of how we would forge a new life together.

Family was shelter from any storm.

Until we lost Therese and *became* the storm.

For the first time we needed protection from each other. Gian took that the hardest. The more Mom tried to protect him from Sebastian's temper, the more Gian felt excluded. Gian was technically a cousin, having joined our family as an infant. Yet in every way that mattered, he was our youngest brother, though he acted as if we'd leave him, as his biological mother had.

When Sebastian lashed out at Gian, I loved and hated them both. Gian took Sebastian's words to heart, which added another layer of gravity to the situation. I didn't want to take sides. None of us did.

Their interactions haunted me.

My parents had recently told me to remember that school should be my first priority. I'd used coursework as my excuse to not return home that weekend. The truth was I didn't want to go home.

I wanted to step outside of my life for just a few minutes. To not be sad, guilty, or angry. I just wanted to forget.

"Another round of shots?" Bob's girlfriend, Ashley, asked as she joined us. The tall brunette was the reason I'd often had to find an alternate place to sleep the year before. Bob swore she was the one for him, but I couldn't see them lasting past college. She was wild, and he was, too, but only when he was with her. His family was a soft-spoken, serious bunch. Away from Ashley, Bob was like them. To be with her—to be like her—he drank. She often joked that sober Bob was a bore.

I would have told him sex wasn't worth the effort he was putting into her, but since I hadn't had sex yet, who was I to judge? Maybe it was.

Ashley ordered tequila shots for the three of us. "Here's to Chris not ditching us for a change."

"I've had a lot going on." I downed my shot as soon as it arrived and welcomed the distraction of the burn down my throat.

"You don't have to talk about it if you don't want to." Bob kicked back his shot.

"Thank you," I said with relief.

"You know what might help?" Bob asked as he put his arm around his girlfriend. "Ash, let's get this guy laid. You must know someone."

"I'm fine," I said with a wave of my hand.

Ashley looked me over. "You've had sex, right?"

I'm sure my face reflected my embarrassment at the truth.

She grimaced. "I'm not doing that to any of my friends." Then a smile returned to her face. "We'll find you someone here."

"Seriously, the last thing I need right now—"

Ashley scanned the room. "Bingo. Blonde sitting alone at the bar. I've never seen her here before, and she looks pissed. My guess? Someone just dumped her."

I followed her gaze, and my breath caught in my throat. As if aware that we were discussing her, the blonde had turned toward us. She looked about our age and every bit as angry as Ashley had guessed. Her long curls were pulled back in a ponytail. Her jeans hugged her ass to perfection. I only had a side view of her breasts, but I bet they were deliciously shaped, just like the rest of her. As my blood headed south, I wondered if her lips would feel as soft as they looked. "If someone did, he was an idiot."

"His loss is your gain." Bob clapped a hand on my shoulder. "Go offer to buy her a drink. This could be your lucky day. She might be looking for a revenge fuck."

I shook my head. "Or she needs someone to talk to."

"Do you want to die a virgin?" Ashley ordered another round of shots. When they arrived, she slid one in front of me. "Life is shitty sometimes, Chris, but you can't let it bring you down. You used to be fun. Yeah, your brother's wife died. We get it. But it's time to suck it up and move on. I'd pity fuck you, but I like Bob."

I exchanged a quick look with my old roommate. I wasn't looking for a pity fuck, especially not from his girlfriend. The awkward moment sent me over to talk to the woman, who turned away at my approach.

"You'll thank me tomorrow," Ashley said in a voice that rose above all other noise in the bar.

I was reasonably certain I wouldn't, but I'd discovered a topic I wanted to discuss less than my family. The glare the blonde gave me as

I sat down next to her would normally have been enough to send me right back to the table with Bob and Ashley, but I was beginning to feel those shots.

"Hi," I said. "My name is Chris."

She grunted and shook her head.

We were off to a great start.

CHAPTER TWO

McKenna

I should have gone home.

I don't know what I thought would happen if I went to a bar at night alone, but if the drunk frat boy next to me laid a fucking finger on me, my fist would have connected with his face. I should have punched Noah, but it had taken me a moment to fully process that he'd thought having sex with me and then one of my friends didn't mean we had to break up.

I'd driven all the way to Providence to look Noah in the eye as I told him what an asshole he was. I'd done it, too, just before I'd thrown the necklace he'd given me back at him. Had I known that such an act would give me one good moment of feeling vindicated, followed by hours of asking myself why the hell I'd even wanted to see him again, I wouldn't have bothered.

I didn't know if I was angrier with him for being someone I couldn't depend on or with myself for wanting someone I could. Ever since my father had died, I'd found it difficult to be alone. You know what felt worse than being alone? Fucking someone so you wouldn't be and then having to face the fact that sex didn't mean shit to most people.

I kept thinking I was nothing like my mother, but maybe, in the end, I was exactly like her. Or maybe fucking a bunch of douchebags was how she'd become someone who didn't care about anyone but herself.

Look at me, Mom, following in your footsteps.
You must be proud.

I took a sip of the strongest mixed drink I'd ever tasted. I wasn't old enough to drink, but I had tits and a fake ID. Sadly, that was enough at most places. Usually, though, I stuck to one beer. I shouldn't have even been drinking at all, since I intended to drive home.

Unless I was hoping to wrap myself around a tree.

Noah wasn't worth it. So why did that idea sound tempting? "I'm so fucked up."

I only realized I'd spoken that last part aloud when the idiot next to me replied, "No more than me."

I shot him an ugly look. "I'm not interested."

"Normally that kind of bluntness might hurt my feelings, but I'm currently buzzed. Don't worry, I'm not sticking around. I just need a minute more over here to let those last shots hit my bloodstream, and I'll be numbed to whatever else my friends say to me tonight."

Yes, he was nearing drunk, but he wasn't giving off a creep vibe. He was also pretty good looking in a middle-class, boy-next-door, trying-too-hard way. What was someone like him doing in a dive bar on the wrong side of town? Had he gotten lost on the way to the library? I almost smiled. "Sounds like you've got some pretty shitty friends."

He sighed. "I'd say we're batting about even on who is less fun to be with lately. They mean well. God, I hope they don't want to hit a dance club after this."

"Then don't go."

"That kind of negates the whole decision to hang out with them tonight."

"Sometimes it's better to be alone."

"How are you enjoying that?"

"Fuck you."

He smiled. "Not even if you asked me to. Not tonight. All I'm looking for is sweet oblivion, and if you're alone, you're vulner—vulnerable." He slurred the last word.

"How is that buzz coming? Ready to go back to your friends yet?"

He seemed to actually consider my question before answering. "Almost." He put a fifty down on the table and asked for two more of what I was drinking.

"I don't want a drink from you."

His smile was surprisingly disarming. "Who said they aren't both for me?"

I rolled my eyes, but I was curious about something. "What were your friends saying that you didn't want to hear?"

"The truth."

"Ouch. Yeah, you're better off without those bastards." I was only half joking.

"At least until I hit the bottom of that second glass." There it was, that easy smile again. I didn't want to like him at all, but I found myself not hating that he'd joined me.

The bartender gave us each our next drink. Chris told him to keep the change, then swept both the glasses in front of him. My mouth fell open. "You're seriously going to drink both?"

He wagged a finger at me. "You didn't want a drink from me, plus you shouldn't get drunk alone."

"Because you think I'm vulnerable?" I might have been small, but I was fierce. I didn't doubt that I could kick his ass, because I was not above striking fast and low if I had to. I sat up straighter and waved a hand over my chest and shot him another glare. "Am I wearing a sign that says I want your advice?"

His gaze dropped to my chest. He blinked a few times, then went a little red and returned his attention to the drinks before him. "What was the question?"

I shook my head but had to fight back a smile.

He looked up. He really did have beautiful eyes—dark and so open. Most guys would have already said something in an attempt to impress me. That was how it worked. Men said shit they didn't mean. Women sometimes chose to believe it long enough to hook up.

Still, I felt I needed to be up front. "There is zero chance of anything happening between us."

He shrugged. "You're the only one who keeps bringing sex up. I just needed a place to sit for a minute."

Irritated, I snapped, "To get drunk enough to be able to tolerate your friends."

He brought a finger to his lips. "Not so loud. It's not that I don't want to be with *them*. I don't want to be with anybody." He took a long gulp of his drink. "Not even me."

"I totally get that."

"Really? You'll get over it. Whatever he said to you—wipe it right out of your mind. One day you'll meet someone who matters, and you won't even remember his name."

"This isn't about a guy."

"Okay, because Ashley thought it was."

"Ashley doesn't fucking know me, does she?"

"Nope, she doesn't. So you didn't just get dumped?"

"*I* broke up with *him*."

Chris shrugged. "Then he'll be even easier to forget later. Have a good cry. You'll feel better by tomorrow."

Every word out of his mouth was like nails on a chalkboard. "First, it'll be a cold day in hell before I cry over a man. Second—" I realized something in that moment. "Second, he's not even what I'm upset about." I stopped. "Like I said . . . my head is all fucked up."

"I know how that feels."

His response irritated me. "Really? Did your father die and take with him everything you loved about your life?" Had I really said that?

Was that how I still felt? My hands shook as I realized it was. And why was I vomiting my issues on a drunk stranger?

Chris didn't matter to me. It was unlikely I'd see him again. It didn't matter what I said to him. I could finally say what I'd been holding in. "I never felt alone when my father was alive, but that's all I feel now."

And scared. For the second time in my life, I felt like I'd had all sense of security ripped out from beneath my feet. My father's friends had been good to me, but we were no longer part of each other's daily lives. I hoped to one day remedy that, but I had no idea how.

"Losing someone changes everything." Chris turned in his chair to face me. "This is the first weekend I haven't gone home since my sister-in-law died. I don't want to be alone, but being with people doesn't help either."

My chest tightened. "I know."

"It's been a few months. You'd think I'd have my shit together by now. She was pregnant, not that losing just her wouldn't have been devastating, but . . . hey, don't you hate it when people ask how you're doing but they don't want to hear the truth?"

"Yes. It's been over a year for me. I don't talk about it anymore."

"Because the people who actually do care get sad when you do."

"And you don't like to be alone, so you sleep with people you tell yourself care about you even though you know they don't."

"Or do enough shots of tequila that you find yourself telling your problems to a stranger in a bar."

"Yeah," I mumbled. I wished I'd had the excuse of having had too much to drink. Sadly, I was sober and just in need of someone to talk to. God, I felt pathetic.

We shared an awkward moment of silence after that. He could not have been less like the men I was used to. In the racing world, men swaggered with flashy smiles and used brags as conversation starters. Chris was good looking, but I didn't get the sense that he knew it. If there was anything spectacular about him, he certainly wasn't boasting about it.

I gave him another once-over. He was taller than I'd initially thought. Nice shoulders. His bicep flexed as he reached for his drink, and my heart surprised me by skipping a beat. I bet he could hold his own in a fight. When he looked my way again, I got lost for a moment in his dark eyes.

His voice turned husky. "I'm sorry about your dad."

Something shifted in the air. He wasn't just someone who'd come to sit next to me at a dive bar; he was someone who understood a pain I'd long ago given up trying to articulate. For once, I didn't feel alone. "I'm sorry about your sister-in-law."

He held my gaze. "I considered dropping out of school to go home to spend more time with my family, but I don't think it would help. My brother is so angry."

I nodded. "I can imagine he would be." I still was. Losing my father was the hardest thing I'd ever gone through, and I still hadn't found my footing. "I bet he's scared too. I am. I don't know who I am without my father. I used to be so confident. I knew exactly what I wanted to do. I don't know anything anymore. I don't know if anything's worth it. No matter what I do—I lose anyway. So why bother, right?"

He leaned closer. "That's not what I see in your eyes."

I told myself anything he said would be a line designed to get me to leave with him. He probably couldn't even focus on my face. Still, I leaned in as well. "Really? What do you see?"

"A person with a lot of fight left in them." His gaze was surprisingly steady.

I wished that were true. "Not as much as you'd think."

He cocked his head to one side. "What did you want to do? Before your dad died?"

I hadn't expected the question and needed a moment before I could answer it. "My dad and I had plans to buy a plot of land when he retired. He was a NASCAR driver." I didn't say his name. I hadn't said mine. Neither mattered. "We had this dream of a private racetrack we could buy old stock cars and test them out on. Just me and him. And our pit crew."

"Pit crew?"

I frowned. "The people who refuel, change the tires, check everything during a race." My father's had been so much a part of my life they were family.

"Oh. Cool."

"You don't watch NASCAR?"

He shrugged. "Was that how your father died?"

"No. Heart attack." His question was a valid one, though. Stock car racing wasn't a sport for the meek.

"You need to build that racetrack."

I shook my head. "Without him? I couldn't."

"Why not? Because it's expensive?"

I made a sound in my throat. "That's part of it, but it's a million other things as well. I don't think I could do it on my own."

He traced a hand down the side of my face. "You could. All you have to do is start with what you want to do, determine what it takes to make it happen, then break that down to smaller steps you can take toward your goal. That's what I always tell my brother, anyway. He has big dreams." His hand fell back to his side. "Or he used to."

I touched his thigh, then withdrew when it felt too intimate. "He's lucky to have a brother like you."

"I don't know about that." He didn't seem to notice my inner struggle. "What would you name your racetrack?"

I had no idea.

"Every dream needs a name," he continued, still slurring his words. "Hey, you never told me *your* name."

"Mack." I normally stopped there, but I added, "Decker."

He spread his hands in the air and moved them outward as if stretching a sign. "Decker Park. I like it."

I shuddered as hope fluttered to life inside me. "My father didn't leave me much. I have enough to pay for school, then . . ."

"Buy that land?"

"Maybe, but not enough to do more than that."

He smiled. "If you buy the land, you'll build that racetrack."

He took my hand in his, sending warmth through me. I told myself I shouldn't feel so connected to someone I'd just met, someone who was obviously wasted. He made it all sound so easy. How could he believe in me when I'd forgotten how to believe in myself? "I miss my father so much I ache."

"Then make Decker Park happen." He asked the bartender for a pen and grabbed a napkin. "Show me what it would look like."

I hesitated. Sketching it out felt like a promise . . . one I had to believe I was capable of keeping. "What I imagine would be too much to do on my own."

"You'd need that pit crew."

My heart started thudding wildly in my chest. Could I ask them to join me? Would they? Was that a crazy dream as well? "I would. Some of my dad's closest friends were on his. We try to stay in touch, but they all had to find work and are scattered around New England. This would give us a chance to do something together."

His smile widened. "See—all you have to do is believe it's possible, then focus on making it happen."

My father had said something similar so many times I got goose bumps. Focus. That was what I'd lost when my father had died. I turned away from Chris and sketched everything my father and I had talked about wanting our racetrack to have. I even drew a building where we could showcase my future collection of priceless refurbished stock cars. The facility would require a huge garage. Big enough to impress

NASCAR's top drivers. I imagined Decker Park as an invitation-only facility.

When I finished, I described it all in great detail to Chris. I didn't know if he was fascinated or if his quiet attention was due to a drunken stupor. Either way, once I started talking, I couldn't stop. I told him that my father had taught me how to change out an engine at the age some fathers were teaching their daughters how to ride a bike. I told him how every time I worked on my father's 1967 Plymouth Belvedere, I felt him with me, and I still struggled with the idea of him being truly gone. When I stopped for a breath, I felt self-conscious about how much I'd shared. "What about you? What do you want?"

Another man might have taken that as an opportunity to proposition me, but Chris's eyebrows drew together, and his eyes darkened with sadness. "I want Sebastian to stop drinking. My family has always been close, but we're falling apart. At least, I am. I lost my brother along with his wife. He's drunk all the time—and such an ass when he is. I don't like him anymore, and that's tough because I love him."

"You'll figure it out." I slid down from my seat, stepped between his legs, and hugged him. When I lifted my face from his chest, our faces were close . . . so close.

His mouth claimed mine hungrily, and his hands went to my hips to hold me close. I expected the kiss to be sloppy, but a gentle, hot caress met my lips. I opened to his tongue, which teased its way around mine. I wanted him in a way I'd never wanted Noah. And this was Chris drunk.

Drunk. He shouldn't be. I broke the kiss off and stepped back. He couldn't help his brother if he went down the same path. "You know on an airplane when they tell you to put your oxygen mask on before you help the person next to you?"

He looked turned on and confused. "Sure."

"Your brother needs you to be sober."

He rubbed a hand over his face. "Wish you'd said that like six . . . seven tequila shots ago."

I laid a hand over his heart. His pain and confusion were as real to me as my own. I'd never been what one would call nurturing, but I sought the words to comfort him. "You're going to be okay, Chris. Your brother will too. Do you know how I know that?"

He shook his head. The sadness in his eyes reflected the state of my own soul, and in that moment, I knew what he needed to hear.

"Because I see it in your eyes. You're a good brother, and there's no way he can fail when he has someone like you on his side. You've got this."

It was a really touching moment until he swayed and turned green. "I'm sorry. I think I'm going to throw up."

I took another step back. "Do you need help getting to the bathroom?"

He shook his head, groaned, then hopped off his stool and rushed away. Alone, I looked around and realized two people were watching me from a nearby table.

I could have given in to the embarrassment that was nipping at my heels, but instead I raised my chin and walked over to them. "Your friend is getting sick in the bathroom."

"Oh, shit. Ashley, I'll be right back," the man said.

"Didn't you say you had his family's number? Call them. We told my friends we'd meet them," she said with a pout that made *me* want to throw up. Those were his crew? No wonder he needed time away from them.

I was about to say I'd get Chris home, but the man was already talking to someone on the phone.

"His father's on his way," Chris's friend said before taking another swig of his beer and turning his attention back to his date.

I walked back to the bar but didn't sit. I'd barely touched my drink. There was no reason I couldn't drive back to my dorm.

No reason besides a need to make sure Chris was okay. I asked for a glass of water, then retreated with it to a booth in the corner of the room. When Chris emerged from the men's room, he returned to where we'd been sitting, then looked around.

I stayed where I was.

We'd had a good talk, but we weren't friends.

I'd come to the bar angry, looking for a distraction, but I'd found something I'd forgotten the importance of—focus. I knew what to do now.

The mistakes I'd made faded away. On the racetrack, all that mattered was what was before a driver. I saw my path clearly, and it didn't include another Noah. Or a Chris. Purchasing a lot of land would be just the start. Reaching my goals would require everything I had.

Chris stumbled back to the table where his friends were. Thankfully they didn't seem to know I was still there. He kept looking around, but the shadows concealed me.

A little while later, an older version of Chris walked into the bar. He looked tired and concerned but not angry. After helping Chris to his feet, he said something to his friends, then walked him out of the bar.

I sat nursing my glass of water for a long time. Listening to Chris talk about his family had reminded me that I had one too. Maybe not a biological one, but people who cared and who I should have made more of an effort to stay in touch with. I called my father's best friend, Ty, and told him where I was. Even though I assured him I'd only had a sip of my drink, he made me promise to stay where I was until he came for me.

Normally I would have protested, but I wanted to tell him about Decker Park and the steps I had already come up with for exactly how I'd make it happen. As I waited, I wondered what Chris would remember of me and our conversation.

We might not have been meant to be, but I'd always be grateful to him for giving me back a piece of myself.

CHAPTER THREE

CHRISTOF

The only thing less fun than asking my father to pull over on the way back to my dorm so I could throw up again was later realizing he was settling himself in a chair beside my bed because he had no intention of leaving. If he was with me, that meant somewhere out there Mauricio was babysitting Sebastian. I was doing the opposite of helping my family.

The room spun. I laid my head back and groaned. "I'm sorry, Dad."

"We'll talk about it tomorrow," my father murmured.

I wished he would yell, but he didn't have to. I knew exactly how much I'd disappointed him. "You don't have to stay."

"Sleep it off, Christof. I'm not leaving until I'm sure you're okay."

Mack's voice echoed in my thoughts, telling me I was a good brother and that I could handle this. I promised myself I'd do better— starting tomorrow. "Do you believe in love at first sight, Dad?"

"Yes, but I wouldn't trust your vision tonight."

He made a valid point, but only because he hadn't met her. "Her name was Mack. When she talked to me, it was like she was touching my soul."

"Oh boy."

"I'm going to marry her someday."

"I'm sure you will."

"She knows so much about cars. I should learn about them. We could fix them together. Do you know how to fix a car, Dad?"

"No idea. Go to sleep, Christof."

"I mean it, Dad. She's the one." I brought a fist to my forehead. "And she met me like this. I kissed her, then ran off to throw up—do you think that's why she left?"

"I imagine there might be a correlation."

I closed my eyes and threw an arm over my face. "I should have asked her for her number. How am I ever going to find her again?"

"If she's meant to be, she'll come back to you."

"Dad?"

"Yes?"

"I'm going to throw up again."

I didn't realize how fast my father could move until I sat up and bent forward. With ninja speed he had a bowl in front of me just in time.

I still had some growing up to do, but I knew who I wanted to be when I did. He had high expectations of us, but when we faltered, he was always there to pick us up. I had the world's best father. I would have told him that, but after I handed him the bowl, I passed out.

CHAPTER FOUR

ABIGAIL CORISI, DOMINIC CORISI'S WIFE

Seven years later

Desperate times called for desperate measures.

Abby waited in the solarium for a woman who was nearly as powerful as her husband. There were people who watched the news, people who were discussed on it, and then people who were so influential they controlled the media.

Had anyone told Abby that she'd meet a sinfully rich man, fall madly in love with him, and leave her simple, middle-class life for the craziness of his world, she would have said things like that didn't happen.

They did, though.

And that life had been good—so good—until recently.

A noise behind her brought her attention to the doorway, where a frail older woman made her way toward her. "Mrs. Corisi."

Abby took a step toward her. "Thank you for seeing me. Please call me Abby."

The woman stopped a foot in front of her, gave her a head-to-toe perusal, and said, "I'd rather not. You may call me 'Your Royal Highness.'"

"Of course." Abby nearly coughed in amused surprise. Delinda Westerly had had a reputation for being starched and formal before she'd married King Tadeas of Vandorra. Although the king had officially stepped down for his son, Magnus, to rule . . . no one dared tell her that she wasn't actually the queen anymore. Thankfully, their mutual friend, Alessandro, had prepped Abby well on how to handle her. She curtsied. "I appreciate you taking the time to speak to me."

"Yes, well, before you thank me a third time, I only agreed to meet with you because Alessandro is one of my dearest friends." She turned to one of her house staff, who was hovering in the doorway, and said, "Please bring us some tea and a tray of something light. I doubt our guest will be staying very long." Her attention returned to Abby. "Now, let's take a seat so you can tell me what it is you think I can help you with."

Abby sat across from the woman and smoothed her hands down the front of her dress. She wasn't normally intimidated by anyone. Her social circle was full of people who thought they were powerful, but few wielded the influence of this woman. As it had for Dominic, that power had brought her both loyal friends as well as enemies. Hopefully that experience would make her a sympathetic ear, because Abby needed her help. "It's regarding my husband."

"I'm far from a fan of the man."

That much Abby knew. If another option had been available, she would have leaped at it. "I am. I love him more than I ever thought I could love anyone. I'm not blind to who he was before he met me, but for over ten years he has been a good husband—a loving father to our daughter. His companies are socially and economically responsible."

Delinda gave her a long look before saying, "My dear, at my age I find dancing around a topic a tedious waste of my time. You would not be in my home if I didn't know exactly who Dominic Corisi is and how he conducts himself."

Her staffer appeared at the door and discreetly rolled a tea tray into the room. He poured a cup for both of them, asked if they required anything more, then made a polite retreat.

Abby picked up her tea but didn't take a sip. Seeking out the help of someone who wasn't invested in the outcome but could be trusted had made sense when Alessandro had suggested it. She wasn't sure anymore.

To Dominic, involving anyone in his business might feel like a betrayal.

Everyone brought some baggage from their childhood into adulthood; Dominic owned his. He'd been open with her about how his violent childhood had lit an ugly rage within him that he suppressed but that not even her love had extinguished. He kept that side of himself hidden away from her and their child. His own father had beaten him brutally, but in all the time she'd been married to him, Dominic had not so much as raised his voice to her. Their daughter, Judy, thought her father was the sweetest, most mild mannered of men.

Abby feared she might one day lose him to his dark side. She cleared her throat. "It has recently come to my attention that my husband is buying up properties in Montalcino, Italy."

"And?"

She swallowed hard. "It began after he went there to see his family. He's been pulling away from me ever since that trip." Abby gripped her hands in her lap. "I need to know why he's investing so much into that town."

"You think he's found another woman?"

Abby gasped. "No, that's not what this is about." *That would almost be easier.*

Delinda tapped her nails on the arm of her chair. "Clearly this is a difficult time for your family. Have you considered couples counseling?"

"I'm not here for advice—I need your help," Abby said with a firmness she hoped would prevail.

"I'm still at a loss for how, though I sympathize."

Deep breath. Just do it. "If I were in trouble, Dominic would move heaven and earth to save me. My heart tells me he's about to do something he'll regret. He's hurt. He's angry. He needs someone on his side who can stop him before he goes too far."

After a long moment, Delinda said, "I'm sorry; I know enough about your husband to agree that you have every reason to be concerned. What you might need to face, my dear, is that a leopard cannot change its spots. If it's protection from him you require, I could set something up for you, but that's as involved as I'll agree to be."

Abby shook her head. "Alessandro said if anyone could understand this side of Dominic, it would be you."

"I have no idea why he would have said that."

"He said you know what it's like to hold anger, to make mistakes because of it, and that those mistakes nearly cost you your family."

"I shall have to speak to Alessandro regarding how freely he discusses my private matters."

Delinda's wall wasn't coming down. It was time for Abby to play her ace. "He said no matter what you did, he never gave up on you. I won't give up on Dominic. This isn't just about stopping him. I want to help him through it, to show him there's a better way. I'd normally use our own resources, but our people are loyal to him, and I don't want them to feel they need to choose a side." Nothing? Alessandro said if all else failed—"I also need someone who isn't intimidated by him."

A spark lit in Delinda's eyes. "Trust me, I am not afraid of your husband."

Thank you, Alessandro. You were right about the size of her ego. I hope you're also right about what's in her heart. A lot of people would love to see my husband fail. Dominic doesn't need another challenge—he needs a guardian angel. "That's why I'm here. I realize you have no reason to care about what happens to me or my family, but Alessandro has been like a father to Dominic and me. He said he considers you a second mother. That makes us family."

"Does it?" Delinda made a delicate grunt of doubt. "Did Alessandro suggest you say that?"

Abby smiled. "He did." Like Dominic, Delinda respected blunt honesty.

Delinda sighed. "Alessandro is the reason my family is back in my life. If he loves Dominic, and he says he does, there must be something in your husband I haven't yet seen." She studied Abby's face carefully. "Has he truly been good to you?"

Abby blinked back tears of gratitude as she realized that she might just have found the ally she'd sought. "So good. With me, he's the man he always should have been. Kind. Attentive. Loyal. Supportive. He's taught me as much about love as I have him."

"But?"

To help her, to help Dominic, Delinda would need to know the demon within him. "He survived things no one should have had to. Did you know his father, Antonio Corisi?"

"By reputation alone, and his wasn't a pleasant one. For a long time it was believed he murdered his wife, a horrific circumstance that surprised no one. The shock came when she resurfaced."

Although Abby had found it in her heart to love her mother-in-law for her husband's sake, what Rosella had done remained incomprehensible to Abby. "She left Dominic and his sister with a man she was so afraid of she faked her own death—fearing if he ever found her, he would kill her. She only resurfaced after Antonio died. Can you imagine what it was like to be left at the mercy of such a man while not knowing what happened to your mother? Dominic searched for Rosella, here and in her hometown of Montalcino. His family there hid her even from him, let him believe she was dead. Later, when he found out she was alive . . . he had to reconcile that with the fact that his family in Italy had always known and never told him. That does something to a person."

In a much more subdued tone, Delinda said, "I imagine it would."

"Dominic let his mother back into his life. He has done his best to move on. Last year, however, our daughter had a school project that involved making a family tree. She started asking questions, and when no one wanted to answer them, she went looking for the answers herself. Dominic returned to Italy hopeful and with an open heart. His mother was back. He was ready to reach out to the family that had chosen her safety over his even when he was still a child." Abby sniffed as a wave of emotion forced her to take a moment before continuing. "I don't know what they said to him, but it's tearing apart the man I love. People look at Dominic and think he's invincible—too hardened to feel pain. That's not who he is. He's just a man who thought he'd finally meet his grandmother, only to discover he is somehow still not good enough to be allowed to."

"And you believe that's connected to why he's buying up property in that town? To what end?"

Abby shook her head. "I wish I knew. As soon as he involved Alethea Stone, I feared it was going nowhere good."

Delinda nodded slowly. "I know her well. I had hoped being a mother would calm her ways."

"This time it's not her fault. I doubt she was given much of a choice."

"Why do you say that?"

"Because I know her. I wouldn't be aware of any of this if she didn't want me to. Whatever they're doing, she feels it's wrong, and she wants me to stop it. Will you help me?"

There was a long pause, and then Delinda said, "What would you have me do?"

"Have you heard of the Romano family? They own a chain of stores in New England."

"The name sounds vaguely familiar."

"They're actually doing very well. I'm surprised—"

"My dear, Tadeas and I have commitments on both sides of the Atlantic. If there is something you think I should know about the family, spare the theatrics and simply say it."

"Camilla Romano is Rosella's sister. Basil Romano, her husband, is also from Montalcino. Why have I never heard of them? Dominic has family who live in New England, driving distance from us; why wouldn't they reach out to him?"

"Perhaps they haven't seen the side of him you have?" Delinda's voice had a chill to it.

Abby scrambled to draw her back to her side. "Maybe, but it has to be more than that. Alethea left their name on a sticky note in my makeup bag. Don't you see? They must be the key to fixing this."

"As would having a good long conversation with your husband."

"You think I haven't tried? In the ideal world that would be the answer. But guess what? Happily ever after is hard work. I came to you because Alessandro said you would understand that, in the end, all that matters is family. Yours. Mine. Dominic's. Please. Find out anything you can about the Romanos. I would, but Dominic would instantly know what I was up to. Help me stop Dominic before he does something he'll regret."

"He won't be happy with either of us."

"Not at first, no. But since he can't hear me right now, I'll need to show him how much I love him."

Delinda nodded and pulled out her phone. "Tadeas? Cancel our water bungalow in the Maldives; we may be heading over to Italy, but first . . . where are the Romanos?" She met Abby's eyes.

"Connecticut."

"We need to go to Connecticut. I hear there is a family there who would benefit from a little *royal* intervention." She chuckled. "Of course I do. Why become a royal if one isn't going to have some fun with it?" She blushed. "Well, yes, there's that, as well. I still have company with me, but I'll call you as soon as she leaves. Abigail Corisi. You'll like her. She's surprisingly articulate." In response to something he said, she laughed again. "She asked to see me, not the other way around. You're so bad." She held the phone away from her face. "I don't know how I survived eighty-plus years without you reminding me to behave. Yes. Yes. I love you as well. See you in a little bit."

After ending the call, Delinda shook her head at the phone, even though she was still smiling. "Husbands."

"They're worth fighting for." Abby's throat tightened with emotion. Nothing mattered more than family, and the woman before her had just agreed to help save hers.

Delinda lowered her phone. Her expression became more serious. "The good ones certainly are. Dominic is one lucky man."

"Thank you, Delinda," Abby said as if she'd been given permission to call her by her first name. A decade with Dominic hadn't made Abby meek. The opposite, in fact. A weak man tried to control his wife. Dominic had always encouraged Abby to value her own voice and said her strong will was part of why he'd fallen for her in the first place.

She prayed he'd feel the same when all of this was said and done.

Delinda wagged a finger at Abby, but her smile returned. "Well, okay, then. Don't just sit there sipping tea. What will your role be in all this?"

CHAPTER FIVE

CHRISTOF

Entering Southwick, Massachusetts

I could have gone around the town. Neither of my older brothers would have chosen the thirty-five-mile-an-hour route home, but I preferred getting to know an area, and that didn't happen by sticking to the highways.

So far the place didn't look much different than any of the small surrounding New England towns. The narrow road was lined by trees on both sides, as well as the occasional rock formation that had been sliced away.

I drove past homes with large yards that opened up to grassy hills and fields. Still nothing impressive, or at least not relevant as far as my reason for being on the road that day. I was scouting out store chains interested in working with the Romano Superstores, a role I'd recently taken on for my family's business. The days of our company entering a market, demolishing the competition, and celebrating the win were over. Our new mission statement was to use our buying power to partner with smaller chains, stabilize them, implement mutually profitable changes, and move on. Philanthropy as part of a business plan? Our competitors had thought it foolhardy, but the world was changing, and it was time more companies began working together for the greater good.

My phone announced my mother was calling. I answered via voice command. "Hi, Mom. I'm driving. What do you need?"

"How was your meeting?"

I smiled because she'd used the same tone when I was much younger and she'd asked how my day at school had gone. Even though I wasn't her youngest boy, she often treated me as if I were.

"It was good. Complicated. The area has a lot of promise. The owner of the regional chain is eager to work with us. I have some number crunching to do before I make my suggestion to Sebastian. The market isn't growing at a rate to justify our involvement." In other words, there might not be any profit in it for us. As the eldest Romano son, Sebastian was acting CEO, though, and the final decision would be his.

"Are they in a difficult spot?"

"They soon could be. They're slowly losing ground. I'd give them four more viable years before they close. We could turn that around, but it would take some major changes on their part and a substantial time investment on ours. If we break even, it would be nice to see them succeed. The family has done a lot for their community. More than they could afford to, but after seeing where their stores are located, I understand why they can't turn a blind eye. It would be nice if we didn't either."

Approval rang in my mother's voice. "Have I told you how proud I am of all my sons? When I think about Romano Superstores starting with the one convenience store your father and I ran on our own—it's still so difficult to believe what you boys have made it into."

"Dad would say it's also unnecessary." To make my mother laugh, I did an impression of my father's voice. "Back in Italy, all I had was one store, homemade wine, and my family, and I was happy."

My mother laughed, as I'd known she would. "He was. We all were." After a moment she added, "Do you miss working in the office? I know you had a good circle of friends there."

"Mom, it's fine."

"I didn't say it wasn't. I'm asking how you feel about the change."

"I'm where I need to be. Sebastian's priority is to stay closer to home with Heather and Ava. He's earned the right to. Mauricio too. I've never seen him happier than he is designing prosthetics with Wren. Now that she's pregnant, he doesn't have time to do double duty. It made sense for me to step up and take over project evaluation."

"Well, start learning to delegate now, because Gian is going into medicine and won't be there to take over when you start your own family."

I coughed on that. "Mom, that's not something either of us will have to worry about for a very long time."

"You're not getting any younger, Christof."

We'd had this talk before. I knew how to shut it down. "You're right; I'll get right on proposing to Amanda. Or Katherine. Or Adeline. Any one of them should be fine."

"I wouldn't know—you've never introduced me to them."

"And what does that tell you?"

My mother clucked. "That you're dating too many women."

"And they're dating just as many men. That's how things work nowadays. This isn't the old country, Mom."

"Are you trying to raise my blood pressure?"

I chuckled. Maybe a little. I could also be sweet, though. "If I ever do meet the right one, you'll be the first to know. I promise. But for now I'm happy with my life the way it is."

She sighed. "It's a mother's job to worry for her babies."

I could have protested. No matter how old any of us got, she'd never stopped calling us her babies. It was impossible to resent the term, though, because my brothers and I had amazing parents who loved us unconditionally.

Just as important, our parents were as good to each other as they were to us. That was probably why I didn't rush into serious relationships. I wasn't at all tempted to settle for less than the healthy partnership my parents had.

Plus sex without commitment wasn't necessarily a bad thing. Not that I would ever dare say that to my mother. Especially not if we were in her kitchen and she had a wooden spoon within reach. "I know and I'm fine. Really, it's good for me to see this side of the business as well." Just then I noticed steam escaping the hood of my car. Shit. "Mom, I have to go."

"Something wrong?"

"Mack's engine is overheating. Nothing big. I'll pull over and give her a rest."

"There is always an issue with that car. It's time to get something new, especially now that you're on the road more."

It was another conversation we'd had before and would likely have again. My 1970 BMW Baur Cabriolet wasn't to everyone's taste, but it had been love at first sight. I'd seen an ad for her online, and despite the poor condition she was in, I knew she'd be mine.

My experience with cars before her had been entirely superficial and my knowledge of what happened beneath the hood of one minimal. That didn't stop me from buying her and having her towed to my parents' driveway and then to my own place when I moved out. Working on her still brought me comfort in a way I found difficult to articulate.

I'd painstakingly refurbished her, bumper to bumper, and enjoyed every moment of it. Sure, a new car would be more reliable, but Mack was special. I was meant to drive her.

Just as she was meant to sometimes challenge me. Looked like she was overheating again. Last time it had been because of her thermostat. This time, I had no idea. Life with Mack was always an adventure. "I'm pulling over. I'll text you later when I'm home."

"Yes, please. Your father wants to know if you need him to drive up to get you."

"Tell him thank you but I'm good. I'm sure there's a garage in town. If this isn't an easy fix, I'll have her towed home and grab a rental or call for a car."

"If you're sure."

"Love you, Mom. Bye."

I turned Mack off, got out, slid off my suit jacket, and tossed it on the passenger seat before closing the door and rolling my sleeves up. More than one woman I'd dated had asked if I cared about my car more than I did about them. I'd always laughed the question off without answering.

Those same women also accused me of being too close to my family. They didn't have to say much more than that for me to know we weren't destined to last.

Mack calmed me, filled me with a sense of hope. I had the feeling that if I kept driving her, one day something wonderful would happen. It wasn't something I could explain, so I didn't bother to try.

CHAPTER SIX

McKenna

"Still no date for the CamTech event tonight? Not judging, just asking."

"Still perfectly fine attending on my own." I closed the door of the 1971 Mercury Montego I'd just driven onto a four-column lift and groaned. It was impossible to be irritated with Ty's interest in my love life or lack thereof. He could be a little overprotective, but I didn't consider that a bad thing.

He, Cal, and Wayne were my family by choice rather than blood, and I was damn grateful to have them back in my life. Losing my father had sent me into a tailspin, and I'd pulled back from even them. Thank God I'd come to my senses.

My life wasn't normal. Was there such a thing for the daughter of a NASCAR driver? Mom had been Dad's first and biggest fan, then his baby's mama. They'd never married, but we'd all lived together in a huge house my father had bought at the height of his career. Not rich but comfortable. Early childhood was arguably the most normal part of my life.

I was ten when my mother had announced she was leaving and that I'd have to choose between the two of them because she refused to do the every-other-weekend thing. She never wanted to see my father again, even if that meant not seeing me.

I was furious with her. It took over a decade and more than one visit with a therapist to be able to articulate that. Asking me to choose between two people I loved had felt like I'd been given the option of jumping from a plane without a parachute or staying aboard and crashing into a mountain.

I'd chosen my father because—well, mostly because she'd broken his heart too. He'd been faithful, hardworking, loving . . . just not rich enough. People brought up my mother's name now and then. She was on her third . . . possibly fourth husband and had had enough work done that she looked much younger than she was. She'd never had another child. I'd once asked my father if that was proof that I was a mistake. He'd said miracles like me were unexpected but never mistakes.

I was sure that wasn't how my mother saw me, but I embraced my father's view. I was his little shadow, his treasured miracle. In my adolescence I saw a lot of shit I probably shouldn't have because my father took me everywhere with him, but I wouldn't have wanted it any other way.

His love for me made everything else okay.

It gave me strength every birthday I didn't hear from my mother, every milestone she failed to reach out to me. She might not have seen my value, but I didn't require her validation. I was a miracle. I could survive without her, and one day I'd show the world the reason I was meant to be.

My conviction that my life was part of a greater plan was shaken by my father's heart attack when I was eighteen. He was there in the morning and then gone by the time I returned from school. No warning. No final words. I found him on the floor of his garage.

Part of me died along with him that day.

Dad's pit crew—Ty, Cal, and Wayne—helped me sort through the mess that followed. They tried to get me to enroll in college so I truly could be the successful, independent woman my father had always bragged I would be, but I fought them at first. Eventually, I did enroll, only because I didn't know what else to do. Nothing made me happy. Life didn't make sense. I hated that beneath my tough talk, I felt scared, lonely, and in need of a good cry most of the time. I started avoiding people I'd known my whole life because I didn't like who I was becoming and I didn't want them to see me the way I was. Worse, I clung to people who didn't care about me because I hated being alone.

Then, one night in Providence, I had a conversation with a complete stranger, and it woke me up. He'd been a random meeting and was initially unwelcome. My father used to say many life-changing events were. Like with a tire blowing out or a sudden opening between cars on the track, a person had to be ready to make split-second decisions. In the heat of a race there wasn't time to strategize. A racer acted, adapted, didn't look back.

It was nuts to think Decker Park was a reality only because some drunk guy had echoed my father's advice and believed in me. I'd never shared that story. That lost, uncertain girl who had needed reassurance was a distant memory.

Soon after that talk in the bar, I'd taken my inheritance and purchased land in Massachusetts. That one step forward had made everything else possible. It had allowed me to ask Ty, Cal, and Wayne to open a garage with me, one that focused on refurbishing stock cars. With our combined knowledge of the industry, we flipped cars others overlooked and invested the money into the business. Partnering with a college student had been a risk for all three of them, like so many decisions in the racing industry, but it had paid off for all of us.

Seven years later we were living a dream beyond even what I had imagined back then. Tucked away on eighty acres, Decker Park boasted a 3.4-mile circuit with nineteen turns. We had enough blind corners and altitude changes to challenge reigning NASCAR racers as well as an oval .526-mile banked track where a novice driver could, for a generous price, experience the thrill of any of the retired stock cars in my garage.

We didn't host races, but everyone who was anyone in the international racing world eventually test-drove something on our tracks. Some came for the privacy we could ensure, others for the novelty of the experience. Regardless of what had brought them in the first time, almost all of them returned year after year. I didn't advertise our programs or the cars we offered for sale simply because I didn't have to.

It still gave me goose bumps each time I sat back and thought about how many other directions my life could have gone in. I'd been ready to give up. Everyone had expected me to. The racing world was rife with crash-and-burn stories, as many off the track as on.

But I hadn't given up.

More than once over the years I'd wondered whatever had happened to the man I'd met that night. Had his brother gotten past his grief? Was his family still as close as he'd described? Who had he become?

I could have gone back to the bar to look for him, but I hadn't. Once I'd chosen my course forward, felt the rush of adrenaline that had come with the confidence that I just might be able to do it, there had been no room for distraction.

Sorry, Drunk Chris. That doesn't mean I don't owe you a huge thank-you if we ever do meet again.

"There'll be photographers," Ty reminded me gently, pulling me back to the present. "And a lot of hand shaking."

He didn't have to tell me what my sponsors expected from me at events. I'd gone to them even as a child, although back then I'd been trotted in, shown off, and whisked away to bed. Back then my father had been the show.

So much of what my father had let me see as a child was an asset to me now. My instincts about cars and drivers alike were often correct. Show me a driver who thought about nothing but racing all week, hit the gym to keep his body alert and healthy, and left the party early to get his eight hours of sleep, and I'd bet my savings on him taking the next race—nine times out of ten I was right.

Drunk? Lazy? Sloppy? If they ever won, it was by pure luck.

Focus was everything.

Determination.

Grit—that was what it took to succeed in any business.

Sponsor money overflowed to Decker Park because our facility was cutting edge. I was a valuable guest because I didn't attend many functions. People loved exclusive. CamTech was a computer company that had no ties to racing, but they loved being linked to anything fast or difficult to attain. I represented both.

No one ever said I couldn't smell like my garage while being courted by drivers who wanted an invitation to Decker Park. I liked to think it added a humorous layer of authenticity. *Sure, my nails are perfectly manicured, but breathe me in, fellas, and you'll get where my priorities lie.*

I checked the zipper on the front of my coveralls and made a show of slipping gloves over my hands. "Don't worry, I've got that covered."

With a smile and a shake of his head, Ty said, "I'd go with you, but I have a date tonight."

"Do you know this one's name?"

"Samantha. Or Sara. It starts with an *S.*"

I laughed. "Somewhere between how you date and how I don't, there is a healthy place neither of us will probably ever know." It had been years since I'd even been on a date.

He chuckled. "Ain't that the truth. Speaking of healthy, Cal called earlier. He and Wayne found a man in Key West who says he wants to sell an old Plymouth Superbird. It's been sitting in a garage. No idea if it runs. They're going to take a look at it, then spend a few days in the sun before heading home."

"Sounds good. They deserve a vacation. Plus a Superbird would be a nice addition, since it was banned and there aren't many out there." I turned my attention back to the car on the lift. It was a possible consignment sale, another lucrative service we provided. We only sold the best, though. The jury was still out on whether this one met our standards. "Do you have time to see how honest this seller was with his description? Original paint. No cosmetic modifications. I'm eager to see how much they resisted changing under the body." Tossing a smile at Ty, I added, "You know you're curious as well."

He reached for a pair of coveralls. "Fifteen minutes, that's all I'm giving this. Serenade is cooking me dinner at her place, and unlike you, I care how I smell."

"If I were you, I'd be more concerned with getting her name right," I teased.

"You know they're all *honey* to me," he joked right back.

Sadly, it was the truth. I tossed a flashlight to him. "You're so bad."

"Or so good I'm worth forgiving."

It was my turn to shake my head. In my book there was no such thing. I returned my attention to what mattered. So far the car looked like it had mainly original parts. "You know you're the reason I don't believe anything any man says."

Ty moved around to the other side of the car to inspect it as well. "Nah, you just haven't met the right one yet. When you do, I'll be the last thing on your mind."

"I sure hope so," I said, even though I struggled to imagine myself with anyone long term. Some people couldn't be alone. I was the opposite.

Fifteen minutes came and went, then an hour. It was worth it, though. The car was in better condition than I would have guessed, and I was ready to list it for the seller.

Ty left swearing after checking his watch and realizing how late he was. I had a feeling Sara or whatever her name happened to be would keep his dinner warm for him. Women let Ty get away with far too much bad behavior. Not that it ever led to anything serious. My father, on the other hand, had been a one-woman man, until my mother had ditched him. It was enough to make a person wonder if love existed outside of romance novels.

I'd grown up in a male-dominated industry and had chosen to remain in it because it was what I knew. No, men weren't a great mystery to me, especially not those with money. Most were players, willing to say or do whatever was necessary to get a woman into their bed until another woman caught their interest.

Some were looking for something more serious, but they'd proved to be just as disappointing. Even if they claimed to admire me, after a few dates they'd begin to drop hints about ways I could change or, worse, how they could save me.

Independent did not equal lonely.

Time spent rebuilding an engine wasn't a waste of my talent. I didn't yearn for the day I could afford to have someone else do it. I already could.

This is *my happily ever after.*

I made quick work of changing into a little black dress, touched up my makeup, and brushed through my hair before slipping into my Belvedere. It was one of the few material things my father had left me, and driving it made me feel like he was with me.

As I drove, I spoke to him in my head.

Wish you could have seen the mint condition of the Ford today. Looked like they barely drove the car after it was retired. What a waste.

He didn't answer me. He never had, but I needed to believe he could hear me. No matter how much time passed, there was still an ache.

I slowed when I noticed a car pulled over to the side of the road— overheated engine from the looks of it. My heart beat a little faster as I took in the make and model. A blue 1970 Baur Cabriolet. One of a little over sixteen hundred ever made, and most were still over in Europe. M10 engine, if it had its original. All-independent suspension and front disc brakes. Squared rear lights, a poor aftermarket choice of an upgrade, but not something that couldn't be undone.

I parked behind the car without thinking it through. Regardless of the driver, this little car was worth rescuing.

A man in gray trousers and a starched white shirt held a white rag and looked about to open the hood of the car. His hair was trimmed in a conservative, modern style, and my guess was that we were close in age.

Nice ass. Flat stomach. Broad shoulders. *I bet he fends off the women in his office even though he's already taken. He looks comfortably polished. Men like that are always married.*

As I approached the car, I called out, "Careful. You need to wait for the engine to cool before lifting the hood."

He paused and turned, a slow smile spreading across his face as he looked me over. My body surprised me by warming beneath his gaze. Those eyes—they felt familiar. The pleasure in them faded, and he frowned. "You shouldn't stop for people you don't know. It's not safe—"

"For a woman?" I finished for him, feigning irritation. I didn't like how my body was beginning to hum with anticipation. He was a complete stranger, and I was beyond meaningless hookups.

"For *anyone*," he countered with a serious expression. "It's a crazy world."

"It certainly is." When it came to people, my instincts were usually spot on, but I couldn't read this guy. On one hand he seemed harmless, but why was my heart racing? What was I missing? "Would it help if I said I'm a black belt in karate and know at least a hundred ways to end your ability to have children?"

"Ouch, and not if I was a lunatic with a gun." He smiled and looked me over again. I expected a compliment or a come-on, but instead he said, "You're not a black belt."

I wasn't, but I didn't like that he didn't think I could be. "Want to test that theory?" I bit out. I could kick ass if I had to.

His smile was nearly impossible to resist. "I'll be a gentleman and say no."

A gentleman? Who described themselves that way anymore? "I could take a look under the hood."

"No need." The laughter in his gaze made him too damn likable. A flirt, but not the way I was used to. I could tell he thought I was attractive, but I didn't get the feeling he was about to pounce or say something offensive. He glanced at the hood of the car, which was no longer steaming, then back at me. In a more serious tone he said, "It's probably something simple. Besides, you don't want to get your hands dirty."

I could have told him I not only owned Decker Park but also worked on every car that came through our shop. My expertise was kind of a big deal in the car industry, but I held back. When dealing with the unknown, it was always best to retain the upper hand. "1970 Baur Cabriolet. It's probably a faulty thermostat."

"Switched it out last year." He searched my face. "You know about cars."

"A little." I waited for the patronizing tone men often used when speaking to a woman about something they thought men could do better.

He surprised me by looking genuinely pleased instead. "I've never been one to turn down help. Let's take a look." I joined him beside the hood of his car and dismissed the tingle that shot through me as his arm brushed against mine. It made sense that I was ultra-aware of this man—I didn't know him, and we were alone in a secluded area. What felt like attraction was more likely a healthy dose of I-don't-want-to-die-at-the-hands-of-a-stranger adrenaline.

My breath left me when he raised the hood and revealed what could only be described as a crime against all that was holy in the field of mechanics. Not only had he replaced the original parts, but many of the new bits were not even in the right location. "I've never seen anything quite like this."

In a proud tone, revealing that he'd completely missed the horror in mine, he said, "Right? Once I understood the basics of mechanics, I let myself get a little creative. So far so good. I'm impressed every time she gets me somewhere. Before her, I had never so much as changed a car's oil."

"I believe you." Fascinated, I leaned over the engine. How was it running at all? It wasn't that he'd replaced or repaired so many of the original parts; it was how he'd done it. On closer inspection a lot of his modifications weren't unsafe, but they weren't right either. I imagined how a doctor would feel if they ever met a patient with their stomach where their heart should be and vice versa. Could it work? Yes, but *why*? Despite all that was wrong, the reason for the overheating engine was simple. "You're in luck. Looks like your radiator hose let go."

"You're right," he said, chucking his shoulder against mine. "I love it when it's something I know how to fix. I'll give it a few more minutes to cool, clamp that baby back on, and I'll be on my way. Thanks."

"You're welcome." I gave him a long look as I tried to figure him out. He wasn't wearing a ring. That didn't mean he wasn't married. He found me attractive, but I also felt like I was being dismissed. *Not that I care. I decided long ago that I don't need to be in a relationship to be happy.* "I have an extra clamp in the trunk of my car if you need one."

He turned toward me. Casual. Confident. "I appreciate the offer, but my own trunk is stocked with everything short of a spare steering wheel. This is not our first breakdown."

I believed that as well. Our eyes met, and for a moment I forgot we were strangers. There really was something familiar about him. "Do you live in the area?" The question came out before I had a chance to think about how it would sound.

He wiggled his eyebrows. "Are you asking because you're hoping to see me again?"

"No," I answered as if the idea was ludicrous, then pressed my lips together. It had been a long time since I'd met someone who made me feel young and unsure. It was unsettling but also exciting. "I was going to suggest the name of a reliable tow service if it ends up you require one."

"Of course." My response hadn't lessened the smile in his eyes. "Well, then I'm from Connecticut, but only about an hour or so away. Not an impossible situation if a tow truck felt inclined to attempt the trip."

Clever little innuendo. I tipped my head to one side as my heart raced in my chest. How far was too far to drive for the promise in his gaze? I reminded myself that he likely already had someone in his life. "You don't have one you're loyal to back there?"

He cocked an eyebrow as if accepting an unstated challenge. "I don't, actually. I handle everything myself." After a pause, he raised a hand in protest and chuckled. "That time I was actually referring to not using a tow service."

This time I chuckled—I couldn't help it. "Whatever. No judgment."

"And you?"

"I—" My cheeks flushed, and I looked away. It would have been easy to take this to the next level. There was a time when I would have. I hadn't valued myself as much back then. What was it about this man that made him so difficult for me to walk away from? My phone buzzed then with a text from a friend at the event, warning that people were asking where I was. "I have to go. I'm already late."

He looked as if he wanted to say something, then changed his mind. "Thanks again for stopping to make sure I was okay."

I nodded. *Well, that's that, I guess.* "You're welcome." I turned and made it all the way to my car before giving in to an impulse and striding back to where he was still standing. "I'd feel better if you had my number just in case your car breaks down again on your way home."

He really did have the most amazing smile. "I'd feel better too." He took out his phone and went into his contacts.

I recited my number, then added, "McKenna."

He gave me an odd look, then typed my number in. My phone buzzed with a text message—from him. Christof.

We stood there for a moment, simply staring into each other's eyes. Man, those eyes. I would have bet my life I'd looked into them before. "Check all the hoses before you start her up again. If they're hard and brittle, you might want to replace all of them."

"Got it. Check my hoses."

I hesitated. His tone was playful, but he was still letting me go. It bothered me that I didn't want him to. My phone buzzed again. I texted back that I was on my way. "I really do have to go. Good luck."

"Thanks. You too."

I walked a few feet away, then looked over my shoulder. Our gazes met and held. I was someone who followed my instincts, but I couldn't justify them this time. Part of me wanted to ditch CamTech and help Christof fix his car. I imagined that leading to us sharing a meal . . . then possibly more. I shook my head. It was crazy to think this could go anywhere. "Don't use my number unless you break down."

He cocked his head to one side. "Okay."

Okay? Fine. I was being an idiot over someone I had nothing in common with. To prove it to myself, I asked, "What do you think of my ride?"

His gaze slid past me to a car anyone in my circle would be able to instantly identify. "Looks fast. Old."

"Do you know the year it was made?"

"Not a clue."

I'd figured as much. Definitive proof that we had nothing in common. I was about to turn away again when he called out, "Hey, what's my favorite board game?"

I searched his face. "There's no way I could know that."

"Unless you asked me and I told you. You have my number. Don't use it unless *you* break down." He was soft spoken, but the look he was giving me was all challenge. I wondered how that would play out in the bedroom.

"Not going to happen." I stood there, unable to leave, unwilling to give in to the urge to stay.

He leaned back against the door of his car. "Don't be surprised when you find yourself calling. Seven out of ten women find me irresistible."

A laugh burst out of me. *Seven out of ten?* The laughter released me from what felt like a spell. I opened my car door. "I'll fight the urge as long as I can. Have a safe trip home, Christof."

"Talk to you soon, McKenna," he said with a grin and a wave.

CHAPTER SEVEN

CHRISTOF

Now that was a woman a man could spend a long drive home thinking about. After reattaching the hose and getting Mack back on the road, I gave myself permission to grin.

She was definitely going to contact me.

Meeting on the side of the road hadn't been ideal. Had we met at a party or through friends, I would have come on stronger. She was drop-dead gorgeous in that tight little black dress, with enough curves to make it difficult to keep my blood above my waistline while talking to her. It felt wrong, though, to show too much interest while she was in a vulnerable position.

I smiled as I remembered how she'd claimed to know a hundred ways to end my ability to have children. Some women might have cursed as they made that threat, but she hadn't. My siblings would love her humor.

It wasn't that we didn't indulge in a bout of profanity now and then, but never around our parents. My brothers and I could have knockdown fights when we were younger and receive little more than a list of shared chores as a consequence, but if we let loose a swear in front of my mother—run. My father had a healthy fear of incurring my mother's wrath. I didn't consider that a bad thing.

Some men enjoyed helpless, clingy women, but I never had. Sebastian's first wife had built her life around his, and I'd endured many a drunken confession from him about how he regretted never asking her what she'd wanted. He saw their relationship in terms of where he'd failed Therese, but in my mind she'd failed him as well. She'd never stood up to him, never said she wanted more. Even that last day, the one he hated himself for, the day she'd asked him to go with her to her obstetrician and he'd chosen a business meeting instead—she could have stood her ground then. Sebastian would have caved. He'd loved her. We all had. Missing her didn't make me blind to how they hadn't been a good fit.

Sebastian's second wife, Heather, an accountant with her own business, was far from afraid of sharing her opinions, and he was a better man for it. Intelligent. Independent. She and her daughter had dragged my brother out of the darkness and back into the world of humanity.

Mauricio's wife was similar—an engineer. Brilliant. Confident enough to stand up to him when he got cocky. Best part? She saw the good in him, just didn't tolerate his bullshit. It was a beautiful thing to witness.

It was easy to imagine McKenna at my parents' table, laughing along with everyone. I wondered what she did for a living. Something with cars probably. A salesperson? No, she didn't give off that vibe at all. A mechanic? Nothing wrong with that, and it would explain how she'd seemed to know right away what was wrong with my car, but I had a feeling she was more than that. She came across as someone who was accustomed to being in charge.

My phone rang with a call from my father. Without wasting time on a greeting, he said, "Am I driving up to get you?"

"Sorry. I meant to call you back. I totally forgot. I'm about thirty minutes from my place."

"You know how your mother worries."

Dad was a worrier as well, but he liked to say it was all Mom. It wasn't like me to forget to update them, though. "I really am sorry, Dad. It won't happen again."

"It's okay. Just glad you got your car started. What was it this time?"

I told him. "Mom thinks I should get a new car, but—"

"Mack is important to you."

I nodded. "Exactly. *You* get it."

"Well, your mother wasn't there the night you met the woman you said 'spoke to your soul.'"

"The night I what?"

He chuckled. "I'm not surprised you don't remember. You were pretty wasted when you told me. Tequila has never been your friend."

"Seriously, Dad, are you making this up?"

He sighed. "Maybe some things are better forgotten."

Life had felt out of control after Therese's death, and I'd turned to alcohol more than once. Tragedies were not supposed to happen to the people I loved. I hadn't known how to deal with the loss of Therese or how it had changed the fabric of my family. I vaguely remembered waking up to my father sitting in a chair in my dorm room, looking so exhausted and concerned I never overindulged again. "No, tell me. I'm curious."

"Her name was Mack. You met her at some bar you were too young to be drinking at anyway. I've selectively forgotten most of the story you told me because there are some things parents don't want to know, but she stuck with me because she stuck with you."

Mack. McKenna. It had to be a coincidence. "What did she look like?"

"You never said. All you cared about was that she was keeping her father's car running to somehow keep him alive. You said you were both sad in the same way, but she said some things that echoed in your soul . . . no, touched it . . . something crazy like that. I thought it was just drunk ramblings, but a week later you bought a broken-down car and named it after her, so I guess she really did affect you."

Holy shit, was that how I'd chosen Mack's name? "Dad, I met a woman tonight—when I was on the side of the road because Mack's engine was overheating. Her name was McKenna. Could she be the same person?"

"Did she touch your soul again?"

I barked out a laugh. "No, Dad. Nothing so intense." But I'd felt a connection to her. I told him how she'd pulled over to make sure I was okay. "I gave her my number. If she calls, I'd definitely like to see her again."

"What did she think of your car?"

"I think Mack was why she stopped. She was driving an old stock car, maybe? I wish I'd asked her about it. It looked old enough to have been her father's car. Dad, what if it was her?"

"Did she say anything that sounded like she remembered you?"

I went over our conversation again with a fresh lens. "No."

"That might be a good thing. You were in rare form that night."

"Right. And you never saw her?" I knew the answer, but I asked anyway. I wanted there to be a glimmer of hope.

"She was gone by the time I picked you up from the bar. Probably left while you were sick in the bathroom." He cleared his throat. "Don't forget to text us when you get home."

"Will do." Before I hung up, there was something I had to say. "Thank you for always being there, Dad. It couldn't have been easy to sit with me like that when you also had Sebastian spiraling. At the time, I couldn't see past how the whole situation was affecting me, but I see it now. I know how lucky I am to have the family I do."

My father's tone thickened when he said, "Drive safely, Christof. I love you."

"Love you too, Dad."

After our call ended, I flexed my hands on the steering wheel and tried to remember the night my father had described. You'd think I'd be able to remember something about a woman who'd "touched my soul." Nothing.

Mack.

McKenna.

I hated that I couldn't remember more from that night in the bar. Not that it mattered if they were two different women. Hell, maybe it would be better if they were.

Later that evening, after updating my parents that I was safe, I lay in bed fighting a strong desire to send a text to the woman who was making it impossible for me to sleep.

I could open the door innocently simply by saying I'd made it home safely. No, too obvious. I'd agreed to only contact her if I broke down. My word was important to me.

Waiting would have been difficult before I'd spoken to my father, but now I had questions I couldn't answer on my own.

Your move, McKenna.

Text, call, smoke signal. I don't really care.

I need to see you again.

CHAPTER EIGHT

MCKENNA

The next day, I pulled to the side of our racetrack, undid my harness, and stepped out of the car I was testing for a client. Nothing like a few laps around the track to clear my head.

"Looked good. How did she feel?" Ty called out as he walked over.

"Smooth. So much better than she handled the first time. Marcus will be pleased."

"Going to keep your helmet on all day?" Ty joked.

"Oh." I unclasped it and took it off. "I forgot I had it on."

He gave me a long look. "Thank God you don't race. Something's on your mind, and whatever it is, behavior like that can get a man killed."

Swinging the helmet from my hand, I quipped, "Then it's a good thing I don't have a dick."

He laughed. "I'm not so sure about that."

I rolled my eyes at him. "Was there something you wanted, you know, besides simply to give me shit?"

He brought a hand up to his chest. "That stings. Yes, I have a question. Why is my phone blowing up with texts from some idiot named Jason and pics of his miniscule package?"

My mouth dropped open, and I slapped Ty's arm with the back of my hand. "He did not send you dick pics. You're making that part up."

With a bland expression, Ty pulled out his phone and scrolled through what could only be described as unflattering images of a semi-aroused penis. Eww. When I stopped laughing, I said, "He was all over me at the event last night. I was tempted to tell him off, but I know how important it is to be on my best behavior. Gross. I knew he was a creep."

"So you gave him *my* number?"

"Oh, come on, that's funny." The look on Ty's face had me holding my side and giving in to another fit of laughter. It didn't matter at all that he wasn't laughing along. "Giving your number instead of mine never gets old."

"Um-hum. You do know I tracked down the last creep you sent my way."

My mouth dropped open again. "You didn't."

"Don't worry, I made it look like an accident. You know how people slip and fall in bar bathrooms?"

That just killed some of the humor. "No, that's not a thing."

"Trust me, it happens. Only this time it was an accident that was accompanied by a lecture from me and my fist. He won't be asking random women to suck him dry anytime soon."

I made a face as I remembered the guy Ty was referring to. "I did not need to know the details of what he wrote."

Ty waved his now-dark screen in my direction. "One more text from this Jason idiot, and I'll give him the meeting he's asking for."

I put my hand on his. "I'm sorry, Ty. I thought it was funny. I won't give anyone else your number. Don't track this loser down. He's not worth it."

"I don't want any of these guys to hurt you, McKenna. That's all. I told your dad we'd watch over you." His eyes misted up.

Then mine did. "And you have. There's an asshole in every crowd, Ty. I just seem to attract them."

"You attract a variety of men, but you scare the good ones away."

I dropped his hand. "Good thing I'm not looking for a man, then."

"It's time you start thinking about not spending so much time alone."

"I'm far from alone. I have you, Cal, Wayne . . ."

"You know what I mean—someone your age."

I raised a hand in protest. "And for your information, I met a perfectly nice man yesterday who seemed quite interested in me and not at all afraid. He was an absolute gentleman. So much so I gave him *my* number instead of yours."

"Really? Have you heard from him?"

Under my breath, I said, "I told him not to call me."

"Excuse me? Not sure I got that right."

"I told him to only use my number if his car broke down again. It was overheating on the side of the road, so I pulled over to see if he needed help."

"McKenna Decker, look me in the eye and tell me you were not alone when you did that."

"He was harmless."

Ty let out a long breath. "You didn't know that. Anything could have happened."

His concern was genuine, and for the second time during that conversation, I was disappointed to have burdened Ty with unnecessary stress. In my mind he would always be larger than life—invincible— one of the heroes who'd swooped in to save me when I'd most needed saving. The reality was his hair was peppered with gray now and no one remained invincible forever. My father had taught me that.

We didn't speak for a moment. I would have apologized, but I didn't know where to start or where that conversation would take us. Ty was a proud man. How he felt mattered to me, and I didn't want to offend him.

"So does this perfectly nice man have a name?" Ty muttered.

"Christof."

"That's it?"

"That's as far as we got. Like I said, I stopped because his car had broken down. I helped him pinpoint the cause. A loose hose. Easy fix. I gave him my number in case it broke down again and went to the CamTech event."

"Okay, now this morning makes sense."

"What?"

"I was worried you blew off that conference call this morning because you were upset about this Jason creep. It's the opposite. You met someone."

"Oh, shit. I can't believe I forgot about the call this morning. Sorry."

"I handled it. We're good. You're allowed to have an off day."

No, I'm not. "Thanks for handling it. Anything I need to get on?"

"Nothing out of the norm. They scheduled some time on the track and asked if we'd look over their cars. They're 2020 models, but they'd still like to get your feedback anyway. You're building a solid reputation for yourself. Your dad would be proud of you."

I sniffed. "I hope so." We started to walk back to the garage together. "Do you ever wonder who we'd all be if he hadn't died? Would I be the same? Would I have gone into racing with him?"

"Hopefully he would have retired by now." Ty stopped and turned toward me. "Do you want to race? There's still time."

I gave his question real consideration. "I enjoy speed but not the competition part. No, I love what I do. I just wonder if—I don't know what's wrong with me today. I feel like there's something I'm missing."

"Or someone?" There was a twinkle in his eye.

"This isn't about Christof."

"Of course it isn't. *Christof.* The way you say his name gives me goose bumps."

I looked skyward for help before starting to walk again. "At least I know his name."

Ty laughed. We were about to enter the garage again when he said, "McKenna, promise me something."

"Sure."

"All joking aside, if you decide to meet up with this guy, I want his full name, address, blood type . . . everything."

"I probably won't contact him."

"You will. Just do this for me."

"You do know that I'm not a child anymore, right?"

"That doesn't mean I won't kill him if he hurts you."

Hands on hips, I turned toward Ty. "He's not going to hurt me because I probably won't even call him."

"Are you lying to me or yourself? I haven't seen you this distracted—ever."

Distracted.

It was a trigger word for me. I smacked Ty's arm again. "You're wrong. I couldn't care less about this guy." See, I hadn't even used his name because he didn't matter.

Ty laughed. "Whatever. Just get me his info."

CHAPTER NINE

CHRISTOF

Sunday dinners were a big thing in my family. Before my youngest brother, Gian, had started at Johns Hopkins in Baltimore, they'd happened only at the home of my parents. Yet for Gian, to prove to him that he was as essential to our family as any of us, we flew down to dine with him. At first we'd rented places, but last Christmas Mauricio had bought a home near the school as a gift for my parents. He'd said it was a practical choice so Gian wouldn't have to live on campus.

Yes, because an eight-bedroom mansion was exactly what every premed student wanted to wander through alone. Gian already had zero social life. He needed more connections, not fewer.

Not that Gian had voiced a protest. He wouldn't.

I wished he would.

Just like I thought we should talk about his biological mother instead of pretending she wasn't my mother's sister. The little I knew was that Aunt Rosella had been mentally unstable and had given Gian to our mother to raise. Her name was not uttered in our home.

Could talking about her lessen how much her desertion affected Gian? I didn't know.

He was one of us, regardless of how it had come to be. If I could give him one gift, it would be confidence in that. Sebastian, Mauricio, and I had all been brats at one time or another. We'd all broken the rules, challenged our parents, fought with each other. Gian never felt secure enough to test the boundaries of our parents' patience. He'd never told any of us to get out of his life, sadly because a part of him thought we might one day do just that.

What Gian was still too young to understand was that family was more resilient than that. Ours wasn't perfect. My brothers and I were each very different people and could get on each other's nerves, but if any of us needed anything, we were right there.

"Do you feel ready for your exams?" my mother asked Gian as she passed him a basket of fresh garlic bread.

"As ready as I'll ever be. I'll do a final review tonight, but I think I'm solid." He took a piece and placed it on his plate before holding the basket out for our little niece. "Ava?"

"Yes, please," she said politely as she reached for one. "Mommy, can I have two?"

Heather shook her head. "Start with one."

Ava's bottom lip protruded a little. "But I really like bread, and if I have to throw one, I won't have one."

I choked on a laugh.

"We don't throw food," Heather said firmly.

Five going on fifteen, Ava waved a hand in the air like my father, and in a tone purely Sebastian's, she asked, "Has she met this family?"

There was a roar of laughter around the table that brought a grin of satisfaction to Ava's face. Attempting a stern expression, Sebastian said, "*She* is your mother and the one who decides your bedtime, so perhaps we should keep our food on our own plates this time."

Ava wrinkled her nose but seemed cheerful enough as the basket moved on to the next person, with her only receiving the piece meant for her stomach.

I leaned forward and lowered my voice. "I've got your back, Ava. I'll take two when it comes around to me. One for me and a spare for you if you need it."

She and I high-fived across the table.

"You shouldn't encourage her," my mother scolded with a smile. To Ava, she added, "Your uncles spent a lot of time doing extra chores together because they thought they could make their own rules. If I see so much as a crumb fly today, they'll be doing the dishes—by hand."

Ava's eyes rounded. "All of them? Even my dad?"

Sebastian gave a solemn nod. "Even me. So let's be on our best behavior, or you'll end up in the kitchen with us."

Sitting up straighter, Ava said, "I'd love that."

Heather intervened. "You and Dad can do the dishes at our house anytime you want."

"Really?" Ava asked in a hopeful tone. "Dad, you hear that? Me and you and mountains of soap."

"Sounds wonderful," Sebastian said in an indulgent tone that warmed my heart. He'd wanted a family for so long, and seeing him with one made me wonder what it would be like to have a wife and child of my own.

I looked around the table. Mauricio and his wife were happily chatting with Gian about his upcoming schedule. Dad leaned over to Mom, whispered something to her that brought a smile to her lips. Sebastian's hand was intertwined with Heather's.

The road to where we were hadn't been an easy one, and tough times were sure to come again, but this was what was important. Not Romano Superstores' profit margin. Not our soaring net worth. In this moment it was easy to believe my father's claim that one store, some wine, and his family were all he needed to be happy.

Mauricio's voice brought me back to the moment. "So Mom said you met someone."

His wife, Wren, took his hand in hers. "He might not want to talk about it."

Grinning ear to ear, he winked at Ava and said, "Has she met this family?"

Ava burst into giggles.

Our father smiled in approval. My mother shook her head, but she was smiling as well.

I sighed. It probably would have been more of a shock if my father had told no one about McKenna. How much he'd told them, I was about to find out. "If by 'met' you mean 'had one brief conversation with,' yes."

"Have you heard from her?" Heather asked.

"Does she really know how to fix cars?" Ava chimed in with excitement. "I want to do that when I grow up."

My head snapped around toward my niece. "How do *you* know about her?"

"Children know everything," Ava said, parroting back a phrase she'd likely heard the adults around her say. She stage-whispered, "Sometimes I pretend I'm asleep. I can hear even with my eyes closed."

"Good to know," I said, then raised my eyebrows in the direction of her parents. Heather made a pained, apologetic face. Sebastian shrugged but added a side nod that I interpreted as saying he'd move forward with more care now that he was aware of her stealthy ways.

Propping her head on both hands, her eyes wide, Ava asked, "Did she really touch your soul?"

"Dad," I said in protest. "You know I'm not even positive it's the same woman."

"It seemed relevant to the story," my father said in defense.

"How did she do it?" Ava persisted. "How did she touch it?"

I didn't want to tread on anything her parents were teaching her, so I kept my explanation vague. I pointed to my chest. "What that means is she said something so beautiful I will keep it here with me forever."

"What did she say?" Ava asked slowly.

Heather put a hand on her daughter's shoulder. "Ava, why don't you tell everyone about what you brought to school for show-and-tell last week?"

Ava pursed her lips and held my gaze. She'd also joined our family in an unconventional way. First Heather had adopted her, and then, after they'd married, Sebastian had as well. None of that prevented me from seeing a lot of Romano in her.

"I don't mind," I said. My family hadn't remained as close as we were by staying out of each other's business. One day, when Ava brought her first boyfriend home and I grilled him mercilessly, this would come full circle. Slowly, parts of the conversation I'd had with Mack were coming back to me. Not enough to know for sure if she was the same woman I'd met the day before, but enough to remember how easily we'd connected. "It was about her father. He died, but the way she keeps him alive in her heart is by keeping his car running."

"Like Wolfie." Ava picked up the stuffed animal that she had laid on the floor by her feet like a sleeping dog. "He keeps my first mom with me."

Heather put her arm around her daughter.

Sebastian bent and kissed Ava's head.

"Exactly like that," I said.

My mother cleared her throat. "I finally understand Mack. You could have said something."

I met my father's gaze. It seemed that he'd left off the part where I'd been too drunk to remember it. I could have hugged him for it.

Mauricio cut in. "I can't believe you don't know if this McKenna is the same woman. There's something you're not telling us. If someone affected me that much, I'd remember what they looked like."

Wren wagged a finger at her husband. "Not necessarily. It's been, what, seven years? I think it's romantic."

"And she didn't recognize you?" Mauricio asked.

"Not that she said," I confirmed.

Mauricio reached for the basket of bread. "It's not the same woman."

My father picked up a plate of antipasto and held it while my mother chose from it. "I believe it is. Have I ever told you the story of how I bought your mother with a cow?"

The slice of bread that bounced off his head was thrown by the only person none of us would chastise. Not even Ava.

Mom winked and said, "Christof, would you mind passing the basket around again?"

With humor and flair, my father moved his piece of bread to her plate. "No need. What's mine is yours, my love. Even if you choose to use it as a projectile."

"Papa," Ava asked, "did you really buy Nona with a cow?"

My father opened his mouth to say something while my mother's eyebrows rose in expectation.

"I'll take this one," Sebastian said. "Nona's family had a farm in Italy. Their cow was old and wasn't giving milk anymore. Papa wanted to do something for Nona's family that would help them, so he bought them a cow as a present. He likes to tease Nona and say it was a trade, but it was just a gift. Like when I give Mom flowers."

While Ava was digesting his explanation, my phone buzzed with a message. Normally I would have ignored it. Phones didn't belong at the Sunday dinner table. I couldn't resist, though, so off to the side I sneaked a look at my message.

Hoping you made it home safely. It was from McKenna. I nearly dropped my phone and, while righting myself, knocked my knee against the table loudly enough to call everyone's attention to me.

"So is it her?" Mauricio asked.

"It is," I answered, bringing the phone above the table.

Wren chimed in. "The first text from her since you met again? This is so exciting."

Mauricio smiled. "If you need any advice, I'm gifted with an above-average ability to understand the female mind."

Not about to let that one slide by, Wren said, "Is that a fact, Mauricio? What am I thinking right now?"

He shot her his most charming smile, the one that used to melt the hearts of women and make them stupid. Nothing. Only when his grin turned sheepish did she smile back.

My mother must have really wanted grandchildren because she said, "Step away from the table if you need a moment, Christof."

I rose to my feet to do just that. I was excited but reminded myself to keep my cool. It was unusual to feel so much, one way or another, about a woman I knew next to nothing about. "I'll be right back."

"Take all the time you need," my father said. I wasn't yet out of earshot when he added, "I hope he doesn't botch this. I really think she could be the one."

"I can hear you, Dad," I called back from the doorway. "And you're making this into a bigger deal than it needs to be. She's just checking that I'm okay."

Stuffed animal still in her arms, Ava ran from her chair to my side and gave my waist a tight hug. "Good luck, Uncle Christof. Do you want me to go with you?"

I ruffled her hair. "Thanks. I've got this."

"Come back to the table, Ava," Heather said.

"But Mom, this is important. She's already *in his heart*," Ava said, pointing to her chest.

Heather took Ava by the hand to lead her away. "He'll be fine, Ava. Sorry, Christof."

Ava's concern was so sincere I bent at my knees until I was eye level with her. Regardless of how my phone call went with McKenna, Ava's concern reminded me that I already had an amazing life. "You know why I'm not worried, Ava?"

She was all eyes. "Why?"

I ruffled her hair again. "Because I believe if we are good to each other and do our best, we all end up where we're meant to be."

"Like me."

Ava was an example of something good coming out of a tragedy. Her first mother had been taken away so young. Heather had stepped in, though, and shown her so much love she'd become a remarkable, resilient little girl none of us could have imagined our family without. I tapped her nose lightly. "Just like you."

A slow smile spread across Ava's face. "Is she pretty?"

"So pretty. But she's something even more important than that."

"What?"

"She's the kind of person who helps someone even when she doesn't know them. Smart and brave. That's more important than pretty."

Ava gave my hand a squeeze. "I hope you marry her, Christof."

"First let's see if she'll agree to meet me for dinner."

"Tell her there'll be cake. Everyone loves cake."

I chuckled and straightened. "I'll keep that in mind."

With that I walked out of the house and into the sunshine as I tried to remember something, anything, from the night I might have first met her.

I reread her message and hesitated before responding. Really, none of it was a big deal. In fact, the whole situation should have felt a bit ridiculous.

Why didn't it?

I chose my first response carefully. I did. Thank you. You were right, it was as simple as reattaching the hose.

Her answer came back immediately. I'm glad.

When she didn't write anything more, I did. I was hoping to hear from you.

You were?

I wasn't used to not knowing what to say to a woman, but I didn't want to "botch" this, as my father had said. I started with a topic I hoped would put her at ease—something we had in common. I'm considering replacing my car's engine. Do you think it'll lower the value of my car?

Yours? No.

I found one that might work. I've been reading about how to do it, and it sounds complicated, but I think I can figure it out, although I might need help.

Are you asking for a mechanic referral?

No, I plan to do it myself—in my garage. I'm inviting you to work on it with me.

When she didn't immediately answer, I wondered if I'd played my cards wrong. Maybe she wasn't as into cars as she'd seemed. I should have led with an invitation to dinner.

You're asking me to drive down to your house and work on your car with you? In your garage?

Put like that, it sounded less like a date and more like a creepy, time-consuming chore. You're right. Bad idea. Let's start over. I'd love to take you out to dinner. Are you free this weekend?
Nothing.
Shit.

CHAPTER TEN

McKENNA

Alone on the porch of the home I'd built in Decker Park, I sat against the railing and tried to sort through my reaction to Christof's invitations. I was reasonably certain he didn't know who I was. It wasn't like I was famous, at least not outside the NASCAR world, so the likelihood that he was angling to take advantage of my expertise was slim.

He hadn't pushed for my number or even to see me again.

Over the past two days I'd thought about our brief exchange a telling number of times. At first I'd dismissed him as too different from me, too conservative, harmless. He should have been easy to forget.

He wasn't.

Twice Ty had caught me standing in the garage, simply smiling, and ribbed me about it. I could brush off the teasing, but last night before he'd left, Ty had said there'd only been one woman who'd ever put a stupid grin on his face, and he still regretted not understanding how rare that connection was.

I'd asked what her name was.

After a long pause, in a thick voice he'd said, "Zoe. I looked for her a few years ago and learned she'd died of breast cancer. And you know what my first thought was? I wish we'd been together so I could have helped her through that. How fucked up is that?"

If we were the hugging type, I would have hugged him then. We weren't, though, so I'd nodded and agreed that life didn't make sense.

I didn't know what it was about Christof that called to me. It could have been that, rather than with the swagger the men in my world often exhibited, his confidence had shone in the ease of his smile, the openness of his expression. He didn't go on and on trying to impress me. I liked that. He was one of those rare people who were comfortable in their own skin, and it made me wonder how he'd gotten to that place.

My father had been that kind of humble. Off the racetrack, he didn't tell people what he did. He raced because he loved the sport. He won because he took racing seriously and surrounded himself with people who were in it for the same reasons. I admired a man who could be good at something without feeling the need to tell everyone how great he was.

It was more than that, though.

On some level I couldn't begin to understand, I felt like I'd just met a man I could be myself with, a man who might one day love me but, more importantly, had the capacity to *like* me.

How the hell had I gotten all that out of exchanging phone numbers over his broken-down car?

He might not have been at all the way he seemed.

For all I knew, he lured all his victims to his garage.

A safer choice would have been to agree to meet him for dinner.

Help him change out an engine? I didn't have time for something like that.

He probably jacked his car up with cinder blocks.

Amateur mechanics could get seriously hurt trying to change out an engine.

I was still debating what to answer when another text came through from him. There'll be cake.

What? I laughed out loud. Was that his go-to move? I had to admit it was unique. I do like cake.

Then say yes.

No to dinner. I'd rather see your garage, but—

But it's a long drive.

Yes.

And you don't know me well enough to want to be alone at my house with power tools.

I laughed again. It's like you're reading my mind.

And who wants to eat cake while working on a car?

You're making all my points for me.

I have the perfect solution, but you'll have to trust me with your address. Before you think it, I'm not suggesting bringing my car to you. I want to send you something to eat while we FaceTime.

Okay, I'll play along. Chocolate or vanilla? Would he know my preference?

Funny thing about me—I'm not really a mind reader. The only way I can deliver what you want is if you're brave enough to tell me what you like.

Brave? My breath caught in my throat. He wasn't just talking about cake. I'd never been with anyone so straightforward. No games? No crazy dance around each other as we tried to figure out what the other person was thinking?

Could a relationship be that simple?

I like ice cream cake. Especially whatever that chocolate crunchy layer is.

Perfect. All I need now is an address and a time.

I texted him my address before I had time to change my mind, then told him I was free on Wednesday afternoon. Or evening if that worked better.

Let's do four o'clock so there is still good lighting. I'll call you. We can start by looking at my setup, come up with a list of anything I should purchase for this project, and then I'll show you the engine I'm considering buying.

Sounds good. Talk to you then.

Looking forward to it.

Me too.

CHAPTER ELEVEN

CHRISTOF

All conversation ended when I walked back into the dining room. I retook my seat before putting my family out of their misery. "We have a phone date on Wednesday."

"A *phone* date?" Sebastian asked as if I were speaking a foreign language.

I picked up my cutlery and sliced into my chicken. "We're going to work on my car together, over the phone. It'll give us time to get to know each other before going out on an in-person date."

"That sounds sweet," Heather interjected.

"Or a waste of time. I would just drive up to see her," Mauricio said with a shake of his head.

Wren hugged her husband's arm. "Let your brother do this his way. If she said yes, she must have liked the idea."

Although I appreciated the support of my sisters-in-law, it wasn't necessary. My brothers and I often disagreed, but that was another way we remained close. We never had to wonder what the others were thinking. And thankfully, there was no expectation of following the advice that was so freely given.

There was someone I did need to thank, though. "Hey, Ava, the cake idea was brilliant. It was touch and go there for a minute, but I told her there'd be cake, and she said yes."

"I knew it!" Ava exclaimed.

The amusement-filled lull that followed was broken by my mother saying, "I also have news. I was invited to a high tea fundraising event on Martha's Vineyard by the queen of Vandorra. I didn't know there was such a thing, but apparently our family made the list. Would anyone like to come with me?"

Not surprising. Money was money. Tea with royalty, though? Hard pass for me and, if my brothers' expressions were anything to go by, for them as well.

"I love tea parties," Ava said. "Mommy, can we go? Please?"

Heather asked, "Are children welcome?"

My mother smiled at Ava. "I'll tell them we can only attend if you can come too."

"You really mean it?" Ava asked with wonder.

My mother reached around my father and took her granddaughter's hand in hers. "We Romanos stick together."

"Then consider me and Ava in," Heather said with a huge smile. Sebastian truly had chosen well.

"I'd love to go as well," Wren added. "I've never been to a high tea. Sounds fun."

"I would," I said, "but I have a thing that day."

"Yes, me too," Sebastian added.

Mauricio chimed in, "The kind of thing we all wish we could get out of but sadly cannot."

Only Gian remained silent.

With a chuckle my father said, "I'd love to go as well, Camilla, but I can't leave my sons on their own to handle this thing."

"Really?" My mother made a tsk sound. "You're lucky I adore all of you. Gian, would you like to come?"

I tossed a napkin his way. "He can't; I need his help that day."

The smile Gian shot me was full of gratitude.

"Well, then it's just the ladies." My mother beamed.

Conversation flowed easily after that. Later, we helped clean up, then moved to sit outside to watch Ava play fetch on the lawn with my parents' dog, Sara. My father joined me on the steps of the house.

"I like that you're taking it slowly with this one, Christof. Friendship is a good foundation for any relationship."

"This might go nowhere, Dad."

"I have a feeling about this one."

I shot him a side glance. "Shouldn't I be the one saying that?"

"You already have . . . in every way that matters."

"Sorry?"

"Whether you see it or not, you've already brought this one home. She matters to us because she matters to you."

I leaned forward, resting my elbows on my knees as my father's words sank in. McKenna's name wasn't the first my family had brought up in question at the table, but I always shut down those conversations as soon as they began. Sometimes with a joke, other times simply by moving on to another topic. I'd included my family in this relationship before it even was one. The realization spooked me a little.

My father continued, "Of all of my sons, you're most like me. Do you know how I met your mother?"

"You both lived in the same town in Italy."

"Yes, and we were friends. I asked her out a hundred times, and she turned me down. I wasn't the best-looking man in town, the richest, or even the smartest, but I loved her."

I straightened and gave my father a long look. "Is this you breaking it to me that I'm ugly as sin?"

He chuckled. "Not at all. I'm agreeing that friendship is a good place to start. Life can throw you some unexpected zingers, knock both of you to your knees, but if you are also friends, you help each other back up and go on—together."

I wasn't sure why he was saying this now, but I nodded because I didn't know what he wanted me to say.

He wasn't done yet. "People have this idea that love has to be perfect to work. It doesn't. It has to be strong enough to survive the imperfections."

"I'll remember that." I stood. "Thanks, Dad."

"Your brothers mean well, but trust your instincts."

"I will, Dad."

"And don't take too much advice from Ava. I'm pretty sure she still eats her boogers."

I coughed on a laugh. "Duly noted. Thanks for the pep talk, Dad, but I've got this."

After a moment, he added, "It doesn't really matter if she's the same woman you met before, but I hope she is."

"Me too."

CHAPTER TWELVE

McKenna

It had unexpectedly taken me a long time to decide what to wear to my phone date with Christof. I considered wearing my coveralls, but they all had the Decker Park logo on them, and I wasn't ready to divulge that much yet. I'd fought back an urge to wear a dress, which, once I realized why, was even more unsettling. My heart was racing at the idea of seeing him again, and I wanted him to be just as affected. In the end I settled on jeans, a plain T-shirt, hair down in loose curls, and just the right amount of makeup to appear I wasn't trying.

I paced my house while waiting for his call, all the while telling myself that I was okay with however it turned out. If he called and we got along—great. If he forgot to call—that was fine too. I didn't know him. There was a good chance that by the end of the call, we'd both have discovered that there really wasn't anything between us.

And that was okay.

I strode into my kitchen. It was bright, open, perfect for a video call. When my phone buzzed, I took a deep breath before answering and holding it up to my face. "Hi."

His smile was just as open and warm as I remembered. "This still a good time?"

I swallowed hard. "Sure. I was just—" God, I'd never been good at lying. I couldn't think of another thing I might have been doing besides waiting for his call.

"You're going to think this is crazy, but I'm actually nervous."

"You are?" *Nervous* wasn't exactly how I'd describe the way my body warmed and hummed as I looked into his eyes.

"My garage has always been my sanctuary. It's my happy place. I've never shared it with anyone before."

I laughed at what I thought was a joke, but when I saw real concern in his eyes, I sobered. "Then I'm honored to be invited in."

"Did you get the cake?"

I opened the fridge and took out the piece that I had cut to defrost. "Right here."

"Okay, then here goes." He opened a door, put on a light, and flipped the image on the phone so I could see the room. I expected to see a dangerous disaster of a space, but my mouth rounded as I took in how clean and organized it was. A painted gray floor, an impressive car lift, chrome shelving. It was a garage I would have easily chosen for myself if my business didn't require a hangar-size building.

His equipment was top of the line. A person could run an actual car-repair shop from the setup he had. I squinted at something in the corner of the room. "What is that?"

"What?" he asked.

"Next to the cabinet on the left. It looks like . . . a robotic arm?" It was impressive in size as well, the kind you'd find on a car assembly line.

He flipped the camera view back and grinned at me. "A gift from my brother Mauricio's friends. They're all technology geeks. They send me all kinds of gadgets that don't work on older cars."

"I'm sorry, back to the robotic arm. What do you use it for?"

"Surprisingly less than you'd think. It's programmable, but all I've used it for is to get me a beer, and I'm not a big drinker."

Enthralled, I sat down at my counter, propped my phone against a vase, and dug my fork into the ice cream cake. His garage was a complete surprise, in some ways more advanced than my own. "I'm impressed. Show me everything."

His smile widened, and he wiggled his eyebrows. "Easy there, tiger. Let's leave some mystery for our second phone date."

I smiled. "Definitely." Then took a bite of my cake. Delicious. I savored it on my tongue just like I wanted to savor getting to know Christof. Talking with him felt that good.

A second phone date. Yes, I could see that happening.

Curiosity got the best of me. "I have to ask. How long have you been working on cars?"

"Since college." He began to walk around his garage again, continuing the visual tour while talking. "I went to school in Providence. Ever been there?"

I felt like I was reaching for a dream I wanted to hold on to, but only bits and pieces remained. "Once, when I was twenty."

He changed the camera view again so we were facing each other. "I took college seriously, more than my other siblings. I knew the sacrifices my oldest brother made to pay my tuition. I was still in college when his first wife died, and I didn't know how to handle it. My family was always where I found my strength. When they started falling apart, I did as well. Then one night I met this woman at a bar . . ."

I got goose bumps, and for a moment I was transported back in time. "I remember you."

"Let me start by apologizing for anything stupid I might have said that night. I was pretty drunk."

The sophisticated man I'd met on the side of the road bore little resemblance to the boy I'd met in a bar seven years earlier. "You weren't stupid; you were sad. And then sick. Your father picked you up from the bar. Tell me you're no longer friends with the people you were with that night."

"They fell to the wayside after college."

"Good." I had to know. "Did you recognize me yesterday?"

He made a pained face. "No. I don't remember much about that night in the bar."

"But you remember me?"

"Yes and no." He looked so uncomfortable with the question I almost felt bad about asking it. "My father remembered you first. Apparently I told him about you."

Interesting. I didn't know if I should be insulted that he'd forgotten me or flattered that he'd spoken about me enough that his father remembered me.

"Your name was Chris," I said.

"It was a phase. I was born in Italy, and I thought Americanizing my name would help me blend in better."

"Is blending in important to you?"

"Not anymore. I wish I could go back and tell my twenty-year-old self that so much that I thought was important doesn't really matter."

"I completely understand that." Something occurred to me. "You could have lied about not remembering me. I wouldn't have known."

"I would have."

I was drawn again to his quiet confidence. Boasting was the tactic most guys I met used to lure me in. Christof was the real deal. The elusive nice guy. I'd heard they existed but hadn't yet met one who wasn't already taken. "You're not married, are you?"

"Would I be looking to date you if I were?"

"Maybe, so the question stands."

"Wow, okay, fair enough. I'm single. If you require more proof than that . . . I guess I could give you my mother's number. She definitely wouldn't lie for me."

I chuckled at that. "That sounds like a bluff if I ever heard one. What would you do if I took you up on it?"

"I've got nothing to hide. If you want to pause our date to have a two-hour conversation with an overly protective Italian mother who will probably start calling you daily to check in once she has your number, that's on you. My parents are amazing people, but they have a flexible concept of boundaries. Don't tell my mother you're hungry if you don't want her to show up with more food than you could eat in a week."

A mother like that was so foreign to how I'd grown up I couldn't imagine it. Even my father, whom I held in my mind as an above-average parent, hadn't been what one would call nurturing. Had I called him and told him I was hungry, he would have asked me if my arms were broken, and we would have laughed.

I tried to imagine me cooking for children of my own and couldn't. My refrigerator was full of one-step dishes or leftovers from restaurants. Was it wrong that I was half-tempted to actually call Christof's mother and claim I was starving just to experience what it was like to have someone show up with a bunch of Tupperware full of food? "Do you cook?"

"Yes, but don't tell my brothers. Mom only had boys, and a lot of her recipes were orally passed down from generation to generation. She'd been teaching Therese before . . . well, anyway, over the years I've compiled them into a database and learned the little tricks and tips that are essential for them to come out like she makes them. I don't want to brag, but I've cooked for my friends, and one of them circled back when he opened a restaurant of his own and offered to buy my recipes. I refused because . . . I guess you could say I'm the keeper of the family secrets."

"How many siblings do you have? You've mentioned two so far."

"Three brothers: Sebastian and Mauricio are older than I am. Gian is nineteen and studying at Johns Hopkins. My parents are thrilled that we'll have a doctor in the family in time for when they start to need one. Two sisters-in-law, Heather and Wren. One niece and two more babies on the way. How about you? Big family? Small one?"

As he spoke, I remembered more and more from our first conversation, and a warm happiness spread through me. "When you mentioned your older brother, you said he'd lost his first wife. Does that mean he's remarried?" I wanted him to be. I wanted to believe we'd all made it past our sadness.

"He did."

I blinked back happy tears, and my lips quivered. "I've thought about you and your family over the years, and when I did, I always hoped you were able to get him out of the dark place he'd gone to."

"It wasn't me," Christof said. "His smile returned when he met Heather and her adorable daughter, Ava."

I didn't argue with him about it, but my gut told me Sebastian wouldn't have been a man anyone would choose to be with if Christof hadn't stuck by him. "Did you finish school?"

"Yes, although I did spend a lot more time with my family after that drunken night. Why do I have a feeling it had something to do with meeting you?"

My mouth dried as snippets from our conversation echoed in my head. "We talked about a lot of things."

"You told me my brother couldn't fail with someone like me on his side." His voice became thick. "I needed to hear that because at the time I thought we'd both already failed each other."

I nodded, unable to speak for a moment. It was the perfect time to tell him about Decker Park and the part he'd played in encouraging me to make it a reality. I opened my mouth to but ended up closing it again without saying a word.

I didn't know exactly what held me back—fear?

A smile returned to his face. "You kissed me."

I looked down at my ice cream and swirled my fork around in it. "No. *You* kissed *me*."

"Either way, it was spectacular."

I scoffed at that. "And yet somehow forgettable."

He didn't have an immediate answer for that one. After a moment, he cleared his throat. "I remember you drove your father's car because it was a way to feel close to him."

"I still do." He did remember. My gaze flew back to his image on the phone. The connection I'd felt to him the first time we'd met pulsed between us. It was different, though. He wasn't drunk, and we weren't both reeling from a loss. This time there was a primal attraction unlike anything I'd felt before.

"I might have forgotten meeting you, but you stayed with me."

"Really?" I didn't want bullshit from him, but he sounded sincere, and I wanted to believe him.

"Something that made no sense to me before is clear now. A week after we met, I bought a broken-down car, had it towed to my parents' garage, and have been working on it ever since."

"So I inspired your inner mechanic?"

"No, you inspired me. I worked on that car instead of going to the bar with my friends. It made a real difference in what I could handle at home."

Had my words of encouragement really moved him as much as his had moved me? "I'm glad."

"I named her Mack."

"Your . . . *that* car?"

"I know—right? I think she was my way of keeping you close."

I dropped my fork on the table. My throat thickened with emotion. I would have bet my life he meant every word he was saying. What did a woman even say to that? "Wow."

"You're not married, are you?"

Fighting to regain my composure, I shook my head, picked up my fork, and waved it at him. "I'm not, but my crew *would* lie for me. I'd say you could test that, but I recently promised not to give out their phone numbers to any more men."

"I sense a story . . ."

Holy shit, he named his car after me.

Panic set in. It was too much, too soon. I barely believed in love. I definitely didn't believe something this powerful could be real. I forced sarcasm into my voice and mimicked his words from earlier. "Easy there, tiger. Let's leave some mystery for our second phone date." I reminded myself that I was too practical to be swayed by the heat in his gaze. "Show me the rest of this garage of yours. We did say we'd come up with a list of what you need to purchase, but I bet you already have everything you need."

"I used to think so," he said while holding my gaze. "Not anymore."

Had he been there, I would have been in his arms. Maybe it would have been a mistake. Maybe not. Either way, I couldn't have fought the need he lit inside me.

If the situation frustrated him, it didn't show in his expression. He smiled again. "What do you know about programming? You could also help me figure out that robotic arm."

Yes, that was much safer than discussing how much I wanted to strip off his shirt and lick him from neck to navel. "Did you really name your car after me?"

"Ask my mother."

"Is that your answer to everything?"

"I'd suggest my father, but lately he's worse than she is when it comes to trying to marry me off. All sense of boundaries is a thing of the past. My brother met someone, told my father about her, and let's just say they're lucky they were able to work it out."

"What did he do?"

For the next several minutes Christof described how Mauricio had gone to Paris to help a friend but ended up meeting Wren and falling in love. Circumstances had separated them, but, according to Christof, anyway, nothing that they wouldn't have worked out. Unfortunately, Basil Romano, Christof's father, had hired Wren to inspect their sprinkler system and had lured Mauricio there so they'd see each other again. "Then Mauricio accused Wren of only deciding she wanted to see him again after she found out he had money, and it all went downhill after that."

"Oh my God. What an ass."

"In that moment, yes, but not in general. And they figured it out. I was there for that explosive moment, so I have ammunition for when Mauricio thinks I'm being a jerk. In that way, I guess, my father did me a favor."

"They really worked it out?"

"They're married. Happily. They have a start-up company that designs prosthetic arms. Kind of like what I have, I guess, but much, much smaller."

"Wow. I'm impressed. Hang on . . . Romano. Romano Superstores?"

"That's us."

It was a huge store chain and growing. Which meant he was rich. Some might see that as a plus. I met men with money on a regular basis, and it didn't impress me. Most of them let it give them an inflated sense of importance. "So you work for your family's company."

"You sound disappointed that I might."

"I'm not. It makes sense that you would," I lied. I *was* disappointed. He came across as someone who made his own way in life, played by his own rules . . . but maybe that was just what he did under the hood of his car. "Do you enjoy it?"

"I don't allow myself to feel one way or another about it. I'm who they need me to be. For a while I was in accounting, to make sure our books were solid. As we grew, I maintained the ground floor stuff. Hiring for new stores. Coordinating management. Writing policy. Mauricio stepped down from the company, and Sebastian is hanging closer to home with his new wife. They're expecting their second child anytime now. So until the dust settles, I'm on the road scouting out potential preexisting stores to partner with."

Christof made his role in Romano Superstores sound like it wasn't a big deal, but it was a multibillion-dollar company. I had to ask. "Sounds like it doesn't leave much time for you to follow your own dreams."

He shrugged. "Or maybe I'm exactly where I want to be."

"Secretly cooking with your mother." It was an asshole thing to say. I cringed, unsure of why I had gone there. Was it because before he'd entered my life again, I would have said the same thing he had? I didn't like how being with him made me wonder if there wasn't more.

Another man might have been insulted, but Christof simply cocked his head to one side. "Are you giving me shit? On our first date?"

I could have apologized. Maybe I should have, but I grinned instead. "Hold on—you're not a first-date shit giver? Christof, you're too nice for me."

His gaze remained warm and steady. "I don't believe that. I think we were meant to meet again."

His words hung there in a heavily sexually charged moment. I wanted this to be real even as a part of me fought against it. Snarky retorts came to me, but I held them back.

I remembered what Ty had said about me scaring nice men away. What did I want to do . . . spend the rest of my life with men who were so crude Ty felt the need to hunt them down? *Christof might be my chance to get it right.* I wasn't sure I was ready for what he represented.

"If I were there," he said in a husky tone, "I'd kiss that frown right off your face."

Heat seared through me. "I'd let you."

We both took a moment to soak that in.

My phone beeped with a call from Cal. When I didn't answer, he called back. "I should take this."

"What are you doing tomorrow night?" he asked.

My breath caught in my throat. "What do you have in mind?" In that moment I would have said yes to almost anything.

"Phone date two?"

I let out a breath, torn between excitement and disappointment. "Yes. But at seven?"

"Perfect. Talk to you tomorrow."

"Talk to you then."

As the call ended, I saw my face reflected on the screen. I was—glowing.

I returned Cal's call and discovered his persistence wasn't due to an emergency. It wasn't even related to the car they'd just purchased and were shipping up. No, Cal and Wayne had spoken to Ty and now wanted to hear all about Christof.

I didn't know where to begin, so I told them everything.

CHAPTER THIRTEEN

CAMILLA ROMANO, CHRISTOF'S MOTHER

High tea with a royal flair and white-glove service was a first for Camilla. The garden with a view of the ocean had small tables that were spread out in a manner that allowed a large group of women to each enjoy an intimate atmosphere. Camilla had grown up on a small farm in Italy, married a man she'd gone to school with, and never yearned for more than time with him and her four children.

She looked around the table at the newest additions to her family. Heather and little Ava were both smiling and comparing their thoughts on the finger sandwiches. Wren was studying the mechanics of her fancy tea infuser. Knowing that they were enjoying themselves was all that mattered.

Hers was a better life than she sometimes felt she deserved, but she did what she could to honor it. In the beginning, Basil's feelings for her had outweighed hers for him. Over the years, though, his gentle, unwavering support had shown her that her original understanding of love was immature. With him, she had a best friend, a caring lover, a protector, a confidant, someone to pick her up when she stumbled and whose happiness had become as important as her own. They were partners in a way she hadn't thought two people could be, and not a day went by when she wasn't grateful for all the blessings his love had brought into her life.

Rather than speaking to the crowd as a whole, the queen of Vandorra was making her way around the garden to meet with each table. She was an older woman, perhaps in her seventies, of diminutive size but large presence. Camilla watched the ladies at a nearby table fawn over their host. They stood at her approach and curtsied.

Is that mandatory? I wouldn't even know how.

I should have asked how to refer to her. I think it's "Your Royal Highness."

Camilla regretted not asking more questions. She hadn't anticipated actually meeting the hostess. She'd imagined the queen would speak from the front of the room and that would be as close as they'd come to her.

While Camilla's thoughts were wandering, Queen Delinda made her way over to their table. "Mrs. Romano, I'm so pleased you decided to attend."

Camilla rose to her feet and automatically held out her hand in greeting. "Thank you for the invitation. What a lovely event."

As Heather, Ava, and Wren rose to their feet, Camilla realized her faux pas but froze rather than lowering her hand. She wanted her family to be well received and would have bowed, but she was standing too close to the queen. *No, it's a curtsy, not a bow.*

The queen solved the problem by shaking Camilla's extended hand before turning to Ava. "And who is this?"

"Ava Romano," Ava said with a deep curtsy she must have practiced from watching princesses on TV. "I was Ava Ellis, but my mom got married, and now I have a daddy and a new name."

"I'm so happy for you," the queen said graciously. She met Camilla's gaze and winked before offering her hand to Heather. "And you must be Heather."

"I am," Heather said with confidence as she shook the older woman's hand. "It's a pleasure to meet you."

The queen's expression seemed relaxed and warm—this must have been just a regular day for her. She shook the more timid Wren's hand next. "And Wren."

"Yes," Wren said in a gasp while pumping the queen's hand. "What a beautiful place to host an event. You chose well."

"Thank you," the queen said. "Since I've been in the area, I've heard so many wonderful things about your family."

Camilla blushed. "That's very kind to say."

Without missing a beat, Queen Delinda said, "I'm not known for that particular characteristic. Honest, yes. Outspoken, often. In fact, Mrs. Romano, there's a matter I wish to discuss with you if you have a moment."

"Of course." This wasn't Camilla's first charity event, and each one was unique, but taking possible donors aside in such a manner was definitely different. "I'll be right back," she promised her family and made a comical face before following the queen out of the garden and into the main building.

In a private sitting room, Queen Delinda took a seat and instructed Camilla to sit across from her. A man joined them briefly and inquired if there was anything either needed. The queen shooed him away.

"Now that we're alone, let's start again, shall we? You're the reason I'm in the area, Camilla Romano. I meant what I said about being impressed. You and your family are well respected in your community as well as by those you employ."

"Thank you." *Where is this going? Why does this feel like a job interview?*

"I wish I could have met you during more pleasant circumstances."

Camilla's hands went cold. "I'm sorry. I'm not following you."

"I'm sure you have your reasons for not wanting Dominic Corisi to be part of your happy little family, but you soon won't have a choice in the matter. Whatever secrets you're sitting on, I suggest you start thinking about how you want them revealed, because I fear they soon will be."

Camilla stood. "You must have me confused with someone else."

Queen Delinda sighed dramatically. "I am many things, but confused is not one of them. Whether you choose to believe it or not, I'm here to help you."

Frozen where she was, Camilla fought back a panic attack. She was not a nervous person by nature, but there were things she couldn't face—things she'd denied for so long she'd convinced herself they weren't true. Some of the past had the power to unravel her family.

The queen continued, "I'm too old to offer my assistance to someone twice. So make up your mind. Sit back down, and we'll discuss what I know is about to happen and how you should address it, or go, and things will play out without my involvement. Just don't stand there gaping at me; it's not a good look for either of us."

I can't leave without knowing what she's referring to. Camilla took a seat again. "What is about to happen?"

"It appears that Dominic Corisi plans to return to your hometown. He's bought up enough of your family's land that he feels he now has the upper hand. I believe you know why."

Camilla did. She'd seen this side of the Corisis before. Dominic's father had done everything in his power to crush her family. He'd taken their land, their businesses, but they'd never bent to his will. Was Dominic back to finish what his father had started? She wound her hands together tightly on her lap. "I do. He has every reason to hate my family."

"They're his family too."

"Yes. Rosella, his mother, is my sister."

"The grandmother who refuses to see him is your mother."

"Yes and no." Camilla shook her head. "It's not that simple. My mother is his grandmother, but she gets confused now. When I heard Dominic had tried to visit her a few months ago and that my cousins had denied him access to her, my heart broke for him, but I understood why it was for the best."

"Because he's a man better kept at a distance?"

"Because my mother is still afraid of his father."

"Antonio Corisi was certainly an evil man. No one wept at his funeral. Well, perhaps his daughter, Nicole, but she's a softhearted girl."

"My mother calls Antonio *il diavolo*, the devil. She believes he is circling our family, planning to do us more harm."

"How he abused Rosella was a crime he should have been punished for, but Dominic knew the pain of his wrath as well."

Tears filled Camilla's eyes. "My sister has a long record of making mistakes that hurt the ones she claims to love. She left her children with Antonio when she ran from him."

The queen pressed her lips together for a moment before saying, "And ran to Italy, where she faked her own death and changed her name."

"You're well informed."

"Always. When Dominic first went to Montalcino to search for his mother, why did they hide her from him? Her son. Seems heartless, even to me."

Camilla sniffed and blinked a few times quickly. Doors were flying open to a time in her life she'd worked hard to put behind her. "Dominic didn't arrive alone. Antonio had followed him. He told our family if Rosella was still alive, she wouldn't be for long. They had no choice but to maintain the lie."

"I see." After a quiet moment, the queen said, "And since Antonio's death, no one has reached out to Dominic. Not even your family. Is there a piece to this I'm not aware of?"

"No," Camilla hedged. As she'd learned to do with anything that involved her sister, she divulged only what she had to. "I simply have no desire to see my sister again. She's in Dominic's life now, which means he has no place in mine."

"Interesting. I didn't take you for a liar."

Camilla's mouth went dry. "Does there have to be more of a reason?"

With a dismissive wave of her hand, the queen said, "Normally I try to mind my own business. Really, if your secrets don't affect me, you're welcome to them, but since I'm here to help you unravel this mess, I can't accept less than the whole truth. It's my understanding that Gian is also your sister's child, although not from Antonio."

Oh God. Is there anything she doesn't know? "You understand correctly."

"From a man she married while under a false name who died shortly before your sister asked you to raise her son."

How does she know all this? "If you know everything, why are we having this conversation?"

"Because Dominic Corisi can be a very dangerous man. He's hurt and he's angry. Justifiably, in my opinion. Unfortunately, that means he's teetering on doing something that might cost him the wonderful family he's made for himself. Normally I have no pity for his type, but he's become, albeit not by my choice, a member of my own extended family. I care about how this all plays out for him—and, after learning more about your family, you as well. As someone who was once afraid she wouldn't be part of her grandchildren's lives, I can't help but think that Dominic deserves to hug his grandmother at least once before that opportunity no longer exists. I don't know how he'll react to discovering he has a half brother who has been raised mere hours from him, but he should be given a chance to know him as well."

"Ideally, yes." Camilla shook her head, not because she disagreed but because the idea of those meetings happening was overwhelming her. "I don't know. I hear what you're saying, but I can't think right now. All I see is everything I love falling apart."

The queen took Camilla's hand in hers. "It doesn't have to. That's why I'm here. My family was shattering when Alessandro stepped in. He has this unwavering belief that love is always the answer . . . regardless of what the situation is. With my connections, I could stop Dominic in his tracks if I had to. It would get ugly fast, but I'd do it if I thought it would save him from himself. Blunt force is effective, but I've learned it has no place in family matters. You have something more powerful than anything in my arsenal: you have the family he's yearning for. Your sons are fine young men who are loyal and loving. Imagine what Dominic could learn from them."

Camilla gave the queen's hand a squeeze, then broke off the connection. "I want to say yes, but I have so much anger in me—toward my sister, toward the decisions she's made. In my heart I want to put it aside and do what's best for everyone, but I don't know if I'm capable. When I think about the past, I still get angry. Angrier than would be helpful in this situation."

"Could your sons step up? All you're asking is for one of them to prepare your family for Dominic's arrival . . . soften them toward him."

"Even though he's already bought up their land?" Camilla brought a shaking hand to her chin. "That won't earn him a warm reception. I couldn't ask Sebastian to handle this. He and Heather are expecting a child soon, and he'd meet aggression with aggression. I won't put him in that position. He's finally happy again. Mauricio has smoother negotiating skills." Camilla sighed. "He might be able to do this, especially with Wren at his side. Neither speak Italian, though, and this is something that will require someone who can reassure our cousins as well as make sure my mother understands who Dominic is. Gian has been hurt enough by my sister that I don't want him involved until we know if Dominic will accept him. It would have to be Christof. He speaks Italian. He's even-tempered. Kindhearted. He's also discreet."

"Dominic is no innocent, but he's not the devil either. He's going to Italy whether or not you get involved. You have an opportunity to get ahead of the situation and shape its outcome. Tell me, does Christof have someone special in his life?"

"No. Yes. Maybe. He's recently met someone he appears to have feelings for."

"Do you trust me?"

"Not really. No. I hardly know you."

The queen frowned. "Well, aren't you pragmatic? Do you believe in the power of love?"

It was an odd question, but it struck a chord in Camilla. "I do."

"Alessandro once told me that if I wanted a rose garden, I needed to stop planting weeds. Your garden is as overgrown as mine once was. It's time for you to start planting more strategically."

"You've lost me again."

A smile returned to the queen's face. "What if I told you that you could smooth over the Dominic situation and gain yourself a daughter-in-law at the same time? Would you be interested in hearing my idea?"

"I don't believe in meddling in my children's lives."

Queen Delinda laughed with delight. "You're a horrible liar and a sheer delight because of it. I look forward to a time when we know each other well enough to swap stories. For now, though, let me tell you my solution to your problem."

Camilla felt like a first-time skydiver poised to jump, not because she wanted to but because the plane was going down. "Sure, I guess. What do you suggest I do?"

CHAPTER FOURTEEN

McKenna

I'd never been someone who enjoyed talking on the phone. I'd rather do something than sit around talking about doing it. Still, as I sat curled up on one end of my couch, I had to admit I loved the sound of Christof's voice. He'd called at exactly the time he'd said he would.

Reliable. That wasn't something I was used to with men. Well, not men interested in dating me, anyway.

"What was the best part of your day?" Christof asked after we'd exhausted a more general conversation about nothing in particular.

I almost told him about the big-name racer who'd booked a spot for the weekend. Seeing that caliber of driver on my track still gave me goose bumps. I didn't say it, though. Right or wrong, I was still hesitant to really let him into my life. "I fixed a car up for a client who'd gone someplace else first and been disappointed. That always leaves me feeling good about what I do."

"That's awesome. I feel the same every time I complete a task my brothers weren't sure I could handle. Doesn't matter that I'm twenty-seven. They still see me as the little brother who needs help tying his shoes."

"Did you?"

"What?"

"Need help with tying your shoes?"

"Who didn't? 'Bunny ear, bunny ear, send him through a hole. Pop him out the other side, fluffy and bold.' First of all, that doesn't even rhyme. Second, no one should tie a rabbit's ears in a knot. It's a horrible image to fill a child's head with."

"You know, I've never had a man recite poetry to me before. Is that Thoreau? Frost?"

"You never struggled with tying your shoes, did you?"

"Never." *Guess that's what happens when there's no one around who'll do it for you.* "But to make you feel better, I used to be terrified that my mother would get soap in my eyes when she washed my hair. I mean, I'd go flip-out nuts. I'd start crying before she even turned the water on. She gave up on me and cut my hair super short. It wasn't until she left that I had enough to put up in a ponytail."

"You can tell me it's none of my business, but where did she go?"

"My mother? Away. She thought she could do better than my father and went off to try."

"How old were you?"

"Ten, I think. I prefer to look forward, not back."

"That couldn't have been easy."

"It wasn't as bad as it sounds. My father took me everywhere with him. I adored him."

"How old were you when you lost him?"

"Eighteen."

"I'm so sorry you went through that."

"It's okay. It's been a long time. I still miss him every day, but it doesn't overwhelm me anymore."

"You told me about him the first time we met."

"I thought you didn't remember much." I sat up straighter.

"It's slowly coming back to me. Fragments of that night. The kiss is fuzzy, though. Maybe we can do something about that when I see you next."

My face warmed. "Maybe." After a pause, I asked, "What was the toughest thing your brothers asked you to do that they weren't sure you could?" It wasn't my finest question, but I knew it would get him talking and give me a moment simply to savor hearing him.

"Let me see. Toughest. Okay, several years ago, when Romano Superstores was experiencing its first expansions, we weren't popular in every town we opened a store in. People saw us as the enemy of the small, independent store chains—and we were. Sebastian sent me to a certain store we couldn't keep employees in. The town hated what we stood for so much, and they were exceedingly vocal about it. They didn't want their husbands, wives, children, or neighbors working for us. I went in and sorted it out."

He was so even-tempered I could imagine him doing that, but I had to ask, "How?"

"I met with everyone who had anything to say and let them speak their piece. Amazing how quickly people calm down when they feel that their opinion is being heard. The store we replaced had been going under before we forced the close. People had already become dissatisfied with what they had. It wasn't the change they hated as much as the feeling that they had no control over what was happening in their town. I formed a committee of locals and gave them the task of compiling a list of what the community most needed from an employer. Turned out they needed after-school childcare. Once I implemented that program, it was as if we'd always been there. It's one of our strongest stores, not a lot of turnover. I like to think that's because they feel invested in our company."

"I bet they do . . . because you invested in them."

"Exactly. No one expected me to be able to turn that situation around. It was the first time I'd say I really earned Sebastian's respect as far as being a valuable part of the company. Since then I've worked in many different departments, but when there's discord at a store, they send me in."

"And you work your magic."

"Not magic. Like you, I enjoy making things work. Most people want to get along. All I do is look for what's standing between them and their ability to work together. At one store it was a manager who was sleeping with several cashiers. How did he not think that would be a problem?"

"What did you do?"

"I fired him. I'm an understanding person, but you can't fix stupid." I chuckled at that. "No, you can't."

"How about you? You work in a garage, right?"

"I do."

"Is it yours?"

"It is."

"I get the feeling you don't want to talk about where you work."

"Work is work." I should have told him about Decker Park then. Really, he'd played a role in making it possible. I couldn't understand my reluctance, but it won out again.

"Right, and this is a date. Of sorts. Our second date."

"You did feed me again, so I guess it counts."

"I took a gamble that you'd like shrimp scampi."

"I loved it. Wasn't sure I should eat it when it arrived or wait, but it came at five, and I was hungry. It was delicious, though."

He chuckled. "I'm glad. I didn't see too many restaurants that deliver near you, but it sounded good."

"You chose well." On time. Thoughtful. Did the man have a flaw? "If you could change anything about yourself, what would it be?"

Yep, I'd gone there. Nobody was perfect, and the more I found to like about him, the more I worried I was missing something.

"That's an interesting question. I'm at a good place in my life. I'm comfortable in my own skin. I'm far from perfect, but I can look myself in the mirror every morning and not hate the person looking back. I don't know that there's much I would change. Is it a requirement that everyone wants to?"

"Maybe not." The more I thought about it, the more I liked his answer. "I wouldn't want to change much of my life either. I'm finally where I want to be, doing something I love."

"Sounds like we have a lot in common."

"More than I thought," I said aloud, then stopped because I hadn't meant to share that last part. "Now, did you already buy the new engine for your car?"

"No, I could only find something similar and wanted to see what you thought."

"I'd like to shop around a little for you. I bet I could find the exact engine you have."

"I looked."

"We may have different connections. That is, if you're okay with me getting involved."

"I'm very okay with it. I thank you. Mack thanks you."

"I still can't believe you named a car after me."

"Crazy romantic or borderline creepy?"

I laughed. "I'm not sure yet."

"Hey, I'm not the one who took advantage of an inebriated person I'd just met in a bar."

"Excuse me?"

"There I was, drinking my sorrows away, minding my own business, and you leaned in to kiss all my pain away."

"That's not how it went down at all."

"Sure. That's what you say now. There I was, a young, innocent twenty-year-old . . . ripe for the picking."

"Hold on. You really were a virgin at twenty?"

"You weren't?"

"Um. Sure. Yeah. I just assumed men started earlier."

"Do you want to hear about my first?"

"Not really."

"Thank God, because I don't want to hear about anyone you've been with either. How about we both consider each other a fresh slate."

I let out a sigh of relief. "I'd like that."

"But yeah, if I'd been more sober, you might have been my first."

"It wouldn't have gone that far."

"We'll never know, will we?"

"No, we won't." He was teasing, but the subject had me flustered. Lately I'd gotten lost in what-ifs. What if he had been sober? Would anything have happened? Would we have gotten together? Would I have focused so much on him that Decker Park would have never happened?

He must have sensed the change in my mood because he didn't pursue the topic. Instead he asked me what my favorite television show was. From there we talked well into the night about everything and nothing. Halfway through the conversation I changed into my pajamas, brushed my teeth, and crawled into bed. He did the same.

There was something absolutely amazing about his voice being the last thing I heard before I fell asleep.

CHAPTER FIFTEEN

CHRISTOF

Sundays were for family dinners. Saturday mornings, while my brothers occupied themselves with other things, I continued my tradition of spending time with my parents.

I whistled as I let myself into their home, a lightness lifting my steps. The smile on my face could only convey a piece of my almost giddiness. Giddiness I hadn't felt since I'd first heard the purr of Mack's engine. I wondered briefly if our phone conversations were leaving McKenna as revved as they were leaving me. All I could think about was seeing her again—in person this time.

My father was sitting in his favorite chair, likely reading the news on his tablet. "Hi, Dad."

He put his tablet aside and stood. "Christof, I wasn't sure we'd see you this morning."

We hugged. The men in my family weren't afraid to express how much they loved each other. "I figured Mom has a story to tell—after all, didn't she just meet a queen?"

"She did."

"And you know she wants to hear all about McKenna."

My father's eyes lit with interest. "Your phone date went well?"

Before I had a chance to answer, my mother appeared at the door of the living room. "Christof, don't you dare update him without me."

In a few strides I was in front of her, receiving a kiss on my forehead. "I would never," I said with a laugh.

"Come into the kitchen, you two. I have coffee brewing and three omelets freshly made."

My stomach rumbled in anticipation. "How do you always know, Mom? I've been craving one. Are you tapping into my home AI?"

"Sure," my mother joked as we entered the kitchen. "I've moved from barely understanding how to set up mine to hacking into yours. Or, last Saturday you mentioned we haven't had omelets in a while, and I listen when you speak."

I snapped my fingers in the air. "Is that the trick? Listening? Dad, did you hear that?"

"What?" he said with a smile as he poured coffee for all of us. "Did someone say something?"

I set the table with silverware and napkins while my mother slid our omelets onto plates. "You picked him, Mom."

She shot a warm smile at my father. "Best decision I ever made."

After delivering the coffees to the table, my father stopped to give my mother a quick kiss. "What did you say, dear?"

She was smiling as she handed him a plate and waved him away. "Give this to Christof and quit the nonsense."

My father was still smiling when he sat down across from me. "So, Christof, you look happy this morning."

"I am happy. I've spoken to McKenna for the last three nights, and we really get along."

My mother joined us. "So I'm dying to know . . . is she the same woman you named your car after?"

I cut into my omelet, stalling, just to torture my parents a little. Then I grinned and said, "She is. Once I brought it up, she remembered me. I guess I wasn't all bad that night, even though I'd definitely had too much to drink."

"I didn't think you would be," my mother said with confidence. "Drunk just makes a person more of what they are sober. You've always been a good boy."

My father nodded. "You told her and she's still talking to you, so that says a lot. Does she know you don't remember meeting her?"

"I told her, but I actually do remember a lot of it now. The more we talk about it, the more it comes back to me."

"I'm glad you were up front with her." My father exchanged a look with my mother. "Honesty is the cornerstone of a good relationship."

For a brief moment my mother's expression looked pained. "Your father and I don't have secrets from each other, but that's not the case with me and everyone. I was fully prepared to lie to you this morning, Christof, but I can't. I can't send you into this situation blind."

I laid my fork beside my plate and studied the serious expression on both of my parents' faces. "Did something happen?"

My father was the first to speak. "Something is about to. I offered to handle the situation, but Camilla had a plan that sounded like it might work. I agree, though: this way is better."

I raised a hand with splayed fingers. "Could one of you please tell me what we're talking about? Whatever it is, we'll figure it out. We always do."

My mother took a long sip of her coffee, closed her eyes briefly, then returned the mug to the table before answering. "I shouldn't involve you at all. None of this mess is your making."

There was something that happened within a child when they realized they were becoming the caretaker of their parents. I felt a flash of panic followed by a wave of protectiveness. I leaned forward and put my hand over my mother's. "That's not how family works, Mom. Whatever this is, we're in it together."

"I should be able to handle this myself. I shouldn't let my anger and my fear stop me from doing what's right." She blinked back tears, and my heart thudded heavily in my chest. "I'm not as strong as you think I am, Christof. Not as brave or as good of a person."

My father put his arm around her shoulders and gave her a little shake. "Camilla Romano, careful how you talk about the woman I love. If you're not a good person, then the world has never seen one. Good doesn't mean perfect. Tell Christof what's happening, and let him decide for himself."

"I can't tell him everything. I can't." She trembled like I had never seen her do before.

He kissed her temple. "Then say what you can."

She turned and searched my father's face. "I love you, Basil Romano. You are not allowed to die before me."

He chuckled. "Hey, hey, no one is dying anytime soon. Now, let's go back to your crazy plan before Christof starts to think this is about something else."

"Yes, because the two of you are freaking me out."

My mother nodded and turned back to meet my gaze. "I think you should take a fiancée to Montalcino to meet Nona."

I sat back in my chair, confused. This talk thankfully didn't appear to be about anything serious. "I don't have a fiancée."

My mother wrapped her hands around her coffee mug. "If you took McKenna there, you might."

I laughed at that. "Mom, that's not how things work."

"It could be. I've read the storyline a hundred times—two people try to deny how much they want their agreement to be real; then they discover they're meant for each other."

I picked up my utensils and started to eat again. Between bites I said, "Dad, I told you those romances would start to affect her brain."

My father shrugged. "Some aren't that bad. If you haven't had a woman read you her favorite romance, don't knock the experience. It really heats things up."

Still holding my utensils, I covered my ears with my hands. "No. Must wipe image out of my head."

A smile returned to my mother's face. "You and your father love to torment each other."

My father and I exchanged a look. We did. In some ways I was more like my father than my brothers were. He and I understood each other, tended to see things the same way. Even his siding with my mother with this crazy idea: For him it likely wasn't about believing it would work out the way she said but rather that he would support her—right or wrong. If it worked, he'd be the first to congratulate her. If it failed, he'd be right there with her, sharing the blame.

God willing, I'd be that kind of partner to someone someday.

Would that be McKenna? It was too early to know.

Relief flooded in as the mood lightened. "I have an idea. Why don't I ask McKenna out on a real date first? We'll get to know each other. If something serious develops between us, I'll propose, and *then* I'll take her to meet Nona."

My parents exchanged another odd look. "The thing is, I've already told Nona you were coming, and there's a situation unfolding over there that needs your assistance."

"A situation?"

After letting out a shaky breath, my mother said, "I don't even know where to begin. You know I grew up on a small farm just outside of Montalcino."

"Yes, Mom—I've visited a few times."

"Because you connected with your cousins there in a way your brothers didn't."

"Only because I bothered to keep up my Italian. Gian studied it, too, but you never allowed him to go. That's always been hard on him."

"I know," my mother said in a tight tone. "I wanted to protect him from what he might hear."

"And that is?"

"My sister, his biological mother, is very much alive, but she's dead to our family over there. They will never forgive her for bringing so much trouble to our town."

"What kind of trouble?" No one had spoken of it to me there, but I'd been much younger the last time I'd visited. Gian's mother had only been referred to as someone who wasn't mentally stable enough to raise him. No one had ever said where she was, and Mauricio and I had joked that she was in a witness protection program somewhere. The one thing we'd all known was that no one wanted to talk about her. No one.

"Start at the beginning," my father suggested.

My mother nodded. "My sister, Rosella, was always competitive with me. From the time we were little. If I picked up a doll, she wanted it. If I put it down and picked up a crayon, she wanted that as well. I couldn't have anything of my own because as soon as I did, she became obsessed with it. When I was a young woman, a man visited our town from Sicily. Antonio Corisi was rich—powerful. I thought he was my Prince Charming coming to rescue me from my small town." She looked at my father. "I was young and foolish."

He raised one of her hands to his lips and kissed it. "I never saw it that way."

She cupped his face for a long moment before continuing. "As soon as I showed interest in him, my sister swooped in. She slept with him and made sure everyone knew about it. In those days, shame followed sex outside of marriage. Our parents were furious. They demanded he marry her. And he did. She moved to the United States with him, where they had two children, Dominic and Nicole."

"Wait, Dominic Corisi. *The* Dominic Corisi?" Arguably one of the richest, most powerful men in the world. People said he was as close to American royalty as we had. "He's my cousin?" None of it sounded plausible.

In a voice just above a whisper, my mother said, "Yes."

"Why have you never said anything? Why don't we know him?"

"Rosella is also Gian's mother."

"Yes, we know that. Oh, shit," I said as all the dots connected, but into a picture that still made no sense. I covered my mouth at my accidental swearing, but they didn't seem to have noticed. "Gian has other siblings." My gut clenched as I thought about how cheated he'd feel that he'd never been told. "You have to tell him. Is Antonio his father as well?"

"It's complicated. Antonio was not the man I thought he was. My sister suffered great abuse at his hands. When he threatened to kill her, she asked our family in Montalcino to hide her. To do that, they had to fake her death. It was messy and wrong in so many ways. She left her children with the man she feared and assumed a new identity in Italy."

"Dad, this is a joke, right? This kind of stuff doesn't really happen."

"There's more you need to hear, Christof."

My mother continued, "I would never joke about anything so tragic. For many years Dominic and Nicole thought their father had killed their mother. As a young man, Dominic needed proof, so he went to Montalcino looking for her. His father followed him. He told our family that if Rosella was still alive, she wouldn't be for long. So when Dominic asked for his mother, the family lied to him and told him she was dead."

"But she wasn't."

"No, she was very much alive. Under an assumed name, she'd remarried. This time to a vineyard owner. They had one son—Gian. When Rosella's second husband died suddenly soon after Gian was born, Rosella became convinced Antonio had found them and killed him. There was no proof, but Rosella has never been stable. She said she had to go deeper into hiding and she couldn't take Gian with her, so she gave him to me. She made me promise to never connect him to her because if I did, he wouldn't be safe. We moved to the United States and started over."

It was a wild story to absorb. I sat back and simply listened.

"Antonio visited our town in Italy afterward. Each time he was turned away, he found a way to make our family suffer. Businesses were ruined. My family lost their farm. Your father and I have sent money back to help them over the years, but speaking the Corisi name in that town is considered summoning the devil himself. My sister's name elicits a similar reaction."

"Which is why you never sent Gian."

"Yes. Our family blames Rosella for bringing the devil's wrath down upon them." She clasped her hands on the table. "Antonio Corisi is no longer a danger to anyone. He's long dead. My sister reunited with Dominic and Nicole. I had hoped that would be the end of this."

Although these were all important things to know, I didn't understand why my mother was revealing them now. "But it's not?"

"A few months ago Dominic Corisi went to Italy to meet Nona. Our family turned him away. He claims to not be his father, but people don't say no to a man like Dominic. Not twice anyway. He purchased the land our family leases and intends to return sometime soon to—"

"To what?"

"Possibly to demand to see Nona. If so, it won't go well. Even though I haven't been back to Montalcino in a long time, I speak to my mother every week. She thinks the devil is circling her. She won't know the difference between Dominic and his father. And if Dominic is angry with our family, I fear what he'll do if he's turned away again."

"Couldn't we call him and explain all of this to him?"

"There's too much at risk for a phone conversation. You don't understand who you're dealing with. He won't stop this time until he meets Nona. You could go there, though, and smooth things over with the family. I've seen you go into volatile situations and calm everyone down . . . somehow bring them all to a common ground. That's what's needed here."

I digested what my mother had shared while I finished my omelet. "Your voice would carry more weight with the family than mine would."

She looked heavenward as if for strength. "There's too much pain and anger waiting for me back in Montalcino. I'm not strong enough to return and deal with it. I'm still so angry with my sister for so many things. I don't want her or Dominic in our lives if they're only coming to take more from us."

"What would they take? The leased land? Is that what you want to make sure we don't lose?" I saw a greater fear in her eyes and suddenly understood. "Gian. Mom, he loves us. Do you honestly think meeting his biological mother could change that?"

My mother pushed back her chair and stood. "My sister ruins everything she touches. She hurts everyone she loves. I thought I could protect my family from her, but she's returning with a younger, stronger devil, and yes, I'm afraid. I'm sorry. I need a moment." With that, my mother left the kitchen.

I sat across from my father for several long moments without speaking. I'd never seen my mother so upset—or was it scared? Either way it left me with a sick pit in my stomach. "What do you need from me, Dad? How do I make this better for all involved?"

"Even the devil?" my father asked in light challenge.

"I don't believe Dominic is one. I could be wrong, but it sounds like his father left a lot of devastation in his wake."

"He certainly did."

"I can't imagine being told Mom was dead and thinking you did it."

"Only to later have her reappear in your life."

"That's fucked up."

My father didn't appear bothered by my slipup, perhaps because he knew I was shaken by the thought of so much evil having been a part of my family. "I'm sure it does something ugly to a man's head. In ways you can't understand, your mother sees him as a danger to our family."

"He's Gian's brother. My cousin. Your nephew. There doesn't have to be any animosity between us. Has he hurt anyone in the family?"

"Not yet."

"'Not yet' is still a no."

"Then no, he hasn't hurt anyone in the family."

"Why does he want to see Nona?"

My father shrugged. "I don't know."

"I need to ask Dominic that question myself, to tell him about Gian and give him a chance to be a true brother to him."

"Then I suggest you fly to Montalcino and meet him."

"How does Mom know he plans to go?"

"A source close to Dominic reached out to your mother. Together they hatched the whole fiancée scenario."

"I can't believe you thought that was a good idea."

"Your mother has always been on my side. I could give her no less."

"Can you imagine how that would have gone over? 'McKenna, I know we haven't so much as gone on a real date yet, but would you like to go to Italy with me for a few weeks? Just a little international family drama. I should warn you that this will either be fun or full-out war, and we need to pretend to be engaged.'"

"It would definitely give you something to bond over."

I whipped my head around to look my father in the eye. "Don't even try to make it sound like it is a good idea."

"Imagine the story it would be for your children."

I stood. "Children? Dad, McKenna and I get along on the phone, but I don't know anything about her really. I couldn't tell you what her favorite song is, if she brushes her teeth twice or ten times a day, or if she even wants children."

"You'd know all of that if you spent a couple of weeks at Nona's with her."

I wagged a finger at my father. "Senility is setting in early."

My father stood and pocketed his hands. "All I'm saying is the idea has potential. Nona's excited about your visit. Your cousins are too. Nothing like an impending wedding to put people in a good mood."

"This is insane. You realize that."

"It might be an opportunity to quickly see if McKenna has what it takes to be a Romano."

"Or to scare her off. There's no way I'd ask her to do this. First, there are too many unknowns. Second, I'd have to tell her everything because I won't lie to her. Third . . ." I wondered what McKenna would think of Nona and my Italian relatives. Did she speak any Italian? Was she good at role play? Zero to two weeks together. The whole idea was crazy. "Dad, you said Dominic could be dangerous. I won't risk McKenna's safety."

"He's not that kind of dangerous. Your mother is afraid of him, but only because he represents a time in her life she wants to forget. McKenna would be in no danger. In fact, she might be the key to smoothing everything over. An invitation to an engagement party would be an excuse to invite Dominic rather than wait for him to arrive on his own."

"I'll go to Montalcino, but there's no way I'm asking McKenna to get involved in this."

"If she is the one, this might be her only chance to meet Nona. Every year she's with us is a gift."

I started toward the door. "That's low, Dad, and I am not that easy to manipulate."

"Call me when she says yes."

"Not going to ask her," I called over my shoulder as I made my way out of the kitchen. I stopped at the bottom of the stairs. My mother hadn't reappeared. I wanted to go to her and tell her I would fix all of this and that everything would be okay.

But I'd never lied, and I had no idea how this was going to play out.

CHAPTER SIXTEEN

MᴄKᴇɴɴᴀ

Late Saturday morning I had just stepped out of my coveralls when my phone beeped with a text message. Morning Mack.

I smiled. It hadn't taken me long at all to become addicted to hearing from Christof. Since I've never had a man name a car after me, I can't decide if calling me Mack is a compliment or not.

I could call you honey.

Or you could keep your testicles. During our last long phone conversation, I'd told him about Ty's practice of calling all of his dates that.

Not every woman can work a testicle threat into a conversation. I like your style.

I decided it was best to change the subject. How was breakfast?

Amazing. Overshadowed, though, by an interesting conversation I had with my parents.

About what?

This is one of those stories that is better saved for when you know me and my parents better so we can laugh about it without you thinking we're all crazy.

He'd brought it up, so he obviously wanted to tell me, but I let that slide for now. More important was the fact that his plans for us included me getting to know his parents. Men had said something similar to me in the past, but it had always been a line—a carrot dangled in hopes that it would get them laid faster. When Christof said it, it felt sincere.

Ty says he wants to meet you before we go anywhere.

I'm fine with that.

He might threaten your life.

Hard to scare a man with older brothers. He doesn't plan to tickle me until I piss myself, does he? I'd much rather be punched.

I laughed out loud. I'll pass along your preference to him.

Are you free tonight? I could drive up. We could grab dinner somewhere.

I inhaled sharply, gripped my phone, and walked to the garage office, where Ty was ending a business call. As soon as he was free, I said, "Christof wants to come see me tonight."

Ty moved to sit on one side of his desk. "Are you asking my permission, or do you need a refresher talk about how things work?"

I rolled my eyes and paced his office. "What's wrong with me, Ty?" I gave my belly a pat. "I have a nervous, queasy feeling in my stomach. My hands are sweaty. My heart is racing."

He folded his arms across his chest. "Your dad got like that before a race sometimes. It's how he knew he'd win."

"This isn't about sex, Ty."

He chuckled. "I didn't say it was. You're talking to someone who used to burp you, McKenna. This guy is different. What are you afraid of?"

I sat heavily in the closest chair. "I *am* afraid. Holy shit, since when is this me?"

"Since you met a man who might matter?"

I was back on my feet, pacing again. "He can't matter yet. All we've done is talk on the phone. For all I know I won't even be attracted to him when I see him again. Oh my God, what if I'm getting attached to a man I won't want to have sex with?"

"Slow down there. You don't find him attractive?"

"I did. That doesn't change, right? It's just that . . . he's different from the men I've dated. He's so—real. More real than I've been with him. We've talked for hours and hours, but I let him think I'm a mechanic with a small shop. What if he comes up here and seeing Decker Park changes everything?"

"Are you afraid he'll be interested in you for your money? He's a Romano. They're rich."

"I know that." *So what am I worried about?* I let the truth spill out with someone I knew wouldn't judge me. "Ty, every weekend his family gathers for Sunday dinners. Do you know where he was this morning? With his parents. His *parents*. He's a good guy. He and his mother swap recipes on Saturday mornings. Does that sound like someone you can see with me?"

"No, you need an asshole."

I stopped and shot Ty a glare. "You're not helping."

"Because you're not making any sense."

As what I was worried about crystallized, I blurted it out. "I'm not the kind of woman a man like him goes for. In two dates, tops, he'll want to change me."

Ty frowned. "I see. This isn't about him; it's about you. You think you're not good enough for him."

I sat back down. Was that it? *No. And yes. Mostly no.* "I like who I am. I'm proud of what I've achieved. I love my life."

"But?"

"But Christof is the kind of guy who still opens doors for women. His mother never worked. She's one of those stay-at-home, have-cookies-ready-after-school paragons. What would I have in common with his family?"

"Him?"

I didn't like the amusement in Ty's eyes. "I wouldn't even know how to be part of a family."

"Because you don't have one?" With that Ty stood up. "I'd say I'm insulted, but that would only add to your freak-out. I don't know Christof or his family, but I do know that nothing is ever as perfect as it looks from the outside. I'd bet my life they're just as messed up as you are. You're worrying over nothing."

I stood back up and reached a hand toward him. "I didn't mean that you're not—"

Ty held both hands up for me to stop. "We're good. You want my advice? Christof sounds like a great guy. You should give him a chance. He might not want to change you because, and I'm just throwing this out there, some guys like intelligent, successful women."

"I'm sorry, Ty. You know I love you."

He nodded. "I wouldn't be here if the feeling wasn't mutual. Now get out of my office—I have calls to make."

I hesitated. "I told him you'd want to meet him before we went out."

"I do."

I smiled. "He said a man with older brothers is tough to intimidate, but for future reference he prefers to be punched rather than tickled until he pisses himself."

Ty laughed. "I like him already. Tell him to come on up. I'll hang around until he gets here."

I turned to leave, then stopped just before I did. "Be nice to him, Ty. I don't know why this one's important, but he is."

"Gotcha, so I'll meet him at the gate with my shotgun instead."

Shaking my head, I walked back into the main area of the garage.

I groaned as I remembered how I'd made it sound as if I didn't have a family. I knew how lucky I was to have Ty, Cal, and Wayne in my life. I'd been referring to the two-parent, dinner-on-the-table, put-money-in-a-jar-if-you-swear kind of arrangement.

I called Cal and asked him to put Wayne on the phone as well. I naturally turned to them when anything in life fell out of alignment— no different from pulling into a pit and signaling that something needed looking at. "I think I hurt Ty's feelings. Could the two of you call him tonight? Check in on him?"

"What'd you say?" Wayne asked.

I didn't pretty it up. No need to. This was my crew. "I didn't mean it the way it sounded, but I hurt his feelings. You know how sensitive he can be about any suggestion that we aren't family." Ty came across as tough, but the only family he had was Cal, Wayne, and me. A fact that didn't seem to bother him unless someone brought it up. "I feel horrible. Did he tell you the name of the woman he went out with last weekend? Maybe I could track her down and see if she'd ask him out tonight. I don't like the idea of him being alone."

"Ty's fine," Wayne said. "He knows you love him."

Cal chimed in, "And I wouldn't stick your nose into his love life. You know he doesn't like that."

"As if that has ever stopped any of us," I joked.

Cal and Wayne laughed. Cal said, "True enough. Don't worry about Ty. Wayne and I are almost home anyway. We decided to head back a day early. We should roll in around three o'clock. We'll clean up, then drag him out for a drink."

"I'd say I'd go with you, but I might have a date tonight."

"With *Christof*?" Wayne asked, dragging out the name in light mockery of how they thought I said it.

"Is he picking you up?" Cal cut in.

"Yes. I think so. Not sure. I haven't answered him yet."

"Way to leave a guy hanging. Poor Christof," Wayne joked.

"I should just say yes. I'm making this into a bigger deal than it is. All we're doing is going to dinner."

"I want to meet him." Cal sounded too enthusiastic about the idea.

"Me too," Wayne added.

"Ty said the same. Promise me you'll be nice to him."

Wayne laughed. "When have we ever not been nice to Ty?"

"He's our bud," Cal said in a tone that revealed they were having far too much fun with this.

"I will kick all three of your asses . . ."

"Did you hear that?" Cal asked.

Wayne said, "So is she saying we shouldn't tell him all her most embarrassing stories?"

"Stop," I ground out. "Don't mess this up for me."

When Cal spoke again, his tone was gentle. "We're kidding, McKenna."

"I know you are." I sighed. They weren't the problem. "God, I'm not used to being nervous. I get all fluttery and weird when I talk to Christof. I'm pretty sure I'm going to fuck this up."

Cal cooed, "Wayne, is this the most adorable thing you've ever seen? Our little girl is all grown up and falling in love."

"I'm not falling for him," I countered.

Wayne couldn't *not* be a ballbuster. "No, she's *fluttering* for him."

"Goodbye," I said firmly. "Drive safely. If you're here when he is, I'll introduce you."

"Oh, we'll be there," Wayne promised.

I ended the call with that. The conversation was headed nowhere productive. After a moment, I reopened my messages and realized a good amount of time had passed without me answering Christof.

Too long?

I did want to see him.

Despite the jokes, I also wanted him to meet my crew.

I scrolled to the last message, and my stomach did a nervous dance. *I really am fucking fluttering. I need to calm down. We might go out and discover we aren't as compatible in person as we are on the phone.*

I was tempted to arrange to meet him somewhere away from Decker Park. Talking to Ty had helped me understand why, and I hated that part of me was certain Christof wouldn't like the real me.

Oh God, I'd never understood women who pretended to be stupid around men, but there I was half considering concealing my successful business from a man I really liked. Because being able to support myself in a male-dominated profession made me less of a woman?

Some men thought so.

Would Christof?

If he couldn't accept me the way I was, wouldn't I rather find out early and end it fast, like removing a Band-Aid in one swift move?

I stared down at the phone without typing. I hadn't gotten where I was by second-guessing what I wanted. Success in anything was the result of careful preparation and then unshakable focus.

Decker Park was proof of the validity of that philosophy.

What was Christof?

At first I'd thought he was the distraction I was supposed to avoid to survive. After getting to know him more that week, I was beginning to think my life had room for more than one goal.

Christof was the first person to make me yearn for more.

Some relationships lasted. Didn't they? Wayne and Cal had been together as long as I could remember.

Love shouldn't require a person to change who they were.

I wanted to be myself with Christof.

With that in mind, I typed: Is five o'clock too early? I'd like to show you around my garage while it's still daylight.

He must have been typing as I did, because his incoming text dinged as mine posted. If you're not ready, we can keep talking on the phone and go out next weekend. I can go as slow as you need me to.

Those were words no one in the racing world ever uttered. My lips twisted in a wry smile. What did it say about me that I didn't know what to do with a nice guy?

Today is fine. See you at five.

CHAPTER SEVENTEEN

CHRISTOF

The map app on my phone provided more information than I was prepared for when I entered McKenna's address. Decker Park. Her house was situated on an impressive racing facility.

One that shared her last name.

Did it belong to her family? She'd said she owned a small garage; there was nothing small about two professional-caliber racetracks and a building the size of a factory that abutted them.

I had been completely honest with her every step of the way. I didn't like that she might not have been the same with me.

The drive up gave me time to overthink the situation.

On the other hand, I was happy for her if she'd found a way to make her dream a reality. She had even gotten her pit crew, from the sounds of it. More memories came back from our first meeting. The napkin. Her sketch. I could almost hear her describing how she wanted the place to be.

Holy shit, she'd done it. No wonder she'd said there wasn't much she'd change about her life. She was living her dream.

So why hadn't she told me? We'd talked every night—seemed like something that big would have come up. Unless she didn't want me to know.

Why lie? Why suggest all she had was a small garage?

My guard went up for the first time since meeting her. I was the type who trusted people until they gave me a reason not to. If she'd lied once, what else wasn't she being honest about? It was a potential game changer for me.

I pulled up to the security hut at Decker Park's main gate. It was as grand as the entrance to any of the country's largest racecourses, but it lacked the commercial feel of them. This was something different. Something private and elite.

The security guard checked my ID, then took an extra moment to look me over before handing it back to me. "Welcome, Mr. Romano. Miss Decker is at the main garage waiting for you. Go straight up this road, then follow the signs at the top of the hill."

"Thank you," I said as I secured my ID back in my wallet.

"Nice wheels," he said before he withdrew and closed the window between us.

Thanks.

I parked my car outside what I surmised was the main garage—a large concrete-and-metal structure. My guess was it was eighty thousand square feet. Enormous. The arched entrance was flanked on one side by a row of roll-up doors, some of which were open, others closed. The other, mostly glass side appeared to be a car showroom.

"Christof," McKenna called out from one of the open garage doors. She made her way toward me, dressed in bright-yellow coveralls, her hair tied back in a ponytail, with a smudge of grease on her cheek. Her chin rose as she met my gaze, as if she was daring me to comment on her attire.

I thought back to the younger McKenna who had worried she didn't have whatever it had taken to make this place. Why wasn't she meeting me with a huge smile, proud of her accomplishments and excited to show them off? I searched her expression and waited.

She stopped barely a foot from me, and her eyebrows came together, lending her an air of uncertainty. Neither of us were smiling. We stood there in a silent standoff, each waiting for something from the other.

She blinked first and waved a hand in the air. "So this is my place."

I simply held her gaze. I wasn't the kind to accuse or corner, but we both knew she'd misled me. I'd been all in, but this had the potential of being the last time I'd see her. To move forward, I'd need to know lying wasn't the norm for her.

She sighed and looked away. "Obviously it's not a small garage."

"Obviously."

When her eyes met mine again, they were flashing with defensive anger. "Listen, what I don't need in my life is another judgmental prick. This is me. Love it or leave it. I'm not some damsel in distress waiting to be rescued. I love working on cars. I love my unorthodox family and spending most of my day in the building behind me, covered with grease, smelling like old leather and oil. I don't need you to approve of how I live my life. So take a good look at me. This will be me a month from now. A year from now. Ten years from now. I'll probably never cook for you. Any child I have, if I ever have a child, will likely know how to swear before they can read and will damn well know their way around a garage."

Relief flooded in. Protecting Decker Park hadn't been a lie so much as a defense mechanism. Someone had hurt her, not seen her achievement for what it was, and she was afraid I wouldn't either. I could work with that. A smile twitched at the side of my mouth. "That's a lot to unpack. What makes you think I would want to change you?"

Her frown deepened. "All men do."

"Then you've been with the wrong men."

She shook her head as if she couldn't accept what I was saying. "Don't feed me bullshit, okay? If you've got a problem with any of this, could you save us both time and say it now? If you're honest, I might still fuck you."

My eyebrows shot up. I did value honesty, and modern women weren't afraid to say much, but she'd still rocked me back onto my heels. She and I handled things differently, but I didn't consider that a bad thing. She didn't look about to fuck me; she looked like she was panicking. A thought occurred to me. "Are you nervous about our first real date?" When she didn't answer, I added, "Because I was more excited to see you again than I've been about anything in a long time, but I'm nervous too. I'm not a prick, though, and not about to apologize for things I haven't done. Did you lead me to believe you had a small garage because some douchebag before me made you feel bad about being successful? Or didn't like the idea of a woman working on cars? Maybe both?"

Her mouth opened and closed, without her voicing a word. Finally, she ground out, "Yes."

A slow smile spread across my face. It was what I'd thought. In a light tone, I said, "Did I mention that I'm not a prick? If we start with that, the rest of this takes care of itself."

Her face flushed red. "And this is why I don't date."

Interesting. And promising. "Do you know what would wipe the last few minutes right out of my head?"

Her head cocked to the side, and her eyes narrowed slightly. "What?"

My mood was definitely improving. Talking on the phone had been wonderful, but my body was so aware of hers it was nearly painful. I stepped closer. "A welcome kiss. It would have to be a good one, though. You know the kind that makes you forget for a moment where you are?"

She moved closer as well and placed her hands on my shoulders. "That would be quite a kiss."

I gripped her hips and pulled her against my excitement. "I'm optimistic we could pull it off."

She rose onto her tiptoes and dipped my head toward hers until our mouths hovered near each other. Her breath became a tickle on my lips. "I *am* nervous about our first date."

"I have a cure for that," I said in a deep growl.

She met the kiss halfway and with a boldness that wiped my brain clean of everything beyond how good she felt in my arms. Her mouth opened to mine; our tongues swirled and teased. Her hands gripped my shoulders as my dick pulsed against her. I could have fucked her right then. She moaned against my mouth, sounding like she was thinking the same thing.

I'd been attracted to her the day she'd come to my aid on the side of the road, but after getting to know her better, my attraction to her was deeper. Yes, I wanted to claim her, but I also wanted to kiss away her worry. She tasted like sunshine and possibilities, and as crazy as it seemed, I saw our future children. A boy and girl. Saw them as clearly as if someone had shown me a photo of them. I shuddered against her.

"We could wait for her to bring him in and introduce us," a male voice said from nearby, pulling me back from heaven. I broke off the kiss and stepped back from McKenna, leaving us both breathing heavily.

Three men—two in coveralls, one in a suit—joined us. The tallest of them, the one in the suit, said, "No, I'm sure he won't mind meeting us before he makes himself . . . at home."

McKenna put a hand on my upper arm. "Hi, guys. This is Christof Romano." She waved a hand in the direction of the three older men. "Christof, this is my crew: my friends and business partners, Ty, Cal, and Wayne."

I shook all three of the men's hands, although not nearly as roughly as they shook mine. "Nice to meet you."

"We thought we'd show you around." Wayne nodded toward the building behind them.

"That's not necessary," McKenna said quickly.

This was her family. They were obviously protective of her, and I respected that. "I'd love a tour." If our roles were reversed, I'd definitely want to know what my intentions were.

In such situations, clarity was key. I held out my hand for McKenna to take. She looked from me to her crew and back before placing her hand in mine. It was a subtle but not-so-subtle message that I was there for her, not the tour. I wanted to make it clear to her that nothing she'd said earlier had spooked me.

Seriously, compared to my family asking me to smooth things over with *the devil*, McKenna's small freak-out was barely a blip on my radar. She shot me a side glance as we followed the men toward the garage. I bent my head and said, "Do you know how many people have dreams they never follow through on and make a reality? Never let anyone make you feel bad about doing something you love. Especially something you planned with your father."

She blinked a few times quickly. "You remember?"

"More every day. Before I drove up, I checked out a map of this place. It's exactly what you described to me."

Her hand tightened on mine. "Don't sound so surprised. You were the first to believe I could do it. You said all I had to do was determine what was standing between me and Decker Park being a reality, then break it down to achievable tasks. That's what I did."

"You're welcome," I joked with a cocky smile. She way overplayed my role in her success, but it was fun to play along.

With her free hand, she lightly punched my arm. "I'm being serious."

I pulled her closer and gave her cheek a quick kiss. "And I'm grateful for loose engine hoses, because I have a feeling we were meant to meet again."

She tensed, and I regretted possibly saying too much too soon. I'd told myself I'd go slowly with her, but my brain turned to mush around her.

I'd never imagined children with a woman before, and I'd been with enough who'd suggested them. There'd been nothing wrong with the other women—well, not with most of them—but McKenna was definitely different.

My father thought she might be the one.

I was beginning to think he was right.

CHAPTER EIGHTEEN

McKenna

I didn't hear half of what the guys said as we toured the garage side of the building. I was too busy beating myself up for vomiting all of my emotional baggage on Christof the moment he'd arrived.

Hi, welcome to Decker Park, a.k.a. Psychoville.

You might have been sweet to me all week, sent me food, even driven up to take me out on a date, but . . . hold on, buddy. I have some serious insecurities I need to lay at your feet.

But don't worry, if you're honest, I might still fuck you.

Why would I say that?

I groaned.

Christof released my hand to allow him to weave between the cars with Wayne and Cal. Ty stayed beside me. "Seems like a nice enough guy."

"Don't get too attached to him. You should have seen all the stupid shit that came out of my mouth when he arrived."

"He didn't appear that bothered to me."

I wasn't so sure. He might have been hanging around for a one and done. Or was I the ass? "Do I want to drive him off? Is that why I keep saying stupid things to him? I don't get it. I really like him."

"Cut yourself some slack, McKenna. You haven't had a lot of examples of good relationships in your life. Okay, Cal and Wayne, maybe, but outside of them? It's not like I've set an example for you."

I sighed. "It doesn't matter. He's already glimpsed my crazy side. All I can do now is wait and see if it's changed the way he sees me."

"That man is clearly interested in you."

"For how long, though? Is this really worth all the trouble when so few relationships work out anyway?"

"Nothing in life comes with a guarantee, McKenna. You could marry him, and he could cheat on you. He could remain faithful and die out of the blue. Life sucks sometimes."

My gaze was riveted to Ty's. "I was hoping for a little more optimism from you."

"Why? You've already decided it can't possibly work out with Christof."

"I never—" I stopped when I realized how spot on he was. "Do you think I'm too messed up for him?"

Ty put his arm around my shoulders, a first for us, and kissed the side of my head. "No, baby, you're the perfect amount of fucked up."

I swear I heard my father's voice in his in that moment. Tears filled my eyes, and I leaned against his chest. "Thanks, Ty."

He released me and cleared his throat. "Opportunities come to all of us, McKenna, but we often fail to see them for what they are. This guy might be your chance for a real family."

I threw my arms around him then and gave him the tightest hug I could. "I already have one of those." When I released him, I dabbed under my eyes. "Did I tell you he cooks? From scratch. Will you still love me if I get fat?"

Ty chuckled, but his eyes still shone with emotion. "Get?"

I smacked his chest. "And I was going to share some of those home-cooked meals with you. You can kiss that opportunity goodbye."

Christof, Cal, and Wayne returned before Ty had a chance to respond. The three of them were smiling. Christof said, "This place is amazing. Cal said Richie Elliott will be here in an hour. If you're hungry, we don't have to stay, but I'd love to watch him tear up the course."

When his fingers laced with mine, it felt natural and right. Although I'd been excited for our date, I'd been a little sad to miss seeing Elliott on my tracks as well. "I'm sure we could fit both into our date."

Cal sidled over. "Christof was telling us that he refurbished his car. We thought we'd take a quick look under his hood before making our way over to the showroom."

I froze. Cal and Wayne had been on their best behavior, but I doubted they'd be able to contain their mirth when they saw Christof's creative mechanics. "Let's not—"

"I don't get to show my handiwork to too many real mechanics. I'd love to see what you guys think," Christof said before I could persuade anyone that it wasn't a good idea.

Resigned, I followed everyone outside. I held my breath when my crew gathered around the hood of Christof's car and he popped the hood up. They knew he was important to me, but they were also experts in their field. I was good; they were better. I wanted to spare Christof the sting of their advice.

Proud as could be, Christof walked them through what he'd done, explaining it as if to people who might not understand. Their expressions reflected my repulsion when I'd first seen Christof's creative engineering, but they slowly changed as he explained his rationale for where some of the parts were. I stepped closer.

Beginning to look impressed, Ty bent over the hood and asked, "What's that little gadget there?"

"Oh, something I designed to update the air quality in the car. It works better than the original system and, I like to think, better than what they have in new cars. I knew what I wanted, drew up the specs, and I had a friend of my brother make it for me."

"McKenna, look at this," Ty said. "Ever see anything like that?"

I leaned in to check out what Ty was referring to. "No, but it's genius. Takes up so little room. I don't see the cooling system." I meant it. Now that I had time to study Christof's work, I was impressed as well.

"That's it. Small and self-contained."

"Does it actually work?" Cal asked.

"You're welcome to try it," Christof said as he handed his keys to Cal, then stood there, hands on hips, as if showing off a child of his. Cal got in and started the car. Wayne got in on the passenger side.

"Instantly cool," Cal said. "Impressive."

Wayne whistled. "It's really quite ingenious when you think of it. And a simple solution. Can't believe no one has thought of it before. You should patent it. You'd be rich."

Cal elbowed Wayne. "He's already rich."

Wayne shrugged. "Still, it's a nifty little gadget. I'd buy one. Get that patent, Christof, before someone steals your idea."

"I will, thanks," Christof said with a bright smile. To me, he mouthed, "Ingenious." He thumbed toward his chest.

I laughed. I loved that he didn't take himself too seriously. "If we're done oohing and aahing over Christof's car, could we finish the tour? Elliott will be here any time now, and I'm already starving."

After Christof closed the hood of his car, Cal said, "If you ever want help working on your car, I've got time to lend you."

Wayne added, "Me too."

Tongue in cheek, I joked, "Back off, boys—I'm the only one allowed to touch his engine."

"No worries, McKenna," Cal said with a chuckle, then linked hands with Wayne. I watched for any sign that Christof might be uncomfortable around Cal and Wayne. He laughed along with them, and I fell a little in love with him right there.

An intercom announced the arrival of Elliott. I exchanged an excited look with Christof.

I was about to suggest we drive Mack down to the track when Ty put a hand out to halt Christof. "Be good to our baby girl," he said in a low tone.

Christof looked down at me, winked, then turned back toward Ty. "I intend to be. I have a feeling she could kick my ass."

We all shared another laugh, and I went up onto my toes to deliver a quick kiss to Christof. Ty was right: Life didn't come with guarantees. Whatever this was, it might last a day, a week, or forever. The real tragedy wouldn't be if it fell apart; it would be if I let my fears be the reason it never had a chance to be at all. "Come on. I don't want to miss anything."

Christof smiled back at me, not moving at first, and said, "Me neither. I'm glad I came."

CHAPTER NINETEEN

CHRISTOF

After dinner that night I sat beside McKenna on the steps of her house. She looked about to invite me in. I was tempted to kiss her until she did. I held back because what we had between us felt too important to rush.

I raised her hand to my lips and kissed her knuckles. Before heading down to the racetrack, she'd shed her coveralls, revealing tight jeans and a T-shirt that clung to her curves, cleaned the smudge of oil off her face, and added a touch of lip gloss. I thought back to the killer little black dress I'd also seen her in. She was beautiful regardless of what she wore.

"My brothers will all be jealous when I tell them I met Elliott. You looked as excited to watch him go as I did. Does it ever get old?"

"Never," she assured me, leaning her head against my shoulder. "I sometimes wake up and worry this is all a dream."

"That's how you know you're doing something right. You've got a lot to be proud of."

"As well as grateful. I couldn't have done it myself."

"That's true of most things people do. Definitely for me. Everything my family has, we've built together."

She let out a sigh. "I love the way you talk about your family. It's like watching a Hallmark movie. What was it like to grow up in a perfect family?"

I choked on that one. "Perfect? We aren't that. My head is still spinning from the conversation I had with my parents this morning."

"You mentioned they'd said something odd. You don't have to tell me what it was, but I'm so curious I might keep asking you to until you do."

"So I don't have to, but you'll pester me until I cave?"

She raised her head and met my gaze. "Is that wrong?"

I kissed her forehead. "A little."

"So will you tell me?"

"I shouldn't."

"How about now?"

What a little shit she was. I loved it. "I'm not ready for your opinion of my family to plummet."

"Perfectly understandable." She looked away, then back. "How about now?"

"No." Perma-grin was a real condition around her.

"I respect your need for boundaries and privacy."

"Good."

"Now?"

I laughed, and she joined in. "It's a long, complicated story with a twist at the end you won't expect."

"I'm not afraid of complicated or an unexpected turn." She cuddled closer, making me question why I was taking it slow at all. We'd both be just as happy if I threw her over my shoulder and hunted down her bed. Wouldn't we? It was the not knowing that held me back. What if this had the potential of mattering if I was patient? I hadn't waited with most of the women I'd dated. That wasn't what they were looking for. None of those hookups had led anywhere, which I'd been okay with.

I already didn't like the idea of McKenna with another man.

I hadn't left yet, and I already knew I'd miss her as soon as I did. "One of my brothers is actually a cousin."

"Yes, I remember you telling me about Gian. His mother left him with yours to raise."

"Okay, so maybe this won't be as confusing as I thought."

I started as my mother had, at the beginning, when she'd met Antonio Corisi. If McKenna stayed in my life, this might affect her as well. Her mouth dropped open when she made the connection between my family and the infamous Dominic Corisi.

She swore a few times when I described Antonio's crimes against my aunt, her own children, as well as my family in Montalcino. Perhaps because the whole story sounded so over the top to me, it flowed out as if I were speaking of something that had happened to another family.

"Gian is Dominic Corisi's half brother. Do either know?" she asked.

"I don't believe so. Dominic is trying to connect with our grandmother. I can't see him knowing about Gian and not reaching out to him. I wouldn't blame him if he knew and didn't, though." I described how Dominic had been turned away from the family recently.

McKenna's hands went to her heart. "He must have been so hurt."

"Actually, it pissed him off." I told her how he'd purchased the land my family over there was leasing and of his impending return to the town. "That's some near-villain behavior there."

"All because he wants to meet his nona? That's heartbreaking."

"It is, right? Most likely I'll be heading to Montalcino tomorrow. I want to be there when he arrives. I'll meet with him, then convince my family to welcome him for a visit."

She searched my face. "I admire your confidence. I'm still trying to wrap my head around how much hurt there is on all sides of this."

"Hurt, anger, accusations, *and* threats. Like a dog chasing its tail, they're going around and around swiping at each other. If I can get either side to stop, the unhealthy cycle will be broken. I honestly don't know if anyone will listen to me, but I'll try."

"That's all you can do."

"Not according to my parents. You should have heard their idea." McKenna had handled the rest so well. Would she think my parents' idea amusing and dismiss it as I had?

"What did they think you should do?" Her eyes were wide and eager, like those of a child promised an early Christmas present.

"Nothing I'd agree to. My mother told Nona I was bringing my fiancée over to meet her."

McKenna tensed and moved away from me. "You're engaged?"

Whoa. I hadn't expected her to think that. "No. Of course not. In my mother's romance-reading mind, I should ask *you* to pretend we're engaged. We'd fly over, invite Dominic to our engagement party—everyone would be in such a good mood they'd accept him into the family, and we'd all live happily ever after."

McKenna seemed to relax a bit. "A fake engagement."

"Crazy. I told you."

"Did your mother actually suggest me?"

"She did."

"Why? I mean, why me? I'm sure you know other women."

I met her gaze. "I don't usually tell my family about anyone I'm seeing, but I told them about you. It gave my parents the idea that this could start off as a pretense but take us somewhere real."

"We hardly know each other."

"That's exactly what I told my parents."

A frown wrinkled her forehead. "How long will you be in Italy?"

"As long as it takes, but I'm hoping for no more than a week or so."

"I have a business to run. Even if I wanted to do it, I couldn't step away for some unknown amount of time."

"I wouldn't feel comfortable asking you to."

She tapped a hand on her knee. "Where would we even stay? A hotel?" She gave me a long look that set my heart racing. "That's too much too soon."

She sounded more tempted than convinced, and I could hardly breathe. "Way too much." I cleared my throat. "But we'd stay at my nona's house. Separate rooms for everyone until they're married."

After a moment, McKenna asked, "This is your mother's mother?"

"Yes. My father's family moved away, and we lost touch with them. My father said they had a falling-out over my mother, but if he had the chance to do it all again, he would choose her every time. They've been married over thirty years."

McKenna smiled. "That's beautiful. Can you imagine being with anyone that long?"

I let her question sink in before answering. As my father had said, honesty was the cornerstone to a solid relationship. "Yes. Yes, I can. Romanos are like geese. We tend to mate for life."

She laughed. "Most men describe themselves as lions or sharks. Geese? Really?"

Unbothered by her amusement, I took her hand in mine, lacing our fingers together. "Well, let's see. If I were a lion, I'd be looking for you to be one of many. I'd strut around, roar at competing males, while you and my other ladies did all the work. I can't really speak to the mating habits of sharks because there is such diversity in the species. I think I read somewhere that they don't mate as often since their gestation period is so long. Also, they travel long distances to their breeding grounds. So if you're looking for infrequent sex with a loner who travels extensively, I guess a shark wouldn't be a bad choice."

Her eyes were twinkling with humor. "I can't say I've ever thought much about it."

I shrugged. "All I'm saying is that geese are loyal, highly intelligent, as well as extremely protective of their families. You could do far worse."

She gave me another long look. "What do you like about me, Christof?"

The question took me by surprise, but I answered without hesitation. "What is there not to? You take care of people—even strangers broken down on the side of the road. You're intelligent, successful, resilient, and snarky. Confidence is sexier than lingerie every day of the week."

"Most men would have only said I'm beautiful."

I caressed her cheek with the back of her hand. "We've already surmised that you've been hanging with the wrong type. No geese in the stock car world?"

"Not in mine."

I turned her face toward me and gave her a kiss I hoped expressed everything I was feeling. It was tender, hungry, hopeful. I didn't know where this was going, but the more time I spent with her, the more I was certain I didn't want it to end.

I broke off the kiss just as it was starting to deepen. If I wasn't staying, it was time to leave, before I changed my mind. "McKenna, I should go."

We were both breathing raggedly. Her eyes were heavy with desire, and I half expected her to say I could stay. When she didn't, I wasn't disappointed. I took it to mean that she might also see potential in us.

She cupped my cheek with her hand. "You scare the shit out of me, Christof."

A laugh rumbled in my chest. "Funny, being with you has the opposite effect on me. I like you, McKenna, and I like who I am when I'm with you."

"I like who I am when I'm with you too." Her hand shook against my face. "I work a lot. I never take vacations."

"I'm the same." Was that her way of warning me there wasn't room for me in her life? I hoped not. I took her hand in mine and gave it a squeeze. "We don't have to figure out everything today. We can take this slow."

She held my gaze and lowered our hands. "Tell me about the town your family is from in Italy."

Whoa. "Are you considering being my fake fiancée?" I joked.

I wished I knew her well enough to be able to interpret the look she gave me. "No. We already established that it's a crazy idea."

"We did."

"I'm just trying to imagine where you're from."

"Oh, okay. Well, then close your eyes."

She did.

I took a moment to appreciate the beauty of her before I said, "Picture driving up a hill lined by oak trees. They thin out as you go higher. In the breaks between them, you get a view of olive orchards and vineyards. When you begin to enter the town, you think it'll be like any other town in Italy. Traffic. A gas station. Old buildings. Then suddenly stone walls rise up, and the streets become narrow. You park because driving has become too much of a hassle, but walking gives you the chance to discover the small restaurants hidden away. It's an old fortress town. If there weren't Vespas and small cars parked in every available nook, you'd swear you'd traveled back in time. Just when you think you don't belong, a door flies open, and someone calls you over. It's one of my many cousins wanting to feed you or ask you a hundred overly personal questions, then feed you. If they bring out the wine, write off the next few hours because you're not going anywhere."

She opened her eyes. "I'm trying to imagine it, but I can't. I've never been anywhere remotely like that. Do they speak English?"

"In the shops they do. Some in my family don't or won't. Italian is a bond that keeps us connected. Although I will say that when I'm in the United States, I feel Italian, but when I'm in Montalcino, I feel very American."

"It sounds amazing."

"Does it? Don't forget about the looming, angry billionaire and my grandmother, who gets so confused lately she may or may not think I'm one of my brothers."

"How old is she?"

"She's in her nineties."

"I never knew my grandparents, but I used to try to imagine what having one would be like. Do they really spoil their grandchildren? Is it at all like how it seems on TV?"

"Yes and no. Love is complicated. My grandmother went through some tough times, and she has held on to some grudges. I never thought it affected me, but now I see it has. I'm really hoping something I say can reach her and give her some peace."

"I'm surprised your parents aren't going with you."

"It's too much for my mother, which is how I know the wounds are deep. My mother doesn't hide from uncomfortable situations. She takes them on—head-on. Whatever went down between her and my aunt was ugly, and it still affects all of them. All of us as well."

"Why aren't your brothers going with you?"

"Sebastian is waiting on the arrival of his second child. Mauricio is good with a lot of things, but not delicate family matters. And there's too much that could go wrong to involve Gian yet. If Dominic shows me anything promising, I'll have him fly over and join me. They're brothers. They deserve a chance to know each other."

"That's a lot to handle on your own."

"That's the way I roll for now. Unless pretending to be engaged while putting out family fires sounds like a good time to you."

"It does sound intriguing. Would going with a fiancée really make it easier?"

My heart started to thud in my chest. She was actually considering it. Or was she? I couldn't tell. "My grandmother wants to see us all married before she passes, so she'd be delighted. When my brothers brought their fiancées over to meet the family, there were large celebrations. I don't honestly know."

"Ty could cover for me for a week. Especially since Cal and Wayne are back."

"Don't feel obligated to do this."

135

She cocked her head to one side. "You don't want to be fake engaged to me?"

She was busting my chops again. I decided to test how far she'd take this. "I'm in if you're in. We'll use my family's private plane and fly over tomorrow morning."

We sat there, looking into each other's eyes. "Fine, I'll update Ty tonight on what I have going. Our phones will work there anyway, right? In case he has a question?"

"Absolutely." I expected her to burst out laughing and agree that the whole idea was nuts, but she was maintaining a remarkably straight face. "Since it was my parents' idea, I'll borrow one of my mother's diamonds. My family will expect you to have something. We can resize it if we need to there."

She stood. "I need to get packing if we're leaving tomorrow morning."

"Do you have a passport?"

"Of course. It's not like I've never been anywhere."

I rose to my feet as well. No way did she intend to actually do this. "I'll send a car for you."

She nodded and gave me a sweet kiss that confused me even more. "I'll be ready."

I stood there, halfway up her steps, trying to figure out if I'd lost my mind. "I'm really sending a car."

She smiled and opened the door to her house. "I'm really going inside to pack."

"So we're doing this?"

"See you tomorrow." She waved and went inside.

I got into my car and sat there in her driveway.

Did I just get engaged?

Holy shit, she said yes.

CHAPTER TWENTY

McKenna

The next morning I gripped my purse on my lap as the car Christof had sent for me sped along the highway. I hadn't slept much. Several times I'd almost called Christof to tell him I'd changed my mind. Talk about allowing him to become a distraction—*I was leaving the country with him.*

Before packing, I'd called my crew to tell them Christof had invited me to go to Italy with him for a week. Cal had thought it was incredibly romantic. Wayne had agreed and suggested I make time for a little car shopping while we were there. You know, in case I wasn't sure yet what to give him for Christmas.

Ty had wanted more information than I'd felt comfortable giving him. Christof had told me his family's issues in confidence. If he wanted Ty to know, he could tell him the whole story when we returned. I made the mistake of telling Ty that Christof was taking me to meet his family.

"You don't think it's too soon?" Ty asked. "So far I like the guy, but there's no need to rush into anything. I don't know if I feel comfortable with you going."

I was glad I'd left off the fake-engagement part as well. "He's not pressuring me to. He was already planning the trip. When he told me about the town his family is from, it sounded so amazing I wanted to see it. We'll be staying at his grandmother's house. Homemade pasta and wine. The only risk is that I'll come home five pounds heavier."

"Call me every day," Ty said gruffly.

I promised to. I also added, "I'm a big girl, Ty. If any part of this isn't what it seems, I'm perfectly capable of flying my ass home."

Cal chimed in, "I'm proud of you for finally taking a risk with someone, McKenna. I know you're happy on your own, but he's adorable and he can cook. I would have said yes, yes, hell yes."

Wayne said something in the background that wasn't clear enough for me to understand, but I got the gist of it when Cal added, "Not now. I'm saying if I was McKenna. Unbunch your panties. We're fine."

We'd ended the call with Ty telling me to be careful and Cal making me promise not to be so careful I didn't enjoy myself. I was smiling when I hung up.

Arriving at the private airfield brought me back to the moment. Was I crazy to have agreed to go? I was committing to spending a significant amount of time with Christof. Would it affect my business? I'd never stepped away before.

Dressed in jeans and a collared shirt, Christof stood at the bottom of the plane's steps waving. There was nothing threatening at all about him. I waved back. The big smile on his face sent my heart beating wildly.

He opened the door of the car before the driver had a chance to. He offered me his hand, and I took it. "You're really here."

With my head tipped back so I could see his face, I said, "Did you doubt it?"

He cupped my face and gave me a long, toe-curling kiss. It was exactly the kind of kiss every woman dreams of being greeted with. I clung to him, giving myself over to it.

When he raised his head, he growled, "I'm glad you came."

After catching my breath, I said, "Me too."

"Ready to go?"

I nodded. More than ready.

Hand in hand we walked up the ramp, and he helped me step into the plane. Then we made our way to adjacent seats. He buckled me in. I could have told him I was perfectly capable of doing it myself, but with Christof, being cared for didn't feel suffocating.

As we sat there, I thought about the men who had tried to take care of me in the past. Their attention had come with a price. To remain with them, I would have had to give up part of myself. It didn't feel that way with Christof. He wasn't picking at what I was wearing, prompting me on how to behave, or promising how much better my life would be with him.

Was it possible I'd finally found a man I could be myself with?

After securing himself in, Christof said, "I have something for you."

"You do?"

He took a ring box out of a bag on the floor of the plane and flipped it open. A small diamond sparkled from a delicately styled setting. I gripped the arms of my seat. His expression turned concerned. "You know you don't have to do this."

"I want to." It was difficult to sort out where the panic was coming from. He was far from pressuring me. I forced myself to let go of the armrests. "It's beautiful."

"Not impressive in size, but it was passed down to my mother from her favorite aunt. She said that ring was worn first on Aunt Annelise's finger, then on a necklace my uncle wore after she passed away. If there are any vibes attached to it, they're all good ones. That is, if you believe in that kind of thing."

"I don't." Or I didn't. I wasn't sure of much anymore. I removed the ring from the box and turned it slowly so it reflected the light coming in from the window of the plane. "It's better than being cursed, I guess."

He chuckled. "Something tells me you don't believe in curses either."

"I never put much faith in things I can't see."

"I do," he said simply.

Arguing about faith or politics wasn't the way I wanted to start our trip, but I had to ask, "Why?"

Some might have gotten defensive at my question or taken it as an opening to push their beliefs on me, but that wasn't Christof. He took a moment, then said, "The moon isn't visible in the sky right now, but I know it'll be back tonight. It's not gone just because I can't see it. That's how I feel about my faith."

I wasn't a religious person, but the simplicity of his words moved me. I believed my father was with me even though I couldn't see or hear him.

There was no denying Christof showing up in my life again felt too significant to be by chance. No, he wasn't what I considered my type— he was better. Not cocky . . . confident. Solid. So much sexier than the peacocks I met on a regular basis. I slipped his ring on my finger. I had that nervous, nauseated, sweaty-hand feeling that we were meant to do this—together. "Do we have to come up with a story about how we met or anything? What does your family in Montalcino know about me?"

He closed the ring box and replaced it in the bag on the floor. "They know we met when we were twenty and that we reconnected recently. The truth is a good-enough story."

I studied the ring again. "Except for the part about this not being real." I met his gaze. The way he was looking at me would have made it easy enough to forget that part.

"Except that."

I told myself it was crazy to be even a little disappointed at how unbothered he was by something that was playing havoc with my emotions. "Sounds like this should go smoothly enough."

The plane tipped back as it left the ground, and my hand naturally found its way to Christof's. He smiled down at me. "I can't believe you agreed to come, but I'm excited to show you around my hometown. Plus, I've arranged for a surprise for you while we're there."

"A surprise?"

"Did you really think I'd let you take a week off from work to help me without coming up with a way to thank you?"

Warmth spread through me. "What did you come up with?"

"A surprise."

"I don't like surprises. Just tell me."

"No."

My eyebrows rose. "Seriously, I'll still be excited about whatever it is."

"Not saying a word. Consider me a vault."

Challenge accepted. I released his hand, leaned closer, and ran my hand lightly up his thigh. "A vault?"

He sucked in an audible breath and grabbed my hand before it reached where it was headed. "No fair bringing out the big guns, lady, when I'm doing my best to keep my hands off you."

If there weren't an intense sexual sizzle between us, I might have been embarrassed. I wasn't used to men saying no. "Maybe you don't have to."

His nostrils flared, and his hand tightened on mine. "I'm all for telling the attendant to stay out of this area and fucking all the way to Italy, but I've never taken things slowly with anyone, and I'm trying to with you."

I bit my bottom lip and took a calming breath. "You are so different than anyone I've been with. If they said that, I would have called bullshit, but you mean it."

"I do."

I thought of all the times I hadn't waited and didn't like how those memories made me feel. I moved to withdraw my hand, but he held it to his thigh. I said, "I'm not like you. When you pick a real fiancée, you should definitely choose someone more like yourself."

"What is this about?"

I tensed and admitted, "I wasn't a virgin when we met in that bar. Far from it."

He frowned. "McKenna, I don't care who you've been with."

"I just want to be real with you," I growled, and this time I really attempted to pull my hand free.

"Look at me," he said gently.

Fighting back tears I couldn't explain, I did, but my lips were pressed together in anger, and I was just a hair from pulling back and smacking him with my free hand. "What?"

"Didn't we say we'd both be blank slates for each other?"

"Yes." We had. I wasn't sure why I'd even brought it up. Because he wasn't rushing me? Because I didn't want a repeat of how I'd shown him Decker Park? I sounded as defensive as I felt but couldn't help it. "I want to be myself with you. No pretense."

His tone was reassuring. "That's how we should be with each other. Take whatever image you have of who you think I want to be with and toss it out that window. She'd bore me to tears and bring out the worst in me. Just like those guys you dated who didn't bring out the best in you. How could they when they didn't know you? That's all I'm doing, McKenna. I'm not judging. I'm not making promises. All I'm doing is taking the time to get to know you."

My hand relaxed beneath his. He wasn't nearly the pushover his laid-back attitude led people to believe he might be. He was a man with a clear idea of what he wanted. And right then, he wanted me.

All of me.

Not just sex.

I found myself wanting to be whatever it was he saw in me. "I'm not ashamed of anything I've done."

His gaze was steady. "Good, because neither am I."

I let out a shaky breath and changed course. "I can't believe you won't tell me what you're planning."

"That's the definition of a surprise."

"I don't handle those well."

"Really? I couldn't tell." The twinkle was back in his eyes.

"You're an ass."

"Still not going to tell you."

"I no longer want to know."

"Good, because I'm not giving you so much as a hint."

"Fine."

We exchanged a look and both burst out laughing like longtime friends. Still holding hands, like the lovers we weren't yet.

CHAPTER TWENTY-ONE

CHRISTOF

It occurred to me more than once over the next several hours that I could have been handling this all wrong. Some of my friends had been with their wives straight out of the gate, and that hadn't stopped anything serious from developing.

I'd meant every word I'd said about not caring about who she'd been with before me. If Sebastian's journey and loss had taught me anything, it was that it was more important to be real with each other than perfect, and life was too short to waste it living in the past. All that mattered to me with McKenna was how we moved forward together. If we did. I could see how she could fit into my life, but for her the jury was still out on if I could fit into hers.

And that was okay.

Friendship was not a bad place to start. If it led to more, I was sure it would be incredible. If it didn't, I genuinely liked the woman beside me.

I wanted to hunt down every creep who'd ever done less than treasure her, but then again, if they had, she wouldn't be flying off to Italy with me. So if I ever met one of them, maybe I'd thank them.

After I beat the shit out of them.

The thought brought a smile to my face, as did the view of McKenna lightly snoring as she slept against my arm. I was tempted to videotape her and show her when she woke, but I decided it'd be even better to capture her after-sex snore and give her shit for it then.

She'd likely whack me in the head with a pillow and pretend to be upset. Making up, even when there'd been no real offense, could be fun.

As if she could feel my gaze, her eyes flickered and opened. "I fell asleep."

"I noticed."

She straightened, her hands smoothing down her hair. "Sorry."

"Don't be. You were tired."

She searched my face. "Why do you look so amused?"

"No reason."

Her eyebrows met in the middle. "Was I drooling?"

"Not a drop."

Her eyes narrowed. "For such a nice man you've got a little edge to you."

"I never claimed to be nice." My grin was shameless. "This is where I admit to also being gifted at giving people shit."

Her attention went to the ring on her left hand. "Even your fiancée?" she joked.

I nuzzled just above her ear and whispered, "Especially her."

She turned toward me, our lips only a breath away from each other. "That's a dangerous game to play. I hear she gives as good as she gets."

I kept our kiss light and teasing. "I'm counting on it."

She blushed, and had she asked me for anything just then, there was nothing I would have denied her. "We'll be landing in a few minutes."

"Wow, that went fast."

"For you. For me it was a slow torture of you cuddled against me, filling my head with all the ways we could have spent this flight."

She gave me an odd look. "You're the one who didn't want to."

I wagged a finger in the air. "That's where this is uncharted territory for me. I've wanted long enough to ache from it."

She frowned, and I didn't like the way I'd voiced how I felt. I was ready to confess that my brain turned useless around her and apologize for sounding like a horny teenager.

Before I could, she wrinkled her nose at me. "Next you'll tell me geese don't fuck on planes."

I burst out laughing, and all tension disappeared between us. "I don't imagine they do. Although it's something we might want to test in the future."

With laughter in her eyes, she said, "You'll have to get a plane with a bedroom and a shower. Geese like to shower after sex marathons."

"So you're a goose too?" It was a sheer joy to see her laughing again.

"Could we stop talking about animals fornicating? It's putting weird images in my head."

"You brought it up."

"I did. Sorry." Her expression sobered. "So what happens when we land?"

"My cousin will collect us from the airport. We'll drive straight to Nona's. I'll introduce you. We'll eat. Probably meet more family. Then head off to bed at a respectable time. This part of the trip won't be the most exciting, but as soon as I resolve the issue with Dominic, we can do some sightseeing."

She put her hand on my arm. "It actually sounds amazing. I can't wait to see what your family is like."

"I hope they live up to what you're imagining."

Her excitement sent a warm feeling through me. I leaned over and kissed her. Being with her felt so natural. So sweet. How had any man ever walked away from McKenna? I couldn't imagine being able to.

Her expression turned serious after we broke the kiss off. "When you meet with Dominic, I want to go with you."

I shook my head. There were too many ways the situation could go wrong. "It may not be a pleasant meeting."

Her expression turned opaque. "I don't have to be in the same room, but I will be right outside. Think of me as your pit crew," she said in a lower tone. "Whatever happens, I'll be there if you need me."

Oh, I could fall hard for this woman. "I've never had a pit crew. Does this mean I don't have to pump my own gas anymore?"

She gave me a long look. "I'm serious."

I kissed her briefly before saying, "Yes, you can come with me, but I'll need to speak to him alone first. He's been angry for a long time. That won't be easy to break through."

"If anyone can do it, you can."

"I'm going to try."

When the pilot announced our descent, I reached for McKenna's hand again. Dominic wasn't the kind of person to arrive anywhere unnoticed. I had people in place who would inform me as soon as he set foot in Italy.

One step at a time, though. First, I needed to introduce my fiancée to the family.

CHAPTER TWENTY-TWO

McKenna

Montalcino was just as Christof had described it. Although we'd arrived by private plane just outside the town, we were driven up winding roads by one of Christof's cousins, Luigi. I'd never been afraid of speed or fast corners, but I'd admit I closed my eyes and gripped the door handle a few times. How Luigi hadn't yet killed anyone or smashed the little tin can of a car we were in was beyond me.

I was seated in the front seat, which thankfully had a seat belt. Untethered, Christof chatted from the back. The warm bond between the two was fun to watch. Luigi's accent was thick, but I could understand him easily. He and Christof spoke in English, for my benefit, but occasionally, when the conversation sped up, it flipped to Italian before Christof would pull it back to English and tell me what they'd said. None of it was anything I couldn't have guessed. They had differing opinions on who would win the World Cup as well as whose *pinci* pasta I couldn't leave without sampling.

It was my first trip to Europe, so I didn't know what to expect, but our arrival was greeted as if Christof were the prodigal son. Luigi honked and slowed as he went down some of the narrow streets. Windows flew open, and people called out welcomes to Christof.

"Are you related to everyone in town?" I joked.

Leaning forward so his head was between his cousin and me, Christof said, "Enough that dating from this pool has always been too risky. Not that that has stopped Luigi."

Luigi said something in Italian. Christof laughed. A moment later Luigi did as well.

"McKenna," Luigi said, "I need a rich American wife. Do you have a friend for me?"

Christof answered before I could. "Stick with dating your third and fourth cousins. American women can't cook."

My head snapped around, and I shot Christof a warning look. "First, no blanket statements about Americans, please. It's so wrong to clump us together and stamp a stereotype on us."

"So you do cook?" Luigi asked.

A grin spread across Christof's face. I folded my arms over my chest and sat back with a huff. "That's irrelevant."

"Don't worry, beautiful McKenna, Christof is the daughter his mother always wanted. He'll cook for you."

The punch Christof delivered to Luigi's arm caused the car to swerve and almost take out a couple who looked like tourists. I gripped the door handle again. What Christof said to Luigi also didn't require translation to be understood, but Luigi laughed it off.

"How far to Nona's?" I asked. Some of the ride was enjoyable. The teasing between Christof and his cousin was comical. Their banter reminded me of how Ty and I often spoke.

"We have arrived," Luigi announced as he pulled off the road and between two stone walls with skill any race driver would admire.

Christof was out and opening my car door before I had a chance to catch my breath. I took the hand he offered me and breathed in the charm of his family's villa. Cypress trees lined one side of the driveway. Rectangular red clay pots of flowers topped the stone walls. In the distance I could see the tower of the fortress Christof had mentioned. What little yard the villa had was shaded. There were wooden tables and folding chairs sprinkled around the grass. Quaint. Warm. Timeless.

The front door opened, and a small herd of children poured out. The youngest was a girl who looked to be about four years old. There were two more girls slightly older, then two boys who appeared to be in their early teens. Christof greeted each of them, then introduced me. I was still trying to link names to faces when more of Christof's family came out to greet us.

Sofia and her husband, Giovanni. Vincenzo and his pregnant wife, Elisabetta. They were the parents of some of the children, but which ones I wasn't clear on. There was a Mario, a Salvatore, and a Ricardo. Pia, Marcia, and Lucia were their wives, but if my life had depended on it, I couldn't have remembered which man they said they were with.

Behind them, on the arm of a young man, came a petite white-haired woman in a blue cotton shirt, gray skirt, lavender crocheted sweater, and big loose boots that looked like they were leftovers from one of the World Wars. She cupped Christof's face between both of her hands and rattled off the rest of her greeting in Italian, then turned to me. "Wren. You return."

I didn't want to correct her, so I smiled and accepted the kiss she gave both of my cheeks.

Christof put his hand on her shoulder. "Nona, this is McKenna, my fiancée."

Nona's mouth rounded, and she wagged a finger at Christof. "Where is my Wren?"

"With Mauricio, Nona. I'm Christof."

She gave him a long look, then grabbed his face between her hands again. "My Christof." Without missing a beat, she added, "You got fat."

Christof laughed, likely because it was far from being true. "I missed you too, Nona."

Nona shook her head with a response in Italian, then gripped my hands. "You shouldn't be here, Heather. The devil is coming."

Luigi stepped closer to me and said, "Don't be offended, McKenna. Last week she smacked me because she thought I was Salvatore." He nodded toward his amused cousin. "I still owe you for that."

Salvatore didn't look worried in the least. "I am not the one who told her who is coming to town. That, Luigi, is on you."

"I didn't tell her. I told Mario, who told Pia—"

"Enough. I get the idea." Christof shook his head. "You weren't supposed to say anything yet. Remember, I wanted to tell everyone myself."

Luigi threw both hands up in the air. "I saved you the trouble. Besides, if the devil is coming, it's for nothing good. I made sure the whole family is ready to go to battle with you against him. We might not have fancy planes, but we know people who know people. People who make problems disappear."

Voices began to rise in anger.

My hand clasped Christof's. His expression was calm, but there was a tension in him I hadn't seen in him before. "The only devil in this town is the one whispering to you that the sins of a father belong to his son. He's done nothing wrong. All he wants is to get to know us."

One of Christof's cousins stepped closer. "So he didn't buy the land Ricardo lives on? Or the store Pia works at? He's not here to finish what his father started?"

Luigi interjected, "We can't sit back and do nothing while he comes for our homes."

"He's not going to take your homes or your businesses," Christof said.

"You don't know that," another of his cousins retorted.

"I do." The conviction in Christof's voice seemed to settle the crowd. "Dominic is family, and I will treat him as such. I intend to invite him to celebrate my engagement with us."

"The devil is no welcome in my house," Nona said with a vehement shake of her head.

Christof leaned down so his face was closer to his grandmother's. "Nona, he's your grandson."

"Antonio is evil. He's no welcome in my house."

Christof's grandmother's confusion added an additional layer of sadness to the situation. I stepped away from Christof, took one of her hands in both of mine, and said, "Nona, I hear you make the best sauce in Montalcino. It was a long trip, and I'm hungry."

His grandmother's face changed from fearful and confused to animated. She made a tsk sound at Christof. "If you starve your fiancée now, she'll starve you after the wedding. Come, McKenna. You're too skinny to be with a fat Christof."

"I'm in the best shape of my life," Christof protested, but he didn't sound upset.

Luigi added, "Look on the bright side: she called you both by your real names."

As his grandmother led me away, my gaze locked with Christof's. I mouthed, "You look good to me."

He rolled his eyes with a smile. "Thank you," he mouthed back.

At first I thought he was referring to my comment, but the look in his eye told me it was about much more. I'd never felt so connected to a man. Words weren't necessary. I knew he was grateful I'd diverted the conversation.

His family poured from the driveway into the small home. Conversation was loud, mostly in Italian, with a fair share of laughter. I was seated beside Christof at a small table in his grandmother's kitchen, finishing off aubergine parmigiana, when the wife of one of his cousins asked me if I'd ever tried Brunello di Montalcino. I almost said I wasn't much of a wine drinker, but she was already explaining to me the difference between a young and an old Brunello. Did I prefer the taste of fresh fruits or something more candied, almost chocolaty? They also made some themselves; did I want a sample?

I said I wasn't sure because when it came to wine I didn't know. After tasting a variety from several different years and comparing some made by traditional methods to those created by modern methods, I still didn't speak Italian, but I felt fluent.

Talk of the devil Dominic Corisi had vanished. The conversation revolved around how Christof and I had met, how many children we planned to have, and where we were planning on getting married. I let Christof field most of the questions while I continued to sip away at the best wine I'd ever tasted, which ended up being Nona's home brew.

Things became quite animated when Christof said I owned a race-track. Was I really a mechanic? At first they seemed to think it was a joke, but when his family realized it wasn't, I was asked more questions than I'd ever received in an interview.

All the while, I kept drinking. Getting drunk in front of Christof's grandmother hadn't been in my plans, but my glass refilled as soon as I drained it, and I drained it more often than I should have.

I'd only closed my eyes for a minute during a lull in the conversation when Christof announced it was time to show me my room. I hung on to him as he walked me down a narrow hallway to a small room. Once inside he closed the door behind us.

"I like your family," I said with a slur.

"They like you too." After propping me up against the wall, he walked to the twin bed and pulled back the sheet. "They think you're hilarious."

"I wasn't trying to be funny." I brought a hand to my spinning head. "Oh God, this is why I don't drink."

He chuckled and walked me to the side of the bed, easing me down into a seated position. "Well, tonight you did. You kept up with the best of them."

I groaned. "I wanted your family to like me."

Christof bent and removed my shoes. "You don't have to try so hard; they're not allowed to not like you."

I wiggled my left hand in the air. "Because we're engaged."

"Exactly."

I sank back onto the bed, leaving my feet on the floor. He lifted them, straightened me, then tucked a blanket around me. "What happens when we're not anymore?"

He sat on the bed beside me and ran his hand through my hair. "We'll have to wait and see, won't we?"

I stuck out my bottom lip. "Wait. Wait. Wait. You're no fun."

"Say that again tomorrow when you've sobered up, and I'll show you how wrong you are."

I smacked his chest with a heavy, floppy hand. "I bet you're good in bed. Do you have a recipe for sex in your database?" I snorted at my own joke.

He chuckled. "No, but I appreciate the faith you have in my abilities."

"I'm pretty good, myself. I can do this thing—"

He put a finger over my mouth. "I promise to give you a chance to show me soon."

I removed his hand from my mouth. "Don't sender me—" I stopped, hiccuped, and said, "Censor me. I don't need to be censored."

"Tonight you do. Just a smidge."

I made a face at him. "No man will ever tell me what to do."

He was smiling, which irritated me a little. I lived by my own rules.

He tucked my hair behind my ear and said, "I'll make a deal with you. We can take turns being in charge."

I poked him in the chest. "You say all the right things now. No one is that nice. Sooner or later the ugly side of you will pop out."

"Someone really hurt you, didn't they?"

"It doesn't matter. I don't need anyone. I'm fine on my own. If this doesn't last, I'll be okay."

"Of course you will be. You're one tough cookie, Mack." Unflappable Christof was back, but I'd seen what lay beneath. I knew he was worried about his family and if he really could fix the situation between them and Dominic. I really couldn't explain why I was pushing him away when all I wanted to do was pull him close.

Memories of my mother became tangled with our reason for being in Italy. Would Christof try to reunite Gian with his mother? I knew the pain of being left behind and exactly how it felt to reach out to someone who should love you only to discover you weren't worth their time.

I wouldn't wish that on my worst enemy. "Poor Gian. Do you think his mother will want to see him? My mother's alive. Did I tell you that? She doesn't want to know me. She doesn't love me. 'I don't have room for you in my life.'" A tear slid down my cheek. "What kind of mother says that to her child?"

"Don't think about that now. Close your eyes and sleep this off. If you want to talk about this tomorrow—"

My gut twisted painfully, and bile rose in my throat. "I don't want to talk about her ever again."

"Shh, go to sleep, Mack. You'll feel better in the morning."

My eyes were heavy enough to close on their own. "Don't tell me what to do. I'll go to sleep when I want to, not when you—"

CHAPTER TWENTY-THREE

CHRISTOF

And she's out.

Until a few minutes earlier, McKenna had been upbeat, entertaining, and, oh yes, awake. She hadn't been offended at all when my grandmother had repeatedly gotten her name wrong. It had helped, I was sure, that Nona also kept confusing me with my brothers.

I probably should have slowed the enthusiastic wine tasting my cousins had come up with for McKenna. I definitely shouldn't have joined in as much as I had. Although I wasn't drunk, I was definitely fuzzy headed. The introduction of the high-octane homemade stuff should have ended my night, but it was nice to see everyone getting along, and I'd missed them.

I'd known my cousins would love McKenna. They were good people. Most of them survived on what they made each week and had very little savings. They were too proud to take money from my parents but also vulnerable because of it.

Their concerns about Dominic were valid. He could do some real damage if he chose to. I had to stop that from happening.

Hopefully it could be handled without a battle. I had to believe that beneath his anger, Dominic was a reasonable man. No one had a direct number to him, so all I'd been able to do was leave messages with people who said they would have him get back to me.

It was going to happen. It had to. My family in Montalcino, as well as back home, was counting on me.

McKenna stirred in her sleep, and I ran my hand over her hair lightly. Her concern for Gian came from having also been abandoned by a parent. She'd mentioned her mother before, but I hadn't seen the depth of how much the abandonment still hurt her until she'd shared it just then. McKenna was independent and stubborn. I smiled as I imagined what she would say if she knew how protective I felt of her now.

She would probably tell me I wasn't allowed to protect her. I'd suspected sadness lay behind her bravado, and she'd just confirmed it. She kept making it clear to me that she didn't need me because she was afraid of needing another person.

Funny, because when it came to helping people, she didn't hesitate to step in. She just didn't trust others to do the same for her.

I'd prove to her that she could trust me—no matter how long it took. Ava had called it early. McKenna was already in my heart.

I wish we weren't engaged.

It complicated things. Instead of dating, exploring this attraction between us, then taking that leap . . . we had a week or so to get to know each other before she handed my ring back. Or was I supposed to ask for it? This was my first experience with fake engagements. Did they end with a handshake? A kiss? The sex we were holding off on?

Did they have to end?

It felt too soon for many of the questions running through my head. Could I imagine waking up to this woman each morning? What would life with her be like? Were these questions the result of finally meeting the woman I was meant to be with, the natural side effect of her wearing my ring, or the consequence of too much wine? I chuckled to myself.

It was definitely partly the wine.

My smile faded as I thought about how hard this trip already was on McKenna. She'd come to support me but obviously felt invested in the outcome for her own reasons. I should have realized how deeply Gian's story would move her. Was she there for me, or was this an attempt to find her own resolution by helping Gian?

I was definitely overthinking the situation.

Luckily McKenna still slept. I doubted I would that night. I'd given the woman I had feelings for a front-row seat to what could be the implosion of my family.

When I'd heard not just my grandmother but my cousins referring to Dominic as the devil, my confidence in my ability to smooth over the situation had taken a hit. So far Dominic hadn't even agreed to meet with me. My vision of talking sense into him, then toasting my engagement with him at Nona's, was seeming less realistic.

Did toasting my fake engagement with a man who was buying up my family's land as part of some sick power play seem like the best idea?

I wanted my brothers' advice. We'd always taken on the world together. When one stumbled, we gathered, and together we made things right again. Could I do this on my own? Should I?

If I called Sebastian, he would come. Or maybe not. His place was with Heather until their second child was born. If he didn't come, he'd hate himself for not being superhuman and able to be everything for everyone who needed him. No, I couldn't involve him.

Mauricio had stayed with Nona when he and Wren were newly engaged. He would fly over in a heartbeat, but could he keep a secret? The little Italian he knew wouldn't be much help. Would he out me and McKenna, even by accident? It wasn't worth the risk.

Gian.

I quietly let myself out of McKenna's room and made my way to my own. It was late but, with the time difference, not as bad on Gian's side.

He answered on the second ring. "Christof. Mom and Dad just left. How is Italy with McKenna? Does this mean what I think it does?"

"I'm sure it doesn't." I stepped out of my shoes and sat on the corner of the bed. There was a lot I wanted to tell him, but not yet. Not until I confirmed Dominic's character.

"Everything okay?"

Not really. "When I was younger, I took our family for granted. I thought all brothers were as close as we are. I just want you to know how important you are to me and that I will always be there for you."

Gian chuckled. "How much wine did Nona give you?"

"Too much," I concurred. "I hate that you've never been here."

"I understand why I can't be."

"Do you?"

"Nona and my biological mother had a huge falling-out. Seeing me would upset her, and she's battling early dementia."

So clinical. So rational. It still had to hurt. "If she was okay with it, would you want to meet her?"

"She's asking for me?"

The hope in his tone was heartbreaking. "No, but she thinks I'm Mauricio half the time, so that doesn't mean anything either way. There's some real family drama going on over here, things I can't get into yet, but I need you to know that you matter more than however this unfolds."

"You sound spooked. Did you accidentally get engaged to your mechanic?"

His question was based on the knowledge that no one brought a woman to meet Nona until they had something to announce.

Could I make it so Gian would have the same opportunity?

"Something like that. I feel better now, though. I needed to talk to one of my brothers tonight."

"I'm always here for you, Christof." There it was—the bond that had to be able to weather the coming storm.

"You don't know how much that means to me. No matter what life throws our way, Gian, we have each other. Don't ever doubt that."

"Do you need me to fly over? I have classes, but I haven't missed one yet. I can be there by tomorrow morning."

"I'm good, Gian. You're right—Nona's homemade wine kicked my ass tonight. Cell phones should have Breathalyzers to prevent these kinds of calls."

"Don't get married without any of us there."

I laughed. The way things were going, who the hell knew what turn this wild ride would take next. "I'll do my best not to."

"Call me tomorrow. I'll be thinking about you."

Thinking. Worrying. Part of me felt bad about laying some of this on his young shoulders. On the other hand, when it came to family and all the craziness that went along with having one, I was beginning to see that it was more painful to be left out than pulled in. "I will. Gian, I may need you over here. Not tomorrow, but possibly sometime during this week or next. I'll send the plane back for you."

"Are you in some kind of trouble?"

"Not yet. But do me a favor—keep this between us. I don't want to worry anyone unnecessarily."

"You're freaking me out a little bit. What are you not telling me?"

He had a right to know. I debated what was worse—leaving him in the dark guessing or sharing what I knew over the phone. He wasn't a child anymore. If I were him, I'd want to know. "I'm here because I recently learned that you might have—no, that you do have a brother and sister no one has ever told us about. I plan to meet with your brother first, then have you come over to meet him."

"Wait, my biological mother has other children?"

"At least two that I know of."

"And no one thought this was something I should know?"

"It's complicated—"

"No, I'd say it's pretty fucking simple. How long have you known?" It was the first time I'd ever heard Gian swear.

"A couple of days."

"And Mom? Dad?"

"I don't know."

"Why am I here while you're there meeting this *brother*?"

It was a valid question I wished I were more clearheaded to answer. "We're trying to protect you."

"No, you don't think I can handle it. You know what I can't handle? Being lied to." Gian ended the call, and I swore. I tried to call him back, but it went to his voice mail. For someone who'd been tasked with making things better, I was off to a horrible start. I could have blamed the wine, but it hadn't dialed Gian's number. It hadn't been the reason I hadn't taken him aside as soon as I'd learned about Dominic.

Plan A was no longer an option.

Initiating emergency plan B, I called Mauricio. As soon as he answered, I said, "I fucked up."

"By taking a woman you've only had one date with to see Nona? Mom told us. Yeah, I can't see how that could have gone wrong."

That was right—he didn't know I was engaged. I didn't know how much Mom and Dad had told him, but my guess was not as much as they'd told me. "It's worse than that."

"You're obviously upset. What happened?"

"You need to drive down and make sure Gian is okay. Tonight. Right now. Go down to his place." I put a fisted hand to my forehead. I hadn't felt drunk earlier, but now it was hitting me hard.

"Hang on." In the background I could hear Wren asking who Mauricio was speaking to. "It's Christof. Christof, do you mind if I put you on speakerphone? It'll save me from repeating all this."

"No problem." Wren was the best thing that had ever happened to Mauricio, and I already loved her as if she'd been born into our family. "I thought I could do this on my own. I should have called you. There I was thinking you'd ruin things with your big mouth when I proved more than capable of doing that on my own."

"I don't have a big mouth," Mauricio countered.

161

In a gentle tone, Wren said, "Christof, just tell us what's going on. What happened with Gian?"

"It's an onion of shit. I keep peeling back layers, thinking I can make it better, but it gets worse. Were Mom and Dad right to say nothing? Should I have waited to say something? Taken Gian with me? I had a plan, but I don't know that I know what I'm doing. What if I piss off the devil and he takes out our whole family?"

"Breathe, Christof," Mauricio commanded. "First question, have you been drinking Nona's wine?"

"Yes."

"You know that shit is so much stronger than anything we have here. I'm tempted to tell you to sleep this off and call me when you wake, but first I need to know what you said to Gian to upset him."

"Too much. I said too much."

"What does that mean?" Wren asked.

There was no sense in not telling them. To be there for Gian, they'd need to know. "Mom and Dad dropped a bomb on me yesterday and suggested a solution I shouldn't have agreed to. I don't know what I was thinking. Maybe I wanted an excuse to spend more time with McKenna. She thinks I know what I'm doing. What if I don't?"

"I wish I were close enough to smack him," Mauricio said. "You're not making any sense, Christof. Let's start over. What did Mom and Dad tell you?"

To help Gian, there were things they had to know. They knew about Rosella, but I told them how Dominic was related to Gian and how I'd blindsided him with that knowledge. "He said what he couldn't handle was being lied to and hung up. And he swore. Gian doesn't swear."

The silence on the other end of the line made me wonder if the call had dropped and I'd released this tsunami of crap to no one. "Mauricio? Wren?"

Wren answered first. "We're here. Mauricio is just taking a moment. So Dominic is in Italy?"

"He soon will be, but not for a good reason this time." I told them the history between Dominic and the family, right down to how they'd blocked him recently from seeing Nona. "He has every right to be angry and hurt—but I have to stop him before he does something that the family could never forgive. Right now they hate the idea of him, but they don't know him. I have to believe he doesn't want to move forward with any plan that will hurt the family more."

"Does Sebastian know any of this?" Mauricio asked.

"If he does, it's not from me. Mom didn't want to worry him, and I agreed. He's where he needs to be this time. I can handle this." My stomach churned, and I sat up, fearing I might throw up. "I'm such an idiot. Why did I call Gian?"

"He had a right to know," Wren said.

Sounding like he was moving around while he spoke, Mauricio said, "Don't worry about Gian—Wren and I will track him down and talk him through this. When does Dominic arrive?"

"I don't know. I have people watching all the airports in the area. As soon as he touches down, I should be informed."

"Good, that gives us a little time. If Gian wants to be there to meet him, Wren and I will go with him. Meet with Dominic; we'll handle this side."

The room was spinning, and I felt light headed. "Meet with Dominic. Fix everything. Got it."

"You're drunk, Christof. Do us all a favor and put your phone outside your reach tonight."

"I can do this, though, right? I mean, I'm good at situations like this." I felt like the boy who had once turned to a complete stranger for reassurance. Tequila had been off my drinking list for a long time, but now Nona's special brew would be as well.

163

Mauricio sighed. "Christof, this is probably the craziest story I've ever heard in my life. If it was anyone else telling me, I would think they were making the whole thing up. You're good at mediating and bringing resolution to difficult situations, but of course you're not sure what you're doing. No one would be—this is bananas. You're the right one for this job, though. Sebastian would have gone in with guns blazing. How much does McKenna know?"

"Everything."

"And she agreed to go with you on the trip? Wren, tell me if I'm wrong, but I think he needs to marry this one. Seriously, you will not find another woman with that kind of balls." After a moment, he said, "Wren agrees. She's a keeper."

"Are we sure Dominic isn't dangerous?" Wren asked in the background. "I don't like the idea of Christof taking him on alone."

A crystal-clear thought pierced my otherwise-muddled thoughts. "I'm not alone, Wren. I've got a pit crew." Back in the States as well as in Italy. "I've got this now, thanks."

In a softer tone, Wren said, "Christof, this is a lot for you, but it's probably also a lot for McKenna. Keep her safe."

I nodded, then realized she couldn't see me, so I said, "I will. I'm her crew as well."

"I'm not sure what that means, but Mauricio is right . . . turn off your phone now and put it in a drawer. We'll call you tomorrow."

I lay back down on my bed. Almost instantly my eyes began to close. I mumbled, "Text me when you know Gian is okay."

With that, I gave in to the sweet oblivion of sleep.

CHAPTER TWENTY-FOUR

McKenna

As soon as I woke up, I closed my eyes and attempted to wake a second time. No, I refused to believe that I was hungover on my first morning in Italy. If I closed my eyes long enough, when I next opened them, not only would I wake up feeling better, but also I absolutely wouldn't remember getting drunk in front of Christof's family.

Conceding that the pounding in my head couldn't be wished away, I told myself to pull a Christof and forget as much as I could. There was no need for me to remember every stupid thing I'd said, including telling him I bet he was good in bed. I groaned.

Yeah, I'd gone there.

Sober me didn't know which sexual move drunk me had been about to brag I could do, but I half wished he'd let me finish the sentence. Apparently, subconsciously I was incredibly proud of some skill I had. Something worth exploring with him later . . . if he was still speaking to me.

No, really, Christof, this is me being helpful . . . just also a little horny.

There I'd been practically throwing myself at him, and he'd left like the gentleman he was. I couldn't imagine any of the men I'd been with walking away and promising to return when I was sober.

I've had way too much alcohol-assisted sex in my life.

I don't like what that says about me . . . or the men I've been with.

There was a light knock, followed by the door opening. A perfectly groomed and smiling Christof entered holding a breakfast tray.

My hands went to my tangled hair, and then I tested my breath against my hand—*couldn't be worse*. I wanted to tell him to get the hell out until I figured out how to make myself look or feel like myself again, but the expression on his face was so sweet I couldn't.

Fuck it.

I sat up and scooted back against the headboard. "Morning." *Oh, good, my voice sounds deep and gravelly, like a truck stop waitress who's smoked the last thirty years of her life away.*

Soak all this sexiness in, Christof.

He placed the tray on my lap. It was then I noticed yesterday's clothes still on my body. *Perfect.*

He smiled down at me. "Mind if I sit?" He pulled up a chair.

What could I say? I shook my head.

Leaning forward, he referenced what was on the tray. "There's ibuprofen if you need some. A glass of water. Toast in case you're queasy. I didn't know if you wanted to taste some of the local cuisine, so I added prosciutto, some cheeses, a sliced tomato, Pia's homemade yogurt, a croissant from the bakery down the street, and of course coffee strong enough to grow hair on your knuckles. I already had two cups, or I'd join you."

Maybe it was the headache; maybe it was because no one had ever brought me breakfast in bed—ever—but my eyes misted up. "You did all this?"

"It was nothing."

I blinked a few times fast. "You might be too good for me, Christof."

His head cocked to one side, and he frowned. "You flew halfway around the world to help me with a family matter. All I did was slap a little food on a tray and carry it down the hallway. If we're in a contest for who is nicer, you're still in the lead."

He kissed me then. Me with my crazy hair, bad breath, and wrinkled clothes. I melted into it.

When he sat back, he hung his hands between his knees and sighed. "There's something I have to tell you."

Oh my God, he likes me, but he can't handle morning-after-binge breath. I can't blame him—it's a huge turnoff for me too. I opened my mouth to admit as much to him, but he spoke before I had a chance to.

"I called Gian last night and told him he has other siblings and that I was here to meet one of them." He covered his face with one hand, then lowered it. "I could blame the wine, but it doesn't matter why I did it. All that matters is he knows, he's hurting, and I made everything worse."

I found my voice. "No, Christof. The truth doesn't make things worse. It changes things, maybe how things happen, but I can't believe the truth is ever better hidden." In the sober light of day, I was once again grateful my mother had been blunt about not wanting to see me. I had friends who constantly tried to mend unhealthy relationships because they didn't want to give up on them. My mother had closed the door between us—a gift, really.

His smile was tight. "I hope you're right. Mauricio texted me this morning. He and Wren are staying at Gian's house with him for the next few days. He's pissed, but not enough to kick them out. I'm glad he's not alone. I'm torn between staying here and trying to meet with Dominic or going home to Gian. When one of us is hurting, we all are."

I held a hand out to him. He laced his with mine. *I could love this man. Not just a little. The whole damn ever-after shit.* "I can't tell you where you belong, but I'm all in for either if you want me to be."

For a long time he sat there looking into my eyes with an expression I couldn't decipher. If I really could have read his mind, I would have sworn he'd just thought, *I want you to be wherever I am.*

Or that's what I want him to be thinking. For all I know, he's about to ask me if I mind ending this charade early to go home. If his brothers end up coming, will a fake engagement be necessary anymore?

"And you think I'm the nice one." He shook his head. "Confession time—"

Don't be married.

Or in love with someone you wish you'd married.

Or dying.

I could handle almost anything else.

Okay, also don't be a criminal.

I squeezed his hand tight. "You can tell me anything."

He left me hanging long enough that I really started to worry. "I don't know as much about fixing cars as I led you to believe."

I withdrew my hand. "You're a jerk, you know that? I thought it was something serious." The tray wobbled on my lap.

He righted it, then caught my hand and held it loosely between his knees. "Sorry, couldn't resist." His expression tightened. "I'm a little over my head here. I don't know what to say to Dominic when I meet him—if he even agrees to see me. I thought I did, but now that I'm here, I'm not so sure. Sebastian would meet him head-on, back his ass right onto his plane and into the air. He wouldn't care how rich or powerful Dominic is. It'd be all-out war. What if that's what it takes to keep my family here safe? I woke early and just lay there thinking about how much this town has suffered at the hands of the Corisis. Am I wrong to think of him as family? What if all I do by going in soft is give him another chance to take a swipe at these people? They can't win against him."

"But you could?"

"Maybe. I don't have Sebastian's clout, but I have connections to people who might."

"Oh, you mean you know people who know people who make problems disappear." I quoted his family with enough sarcasm that I hoped he saw how wrong I felt that idea was. Christof's confusion was understandable. I felt for his family as well. Their fears were founded in experience. They'd fought this battle before and lost. Winning required confidence, though, and focus. "You're not your brothers. If you try to handle this the way they would, you will fail. You're a good man who believes family is more important than anything else. When you told me your plan would work, I believed it because you did. The only thing you've done wrong so far is doubt yourself."

"I appreciate you saying that, but—"

"Maybe I'm as wrong as you're afraid you might be, but I want Dominic to meet his grandmother. I want Gian to have a chance at a relationship with him—and his biological mother. Your plan is the only way any of that is possible. War doesn't bring people together. You said it yourself—they're caught in a cycle of hurting each other. I believe you're here because you're able to look past everything they've done wrong and see good in both sides."

"I thought I could. When I see the kids and think about how Dominic with all his money and all that power is coming here to take food off their table, steal the beds they sleep in, I don't want that man near Nona. I don't want him near Gian." In a lower tone, he said, "Or you."

I didn't have a fast answer for that one. I had no idea what was in Dominic Corisi's soul. What I did know was that there was another possible loss on the table. I'd seen it a hundred times in the racing world, but for a very different reason. People came into racing because they loved cars and speed. Over time, the lure of money and fame brought them to a place where they could win if they compromised their ideals a little. In the racing world a cheat could bring in a fortune. Taking down an opponent off the track by messing with their sponsors could also tip the scales. It was a heady temptation. Those who gave in to it were forever different, even if they didn't get caught.

Christof could strike first against Dominic. He could align with his cousins and drive him out of town—but those actions wouldn't fit who he was or what he believed was right, and the weight of doing that would change him. "You don't have to worry about me, Christof. I might not look it, but I can throw a mean punch."

He chuckled without much humor. "I bet you can."

I put the tray beside me on the bed and turned so I could lower my feet to the floor. Leaning forward, I laid a hand on his chest. "What does your heart tell you to do?"

He placed his hand over mine. "I want the happy ending."

Whenever we were together, I wanted to believe those were possible. I smiled. "Close your eyes and imagine what it would look like."

He didn't at first.

"This is the advice you gave me when we first met, and it was damn good advice. Now close your eyes." When they were shut, I said, "Imagine that conversation with Dominic. Let yourself be in that moment. Think about what you want him to hear. Think about what would reach a man like him."

"Okay."

I gave him a moment, and then I said, "Open your eyes."

He did.

I continued, "Now just fucking make that happen."

He laughed. "I love you."

We both went awkwardly red.

He corrected, "I mean I love this—us."

That was a lot as well. Too much for me to be able to breathe. I was torn between kissing him and bolting for the door. So I sat there simply staring at him.

He stood. "I bet you'd like to shower."

I nodded. No matter where the day took us, that was a very necessary first step. "Yes."

"The shower is in the bathroom in the hall. There's no lock on the door, but if you hang a shoe on the outside, people know not to go in. I suggest a short shower, though, because the kids don't always respect the shoe."

"Gotcha." I rose to my feet and looked until I'd located my luggage on the floor at the end of the bed.

"McKenna?"

Our eyes met. "Yes?"

His kiss took me by surprise. It started light, then deepened. My hands found his hair. His found my ass. We ground against each other.

When he raised his head, his eyes were burning with the same need that was throbbing through me. "If we were anywhere but here."

I dragged his head back down and kissed him with everything inside me, until I finally took a step back. "Yeah." Decker Park, Ty, and the others felt like another lifetime. It scared me how easily everything else faded to the background when we were together. I needed to clear my head. He stood there, not saying a word, as I picked up my suitcase and headed out the door. "Thanks for breakfast, Christof. I'll eat it after my shower."

He stepped to the door of my bedroom as I made my way across the hall to the bathroom. I had just hunted down a shoe to hang on the doorknob when I heard his grandmother yelling at him in Italian.

His grin made him look years younger. "I'm in trouble. I'm not supposed to be in your room."

"Better go, then," I said with an answering smile. I closed the door and leaned against the back of it. Christof and I were in Italy to help his family through a difficult and possibly dangerous situation. Why did I feel giddily happy?

He'd said he loved me.

I looked down at the ring on my left hand. I'd almost said it back.

Love took time. Months. Years, maybe. It didn't hit like lightning one day into a fake engagement. No, whatever this was, it wasn't love.

Infatuation?

Lust?

Something.

Definitely not love.

CHAPTER TWENTY-FIVE

CHRISTOF

Right in the middle of a long lecture in Italian on how I needed to show McKenna more respect in her house, Nona asked me if I was hungry. When I said I wasn't, she continued to lecture me about how the way I treated my future wife now was how she would treat me and our babies later. Papa, she said, was from another town. He had slept in the barn until their wedding night. With her hands waving in the air, Nona told me she hadn't held the smell against him because everything he'd done, even smelling like cow dung, had been because he respected her. Love, Nona said, started with respect and died as soon as it left.

I sat at her kitchen table nodding politely. I didn't dare smile at the reference to the cow dung.

Nona sat across from me and in Italian said, "I still miss him. I tell him I want to come now, but he says I have to wait. I have more to do here. What more is there?"

The fact that I didn't believe a person could speak with the dead didn't stop me from getting goose bumps. Who knew: perhaps when you were as close to crossing over as Nona was, the veil between where we were and where we were headed thinned. With no one else in the house, I took the opportunity to speak to her about a subject I knew would be difficult for her. "He's right, Nona. You have family who loves you, who want to meet you but haven't yet. You do still have work left to do. You need to save this family."

Her eyes lit with fire. "From the devil?"

"No, Nona. From the fear of him. The man you call the devil is dead. Whatever evil he did should die with him. But your daughter, Rosella, had children who want to know you. Family, Nona. Family who should be at this table with you."

"Rosella is dead to me," Nona said in Italian, then repeated it in English for emphasis.

Dead. I get it.

There had to be something I could say that would soften her heart.

"If my mother made a mistake, would I be dead to you, Nona? I love you. Would I not be welcome here?"

She gripped my hand. "Mauricio, nothing could make me not love you."

I didn't correct her. I laid my free hand over hers and wondered if I was wrong to discuss something so serious with her when she still confused me with my brother. In the past I'd found amusement in it, but there was nothing funny about her confusion. I felt sad for her and for Dominic, his sister, and Gian, who would never know the grandmother I'd had. Still, McKenna's words echoed in my mind. This was the only way that had a hope of ending the fighting. "Nona, I have a brother who is also Rosella's son. Do you have no love in your heart for my brother?"

"Gian is Camilla's son."

"Now he is, but he was Rosella's. Rosella married a vineyard owner. Do you remember?"

Nona's eyes darkened. "I told her to keep Gian. What kind of mother leaves her babies? No daughter of mine."

"Because family is all that matters."

"Yes. Yes. Family. In the end only family matters."

"Gian wants to meet you, but my mother tells him not to come. She thinks you can't love her son because he is also Rosella's son. When Gian heard I was here, his first question was if you wanted to see him. He belongs here, Nona. Papa would want him here." I had no idea what Papa would or wouldn't want, and maybe people went to hell for putting words in the mouths of the dead, but this was too important.

My grandmother's hand shook between mine; a spark of clarity shone in her eyes. "Christof?"

"Yes, Nona."

"Papa does want that."

Thank God. "Then that's one of the reasons you can't leave us. You don't know this, but Gian learned Italian, Nona. He learned it so he could speak to *you*. Could I put him on the phone with you?"

"Yes." It was all she said, but I didn't need more than that to dial Gian's number. It was still early there. He might be sleeping, but at least he wouldn't be in class yet. If he wasn't still furious with me, he'd pick up.

He did. "Four a.m., Christof. Most people wait until at least eight to apologize."

I didn't have time to waste, so I dived right in. "Gian, there's someone here who would like to speak to you."

I hit speaker and handed my phone to Nona, then sent up a request to Papa that he stay with her long enough for her to not say anything that would upset him more.

"Gian?" Nona asked.

In a thick, emotional voice, Gian answered in perfect Italian. "Yes, this is Gian."

When neither said anything more, I interjected, "Gian, Nona would like to speak to you."

There was an audible gasp from Gian's side. "Nona?" What other old woman did he think I'd put on the phone with him?

"Yes, Gian," I said. Then decided to give their connection a nudge. "Nona, Gian is studying to be a doctor."

Nona made a scoffing sound. "I don't like doctors. All they do is tell me what's wrong with me. I know what's wrong. I feel it every day.

Don't be such a downer; tell me what my body is still doing right—it's a shorter list."

Gian answered, "I'll make sure not to be a downer of a doctor."

Nona nodded. "A doctor. We don't have doctors in the family. We have a butcher. It's the same thing, I guess."

This time Gian chuckled. "Hopefully not the same thing at all."

"Your Italian is good, Gian."

"Thank you, Nona."

"Good enough to come to Montalcino, you think? And get my radio back from the man who has been fixing it for a month? Take a week to fix something, you're a hero. Take a month, you're a thief. I bet he listens to my radio every night and loves it too much to return it."

"What do you think, Gian? Would you like to come and help me find Nona's radio? We'll go shake down this repairman together," I said.

"Don't shake him," Nona said. "Alberto is two years older than me. Old bones don't need rattling."

"I would love to come," Gian said. "I could be there by tonight. Mauricio and Wren have a rental plane readied here in case I wanted to go."

"Mauricio," Nona said with excitement. "And my Wren." She gave me a long look. "Christof."

I smiled and nodded. "Christof. Except when you catch me doing something wrong; then it's okay to call me Mauricio."

Nona cackled.

Gian laughed as well.

From the corner of my eye, I caught sight of McKenna in the doorway of the kitchen. I rose and joined her there. "Nona's talking to Gian. He's flying over to meet her."

She stepped forward, wrapped her arms around my waist, and gave me a full-body hug that moved me in a way not many things in my life ever had. "I knew you could do it."

I hugged her against me, tucking her head beneath my chin. "I had help." I looked skyward. *You did good, Papa.*

"Me?" she asked, tipping her head up so she could see my face.

Sure. I nodded. I wasn't about to tell her I'd been referring to a more divine intervention. The talk she'd given me that morning had definitely played into how I'd approached speaking to Nona. Because of McKenna, I'd known what I wanted, and that had allowed me to break the goal down into achievable steps.

Even a mountain was not insurmountable if you took it one step at a time. That was all I was doing: putting one foot in front of the other as I continued toward my goal of getting my family beyond this.

I studied her face. Beautiful, but she always was. She was dressed in casual slacks and a conservative top, with her hair and makeup freshly done. Perfect for visiting with family, but I wasn't surprised. I thought of all the women who might have worn something much more revealing, thinking it would please me, but really all it would have done was make things awkward with my family. McKenna naturally picked up on the vibe of a situation. There was no mystery about why she was as successful in business as she was. "We have the day free; how would you like to spend it?"

She arched an eyebrow, then said, "But I'd settle for a tour of your hometown."

Most of my blood left my brain and headed south. "You should never settle for less than you want. Last night one of my cousins gave me this." I took an old-fashioned key out of my pocket. "It's a guesthouse at the bottom of the hill, cleaned and stocked with food in case our visit requires breaks from Nona's."

She laughed with delight. "Are you serious?"

I repocketed the key. "We're not the first couple to stay here, and if anyone understands the impatience of new lovers—it's Italians."

We spent a heated moment simply breathing each other in. I bent my head until my lips hovered over hers. I was flying high off the breakthrough with Gian and my nona. What better way to celebrate?

"Ouch!" I exclaimed as the wooden spoon cracked across my lower back.

"Out," Nona said in a raised voice while waving my phone in one hand and the long spoon in her other. "Go play outside."

I winced but laughed and retrieved my phone from her hand before translating to McKenna. "She says we should take this out of her house."

She was laughing as well. "I gathered that."

Nona continued chastising us. I was about to repocket my phone when I realized Gian was still on the line. I took it off speaker. "Be on your best behavior while you're here, Gian. This is where Mom learned her ninja moves."

He laughed. "I'll keep that in mind." In a more serious tone, he said, "Hey, Christof. Thanks. I mean that. It was a lot to process, but I know you'd never lie to me."

"It's a highly charged situation, Gian. When you get here, you'll understand why Mom made the decisions she did. She might have been wrong, but everything she did was because she loves you."

"Mauricio and Wren helped me see that. I wasn't happy that you sent them, but now I'm glad you did. I would have still been upset with you this morning if they hadn't come, and I would have missed the gift you just gave me."

I met McKenna's gaze as I answered. "All I did was what you would have done for me. We're brothers."

"I love you, Christof," he said. "I'll be there tonight."

"Love you too," I answered. "Now I have to go because Nona is getting a bigger spoon."

177

CHAPTER TWENTY-SIX

McKenna

Hand in hand with Christof, I stepped out of Nona's villa and squinted as my eyes adapted to the bright Tuscan sunlight. After my shower, I'd called Ty to update him. I left out all the parts of the trip that were confusing and focused on how strong homemade wine was. I told him about Christof's many cousins, his hilarious grandmother, and how warmly I was being accepted.

"I'm half expecting you to return married. I've never heard you talk like this," Ty said.

I laughed his comment off, told him he was confusing my new-found love of travel with something else. Still, his words stuck with me. Especially each time I looked down at the ring on my finger. He still regretted not taking a leap for love. I'd not only leaped—I was still free-falling. I wasn't ready to talk it out with Ty yet, though. I wanted a little more time to pretend this could all work out.

Ty and I had moved the conversation on to business, and the call had ended with a request from him that I call again the next day. I'd promised to.

Realizing that Christof and I were walking rather than getting into a car, I asked, "Where are we headed?"

He spun me to his side, pulled me close, then growled into my ear, "Guesthouse?"

My breath quickened. *Oh yes.* "Is it far?"

"A few miles. We could bike there, but you said you wanted to see some of my hometown as well, so I thought we'd walk, at least until the edge of town."

"Then?"

"Then someone will give us a ride to the guesthouse."

"Someone? Like a taxi?" I didn't see any.

We started walking again. "No need for one here. Worst case, we could make it down the hill on foot. But I'm confident we'll come across enough family along the way that we'll be offered more rides than we need."

As we walked along, I was transported back in time. We stopped at the entrance of the towering medieval fortress. Surrounded by a roped-off lawn, the pentagon-shaped *fortezza* stood tall and proud in impressively good condition. Its towers still looked accessible, and I could only imagine the view they would provide of the area. I wanted to see the inside but was torn. I also wanted to get Christof alone and didn't want to risk anything that would change how he was looking at me as if I was everything to him.

"Would you like to go inside?" he asked.

"Would you?" I parried and then hated how much I sounded like every weak-minded woman I'd ever mocked.

His smile warmed me down to my toes. "I do and I don't. I want you in my arms, right now, but then I also want you to have a chance to fall in love with this town as I did. I don't believe you can if you treat its history like a profile on Tinder, swiping past whatever isn't instantly pleasing."

I put a hand on my hip. "Oh, so you've swiped?"

His cheeks flushed. "Hasn't everyone?"

"And here I thought you were a good boy."

"I don't know why. I never said I was."

I searched his face. "You keep talking about waiting."

179

"With you. I want what my nona had with Papa—what my parents have." I listened in fascinated silence as he told me a confusing story about farms and cow dung and how when something was meant to be, it worked itself out. "Times have changed, but some things don't. My parents love each other, but the respect they have for each other shines through as well. If I ever do marry, I want that."

If he ever does marry.

If.

Oh yes, because regardless of how real the ring on my finger feels, it doesn't represent a promise of anything. "I want the same thing with someone I don't have to give up being me for."

He nodded. "So I'll ask you again, and this time tell me what you want instead of asking what I do. Do you want to see the inside of the fortress?"

I threw my arms around his neck. "I do. I want to see the museum, taste whatever it is they're selling from that shop over there, then make our way to the guesthouse the long way . . . stopping at whatever we both see of interest."

He claimed my mouth then, but I met that kiss with just as much passion as he brought. Could he be as right as he felt? I didn't know, but I let myself stop questioning and just enjoyed the taste and feel of him.

We toured the fortress, then stopped at craft shops and a clock tower, but we passed on stopping in at any wine bars. We were too eager to be alone to spend much time at any of the places, but I loved seeing the town through his eyes. Each time Christof came across someone he knew, he introduced me as his fiancée with pride, as if our engagement were real—both confusing and wonderful at the same time.

I met so many people that day, but there was one who would always stand out in my mind. Her name was Gianna. She looked about Nona's age, with a toothless smile and gray hair piled on her head in a loose bun. She met us at the door of her home with a smile and fresh pastries. It didn't take more than that to lure us in.

When Christof told her I renovated old cars, she kissed the cross around her neck and said she had the perfect wedding present for us. Like a good marriage, it would require some work, she said, but she wanted us to have it.

She led us down a narrow driveway to a small garage where a bright-red convertible two-door 1949 Alfa Romeo Super Sport sat on four flat tires. She said it had belonged to her husband. They'd hoped to leave it to one of their children, but he'd died before they'd had any. So there it sat, waiting to be loved again.

It was dust covered, clearly neglected, and fucking amazing. Forgetting for a moment that Christof and I were not actually headed down the aisle, I ran my hand over the hood of it and said, "We'd name him Chris."

Christof put an arm around my waist and kissed me on the cheek. "I like that. Think he could beat Mack? At least it'd be a fair race. Your father's car would blow Mack away."

I imagined Christof and me doing laps around the tracks at Decker Park. "Wouldn't it be fun to find out?"

"It would." He kissed me on the cheek again then. I would have loved to see the car's engine before we left, but Gianna began to look tired from our visit.

And I came to my senses enough to remember Christof and I were not in need of a wedding gift. I pushed those thoughts back, though, refusing to let myself ruin the rest of our day. After thanking Gianna and promising to invite her to the wedding, we continued our walking tour.

At the end of town Christof flagged down a car that was—surprise—driven by one of his cousins. I was beginning to think the term was used more generously here than back in the States. When he explained where we were going, the man put a hand to his heart and said, "Young love. I would miss it if my babies did not bring me so much joy. I have six now. It's a good number, Christof."

"Six?" I asked, eyes widening. "I was thinking one or two."

Christof shrugged. "She's American, but I love her."

His cousin laughed.

I jabbed Christof in the ribs with my elbow. "You're American too."

His cousin joked, "Not in the kitchen, and I hope never in the bedroom."

Christof laughed along but shot me a silent request to not say— what? Oh, that he could cook. Luigi knew, but apparently, it wasn't something Christof was proud of. Was cooking not considered macho? I held my tongue. He was a man straddling two worlds, and I could respect that.

Respect. I'd never put much thought into what a rare commodity it was. People tended to give it to those they thought were the same as they were, but it quickly dissolved when differences appeared. That was what Christof was acknowledging about this cousin he obviously knew and liked. Christof didn't think he'd still be respected by his family if they knew the other sides he'd shown me.

Did his brothers know he cooked? I hoped so. How sad that Christof couldn't be himself with so many of the people he loved.

We climbed into the back of Christof's cousin's car and sped down a long, winding road. When we stopped, Christof shook hands with his cousin, I thanked him, and a moment later we were left standing in the driveway of a small stone house on the edge of an olive orchard. In classic Tuscan style, it had a tiled roof, vines growing up one side, and stone walls that looked as if they'd weathered many storms.

Perfect. Romantic.

I met Christof's gaze, and my body warmed with anticipation. I licked my bottom lip and let out a shaky breath. "It's beautiful."

Desire shone in his eyes, but there was also a twinge of sadness. "All of this used to belong to my family. Now it belongs to a foreign buyer . . . or maybe even Dominic already. I don't know. Salvatore leases this land, but not for long if I mess any of this up."

I caressed one of his cheeks and turned his face toward mine. "You won't."

He gathered me to him for a hug that at first was more about comfort than sex. "You don't know how much it means to me to have you here."

Against his chest I mumbled, "I feel the same about being here."

He swept me up into his arms then and carried me toward the door of the guesthouse. Only when we were on the stone landing before the door did he say, "The key is in my pocket. Hang on." He juggled me in his arms while fishing around in one pocket.

"Don't you dare drop me," I said.

"Dammit, I just had it."

I brought my hand around to the back pockets of his jeans and stuck my hand inside. "Thought so," I said as my hand closed around the key, then waved it triumphantly in the air.

He stepped closer to the door. "Well, use it; you're not getting any lighter."

My mouth dropped open in surprise. I would have said something scathing, but laughter glinted in his eyes, and he kissed my retort clear out of my head.

Between kisses, I fumbled to unlock the door.

The door crashed open. Christof carried me through it, kicked it shut behind him, then lowered me to the floor in front of him. Our hands feverishly pulled at each other's clothing. I untucked his shirt. He pulled mine clear over my head.

My bra hit the floor a second later.

His mouth worked magic from my neck down to kiss the tips of my breasts, which his hands cupped, before returning to my mouth. That tease sent a shudder through me. I undid his shirt and pushed it off his shoulders.

We made fast work of the rest of our clothing. When his pants hit the floor, he bent to retrieve a foil package from them and tossed it on the couch. "We'll need that later."

I would have answered but lost my ability to speak when he ran his hands up and down my naked body and whispered, "Beautiful."

He paused, giving me a chance to . . . return the favor? Not that I minded. I was a chest woman, and his was swoon-worthy. Chiseled. Lightly haired. Flanked by strong arms, flat abs, and . . . fully excited, the size of him was a delicious surprise. Size wasn't everything, and I wouldn't have walked away from much smaller, but still—holy shit. If he ever had trouble dating, all he'd have to do was whip that sucker out, and someone would go home with him.

I frowned. I didn't like the idea of him with anyone else. I remembered being in a bar once where a bride-to-be had worn a pin that said, *One dick for the rest of my life.* At the time I'd thought it was a passive-aggressive complaint, but maybe it wasn't. Maybe a sex life could be sustained with one dick.

Tucking a finger under my chin, Christof raised my face to his. "No frowning at the merchandise."

When I didn't laugh, he added, "Hey, if you're having second thoughts, I can go cuddle with an ice pack for a few minutes, and we can go back to touring the town."

He was so sweet I almost burst into tears. How could I explain to him that it wasn't that I wanted to wait but that I wanted what was between us to be real—now? I opened my mouth to attempt to, failed to find the right words, then pressed my lips together and simply shook my head.

He pulled me to him for one of his enveloping hugs. "Don't cry, Mack. This is the good stuff."

I sniffed. How perfectly our bodies fit together was insane. I didn't believe in reincarnation or any kind of afterlife, but I couldn't explain how right it felt to be with someone I'd known for such a short time. Soul mates? Rubbish. Still, I'd never felt this way with anyone before. "I don't cry."

He kissed my forehead. "I do. I'm human."

The simplicity of what he'd said rocked through me. This was another glimpse into the real him. It felt natural to let him in as well. "Crying clouds focus. Distractions are career enders."

He ran a hand through my hair. "There was a time I would have agreed with you. I didn't want to feel anything when my family was in pain, but trying to turn it off was worse. I'd rather laugh and cry, love and lose, than feel nothing."

I swallowed hard. If we were being real . . . "Losing is what I fear the most."

"I know."

I wasn't talking about just in business, but he seemed to understand that. "What are we doing, Christof? What is this?"

He hugged me closer and let out a slow breath. "I don't know, McKenna, but it feels too important to not give it a chance. I'll tell you a secret. Sometimes when I look at you, I see . . . forever. I know it's too much too soon. I know we're doing all of this backward, but I have to believe that if we hold on and ride it out, there's a future for us together."

This wasn't a man saying what he thought I wanted to hear to get me to fuck him. He was speaking from his heart, and I wanted to be the kind of person who believed in forever. Could I be? Were we headed for a future together, or a month from then, would he just be another man I'd been with? "Kiss me, Christof. Let's enjoy today and let tomorrow figure itself out."

A gentle smile spread across his face. "I can do that."

Slowly, passionately, he kissed me until I was writhing against him. His hands were everywhere, awaking every inch of me.

I got greedy and impatient. He felt so good, and I was ready for him, but he made me wait. He stepped me back to the edge of the couch, then encouraged me to stand on it. I held on to his shoulders, moved one of my feet to the arm of the couch, and gasped with pleasure as he spread my sex with his fingers and dipped his tongue inside me.

He took his time. I gave myself over to his control, and where he took me was heaven. With his tongue. With his thick fingers. I called out his name as I came.

As I came down from that glorious orgasm, he kissed his way up and down my legs. No rush in this man. Waiting, I was discovering, was its own pleasure.

He kissed his way across my stomach, up my rib cage. All the while his hands explored and tested until he knew just how to make me squirm and beg for more.

He turned me around and spent as much time kissing his way up the back of me as he had the front. Legs spread wide, I gripped the back of the couch and shivered with pleasure each time his breath tickled just before his tongue claimed.

The sound of foil being torn open had me gasping with anticipation. I turned at his command, facing him again, and kissed him deeply. He lifted me, wrapping my legs around his waist.

Our tongues were intimately dancing around each other when he thrust up into me. Oh God, he was fucking perfect. Gentle when a man should be. Strong and bold when anything less would have been a disappointment.

As he thrust deeper and deeper, we continued to kiss as if our lives depended on the connection being maintained. We moved, and my back hit a wall with force. He pounded into me as I clung to him, meeting each thrust with my own. Harder and faster, wilder and wilder. Just when I thought I couldn't take any more, he switched positions, and the pleasure became even more intense.

I came just before he did. We ended with me lying across one end of a wooden table. He stepped back, withdrew, cleaned himself off, tossed the condom in a trash bin, then lifted me back into his arms and carried me to the couch as if I weighed nothing. *Not too shabby.*

I laid my head on his shoulder and took a moment to breathe him in. I'd had good sex. Prior to Christof I would have said I'd had great sex. This was different. It hadn't been just about how he made my body feel. We'd connected.

For just a moment we'd been one.

I made a noise in my throat as I heard my own inner dialogue.

"What's wrong?" he asked with a chuckle.

"You bring out a side of me I'm not sure I like," I said with an honesty that surprised me.

His eyebrows rose, and real concern filled his eyes.

It probably wasn't the best after-sex thing to say, so I quickly added, "When I'm with you, I think all this sappy shit I didn't know I was capable of."

That earned me a quick kiss. "Like what?"

I shook my head. "No way."

One of his hands gripped my side, poised to tickle. "Don't make me."

I grabbed his hand. "Do you know some cultures consider that torture?"

"Tickling?"

"Yes."

His eyes narrowed. "Which cultures?"

Without missing a beat, I said, "Mine."

He nodded. "Mine too. I still want to know, though."

"Really, it's stupid."

"You will tell me."

"I don't think so."

"When you're ready, you will."

"Don't hold your breath."

"Are you ready to tell me now?"

"No."

He looked away, then back, mimicking how I'd done the same on the plane. "Now?"

I laughed. "You're as bad as I am."

"Which is why we belong together."

How honest should I be? This was Christof. He could handle the truth. "That's the kind of stuff I keep thinking."

He smiled. "And it freaks you out."

How did he know me so well already? "Exactly."

"Me too." He tapped my nose. "I was half hoping you'd be a bad fuck."

"What? Why?"

"It's too good between us. There's always a letdown. What aren't you telling me?"

I laid my head against his chest again. How was it possible to feel this good with a man and still get the waves of nauseated nerves? "I'm not giving up my garage."

"Uh, I believe that was clear from day one."

"I'm headstrong."

"Yep, you didn't do much to conceal that either."

"I snore?" I was only joking.

"It's a cute snore."

I tweaked his chest. "I don't really snore."

"You do. One day I'll film it to show you."

"Don't you dare."

"I'm willing to take the heat for it if I think it's funny enough. So, my big bad McKenna, how do you feel about a man who's not intimidated by you?"

I raised my head and met his gaze. "It's nice, actually. It's a relief to be with someone who doesn't want to change me."

"The only thing I'd change is your name."

"Oh no. I'm a Decker. I own Decker Park. No way would I ever change my name."

"You'd change it for me."

"Really?" I asked in a tone heavy on the sarcasm.

"And our little babies. Come on, you wouldn't want them to have a different last name than their father."

"Did you hit your head during sex?"

"It's the only line I'd draw in the sand. I don't understand wives with different last names."

"A name doesn't make a marriage."

"It doesn't make a person either. Would you really not change your name for your husband?"

"Would you really not marry someone who wanted to keep their own last name?"

It was our first real standoff. It felt foolish. We were fighting over something that was completely abstract.

"To me, a name does mean something. Gian is a Romano."

"If he changed his name to Corisi, would he be less of your brother?"

Christof eased me off his lap and stood. "We should get dressed and head back."

Because after-sex cuddling was only for those willing to take on the Romano last name? I didn't voice the question, but it welled up inside me. I started gathering my clothing off the floor and headed toward what looked like a bathroom.

"McKenna?"

I stopped without turning back to face him. "Yes?"

"I don't want to argue with you. I'm sorry."

"Me too." I was sorry. Sorry I might have just glimpsed what would be the reason we eventually ended. "I'll be right back."

I closed the door of the bathroom, laid my clothing on the side of the tub, and took a few deep breaths. His stance made sense. He was a family man. Old fashioned in many ways.

My hands fisted on the edge of the sink. Decker was my father's name. It was one of the few things I had left of him. No man would strip me of it.

I hadn't come to Montalcino believing Christof and I were meant to be together. I wasn't looking to get married. There was no reason we couldn't date, enjoy ourselves during and after this fake engagement, then go our separate ways when the fire cooled. Relationships ended. That was the way life went.

I kicked myself mentally for confusing fake with real and ruining what otherwise had been a wonderful day.

Let it go.

In the end, it doesn't matter.

This was never supposed to be forever.

CHAPTER TWENTY-SEVEN

CHRISTOF

As I dressed, I went over the sharp turn our day had just taken and owned up to my part in it. McKenna was an independent woman. She'd worked hard for everything she had. It made sense that she would want to retain her name.

Why the fuck am I making a big deal out of something that isn't relevant to where we are in our relationship? I'm an idiot.

And I upset her.

My last name was important to me. It was a source of pride. I'd never considered that a wife of mine might not want it. My first impulse had been to say I'd never accept anything else.

Like a caveman beating my chest and demanding that a woman wear my bearskin. I didn't want to own McKenna. I didn't want to change her as she'd said so many before me had tried to.

I'd been doing fine, ready to talk the subject out with an open mind, until she'd asked how I'd feel if Gian changed his last name. It had struck a chord in me and reminded me of my mother's fear of losing him.

My thoughts were torn between what I wanted to do and what I had to do. I wasn't clearheaded, but I didn't want to ruin things with McKenna. I couldn't lie to her and say I didn't feel the way I did. On the other hand, compared to everything that was going on, the whole conversation was ridiculous.

Our first full day in Montalcino, and we'd already had sex. So much for waiting. McKenna would come out of the bathroom soon, and I knew I should say something to make her feel better. Not to smooth it over because I wanted to avoid an argument, but because we'd just shared something beautiful. A wiser man would have kept his mouth shut and simply enjoyed holding her.

My phone rang. I checked it but almost didn't answer when it was an unknown number. With everything going on, though, I didn't want to risk missing a call. "Yes?"

A woman with an American accent said in English, "Christof Romano, it's my understanding that you've been trying to set up a meeting with Dominic Corisi."

My hand tightened on the phone. "Who is this?"

"I'd rather not give you my name, but I can get you in to see him."

Fully dressed, McKenna appeared in front of me and nodded toward the phone.

Silently I mouthed, "It's about Dominic."

She took my free hand in hers and gave it a squeeze.

"I'm in Italy," I said to the woman on the phone.

"So is Dominic. Listen, I don't have much time." She read off an address. "He's conducting business in your area. He travels with more security than the pope, so there's no going in the front door. I'll bring you in the back, take you up a service elevator, and get you inside his office. It's up to you after that."

"I'm not sneaking in like a criminal. How do I know this isn't a prank? Who are you?"

"It's not a prank. It's enough that you know I'm someone who cares about Dominic and who wants him to hear you. Do you want to speak to him or not?"

"I do."

"Then be there in an hour. Tell no one where you're going. Park a few streets over. Enter the parking lot from the alley just after the clothing shop. Come alone."

"I'm going with you," McKenna said.

I shook my head.

The woman on the phone said, "His security team doesn't know you're coming. No extras. Too dangerous. You could get shot if you're not careful."

"Sounds like a shitty plan," I said.

"Do you have a better one?" She ended the call before I had a chance to answer.

I couldn't call her back. All I could do was meet her and trust that she was doing this because she wanted it to work out and not to lure me off to meet Dominic in secret so he could erase me.

"I'm going, even if I only stay in the car. No way are you going into this alone."

"You heard her."

"I did, but you're right—her plan is a shitty one. I am not letting you get killed when we haven't had a chance to make up. You're going to meet this billionaire, talk some sense into him, come home, and finish our argument."

I laughed and hugged her. "She said it'll be dangerous. I can't take you into a situation like that."

"Do you know what's dangerous? Life. From the minute we're fucking born, something is trying to kill us. And you know what? In the end something does. None of us are spared the crash and burn. Honestly I'd rather die dodging bullets trying to save your ass than accidentally stabbing myself to death with a knitting needle in a nursing home."

"Are those the only two options?"

Hands on both hips, she faced off with me. "You know what I mean." She tapped my chest with a finger. "And you agree."

I did. "Okay, you can come as far as the street. That's it. I can't imagine the meeting will take long. If I don't come out in an hour, call Luigi and Sebastian. I'll give you both numbers."

She nodded. "My heart is pounding in my chest and my hands are sweaty, but not in a good way. How about you?"

"Couldn't have described how I feel better than that. Let's go. We don't have much time." I sent a text to Luigi, told him where we were, and asked him if we could borrow his car. He said he'd be over in a few minutes. I asked him to hurry. "Okay, we have a car and a few minutes to wait."

We shared a long look, then said "I'm sorry" at the same time.

She raised a hand to my face. "We're very different people."

"I don't see that as a bad thing."

"I'm freaking out a little," she said.

"I told you you don't need to come." I took her by the shoulders and stared down into her eyes. "I can do this on my own."

"I want to go with you. That's what is scary. None of this makes sense. None of it is a good idea, but I don't want to be anywhere else."

What could a man say to that? I let a kiss try to explain how tangled up she had me on the inside.

I'd never wanted a woman more.

Never worried more that I might not be what she needed.

I wanted to protect her, tell her to sit her ass down and wait for me to return.

Even more, though, I wanted her at my side through this.

Like I said, it was a tangled mess inside this caveman's head.

CHAPTER TWENTY-EIGHT

McKenna

There's a difference between knowing something potentially deadly will hap-
pen and driving to it to speed things up. If I were sitting in a movie theater
watching this unfold, I'd expect a car chase to ensue right about now. Or
the cavalry to arrive.

Neither did.

The ride was painfully quiet. I'd gotten accustomed to Christof
cracking jokes to defuse a situation, but his hands were tight on the
steering wheel, and he appeared deep in thought. I wasn't about to break
his concentration.

When he parked on a side street in a small neighboring town, I
couldn't hold my silence any longer. "Christof."

He turned to me. "Yes."

I wanted to tell him not to do this, but I didn't. When I was little,
I'd tried to stop my father from racing once. A driver had died in a
crash the week before, and I'd been there to witness it. I'd begged.
Pleaded. Threatened. I'd been furious with him when he'd asked Ty to
have someone take me home.

What I hadn't recognized then was the look I now saw in Christof's
eyes—sheer determination. I'd always thought my father was impervi-
ous to fear, but I was beginning to think he hadn't been. He'd been a
man, like Christof, who knew what he had to do and refused to let fear

stop him. That kind of resolve didn't bend before the tears of a child . . . or a woman.

I wouldn't have wanted it to.

More than anything, I wanted Christof to win, as much if not more than I'd ever cared if my father won a race. Christof wasn't walking into that building looking for anything for himself. It would have been justifiable for him to blame both sides for getting themselves into this mess, to step back and say it wasn't his problem.

My mother had taken that path. In her twisted mind she still blamed me for the state of our relationship . . . or lack thereof. She'd never forgiven me for choosing my father.

I couldn't imagine Christof ever putting a child in that position. His view of family and the responsibility each member of one had to the others was so much less selfish.

And forgiving. Family didn't need to be perfect to be welcome at Christof's table. Regardless of the state of Dominic's headspace, he would surely be moved by that kind of selflessness.

Unless Christof is accidentally shot by his security team first. I unbuckled, leaned over, and whispered against his lips, "Be careful."

He kissed me gently, then unbuckled his own seat belt. "I will be. Don't call the numbers I gave you unless a full hour has passed. I can't imagine this going badly enough to involve anyone else, but if it does, get as far as you can from here before you make those calls."

"No matter what happens, I won't leave you."

He gently ran a thumb over my cheek. "You'll have to. If things go south, I'll need you to keep my family safe." He sat back. "None of that is going to happen, though, because Dominic is not his father. The woman who called said she cares about him. He can't be all bad if he has people close to him who want him to reconcile with his family."

"But they're afraid enough of him to require that you slip in the back door?"

Christof acknowledged my comment with a tip of his head.

He moved to get out, and I gripped his arm. "This doesn't change how I feel about women giving up their last names when they marry. It's a ridiculous, outdated practice."

He gave my hand a squeeze. "I'm going to be fine, McKenna. If you want, I'll call you right now and leave the line open. You can hear everything."

"You'd do that?"

"I couldn't sit here waiting for you to return with no way of knowing if you were okay. So yes." He dialed my number. I answered on my phone. "Mute it on your side. Don't get me killed."

I gave him a deep please-don't-fucking-die kiss, then sat back and put the phone on mute. He gave me one last long look, then opened his car door and got out.

As I watched him go, my stomach did a painful flip. My body was shaking. I was nervous, sweaty, and nauseous, and my heart was pounding heavily in my chest. I'd become comfortable with the version of me who didn't need anyone.

I couldn't imagine what I would do if he didn't return to me.

I didn't want to imagine my life without him in it.

My mouth went dry.

My eyes blurred with tears I refused to shed.

Never had I felt so invested in a relationship.

I wasn't sure I even wanted one or two kids, but if Christof came back to me, I'd have a whole litter. *Just don't let him die.*

I can't lose him, not like this.

I took several deep breaths and told myself it had only been two minutes and not a lifetime since he'd left.

If this is love—it sucks.

CHAPTER TWENTY-NINE

CHRISTOF

I put one foot in front of the other and simply forced myself to walk away from McKenna. I knew it couldn't be easy for her to sit back and watch this play out, but the alternative was to put her closer to potential danger.

A tall brunette met me in the alley after the clothing shop. I didn't know what I'd expected, but she was dressed casually and would have blended in well with local tourists. "You look nervous," she said.

I shrugged. "You did tell me I could get shot in there."

She looked me over again. "That won't happen unless you do something stupid. If you follow my instructions, you should be fine."

"'Should be.' Your optimism is far from overwhelming."

She raised a hand with impatience. "We don't have time to bullshit. I'm risking my job, my friends, everything—not Marc, thank God; he's a better man than I deserve—but everything else. I can't fuck this up."

Her growing agitation wasn't a confidence builder. "Are you okay?"

She pointed a finger at me. "You had better be everything I think you are. If you have an agenda beyond helping Dominic finally meet his grandmother, I will personally gut you and strangle you with your entrails."

"Wow," I said with a grimace. "Can't say I've ever received such a graphic threat. I can assure you I come in peace." I shook my head at my own choice of words. *This definitely ends with me getting myself killed.* "I mean, I'm here to smooth things over and help both sides find peace."

She didn't look impressed, and I couldn't blame her. "You're the only hope we have of that happening. We're fucked. Whatever. Follow me."

At the end of the alley, we stopped. She started listing all the places where Dominic's security would be stationed. My jaw dropped open as she went on and on.

I remembered a story Mauricio had shared about how, during his last visit to Montalcino, his landing had been delayed because Dominic Corisi had closed the airport. When he had landed, Mauricio said the airport had been crawling with security. What kind of person required their own militia?

"Is he a paranoid man?"

"No, there's a lot of people who would like to see him dead."

I know some of those people.

"Anything I should know?" My voice rose to a telling high pitch. I cleared my throat and tried again. "Beyond what's gone down with the family?"

"If I told you, I'd have to kill you." She smiled. "But don't worry, he left that life behind."

"Do you know what would make me worry less? If you stopped describing death scenarios for me every two minutes. Unless you think me shitting myself will give me an advantage when I talk to Dominic, I suggest you chill out a little."

"Please don't shit yourself."

"One more death threat, and anything could happen."

She looked me over again, then smiled for the first time. "You're funnier than I thought you would be."

I didn't tell her I wasn't completely joking.

"Let's go," she said. She took my arm as if we were a couple out for a stroll. We walked slowly toward the back of the building. Once through the back door, she told me to be silent. We made our way through several locked storage rooms to a service elevator. The door slid open. She didn't step in with me. "He's on the seventh floor. Second door on your right as soon as you exit the elevator. You'll step into a bathroom that is attached to his office. This entrance was designed so the cleaning staff wouldn't disturb anyone in the office."

"So I'm popping out of his bathroom?" *Sounds like the perfect way to get shot.*

"At least if you need to nervous shit, you're already where you can."

"That's the only way I can imagine this going worse than I already picture it."

She smiled again. "You'll do fine. You've already impressed me. I didn't think you'd actually come." The door of the elevator started to close, but she put her hand out to stop it. "One more thing. Don't tell him you had help getting into the building."

"Right. Ambushing him from his own bathroom was all my idea. Gotcha." Yeah, there was no way this could go wrong.

"Good luck."

The door closed between us, and I chose the seventh floor.

Only because I knew McKenna was listening, I said, "Mack, when we tell this story to our children someday, let's not mention the part where I said I might shit myself."

CHAPTER THIRTY

DOMINIC

They call me the devil.

The man standing by his office window in Montalcino fisted his hands at his sides. He couldn't deny a younger him might have deserved the title. Funny how circular life could be. Coming to Italy had never worked out for him, but there he was giving it one more go.

But this time I'm the one holding all the cards.

A knock on his door announced the arrival of the head of his security team, Marc Stone. "Do you have a moment?" There were few people Dominic trusted; Marc was one of them.

"What do you need?" When Marc didn't say anything, Dominic turned to face him. Something was bothering Marc, and that was never good. "It's not Alethea, is it?"

"It's not."

"I was clear that her part in this is finished."

Marc adjusted the cuffs of his suit, a tell that he was sitting on something Dominic was sure he didn't want to hear. "She assured me she understood that."

Dominic sighed. "Then what is it?"

After clearing his throat, Marc said, "I've worked for you for a long time. I owe you more than I could ever repay."

"But?"

"It's not really a 'but'; it's a question. What are we doing here?"

Dominic would have told almost anyone else to get out of his office, but Marc was as loyal as they came. "I tried to do this nicely. They wanted to do it the hard way."

"Do what? Who is the enemy? I can't properly protect you unless you give me something to go on. Are you building a new headquarters here?"

"Building? No. This is more of a demolition project."

Marc shook his head. "When I first started working for you, you weren't someone I could care about. You were a job, but not one I was proud of having taken on. I've seen you change over the years. You've done so many good things for so many communities. You have a wonderful wife, an amazing daughter. Both of whom love you. Do you know how worried they are about you lately? I'm worried too."

Hands clenching at his sides, Dominic turned away again. "None of you have any reason to worry. When this is done, I'll go home, and everything will return to normal."

"No, I don't think it will. You're headed down a dark road. I know this Dominic, and I don't want to work for him again."

"Go back to the United States, then."

"I'm not going anywhere, but I can't stand back and not tell you that you're hurting everyone who cares about you. Is whatever you want here worth that?"

"Yes," he said tightly. "Yes, it is."

"Okay," Marc said.

"Is that all?"

"Yes. That's it." Marc's phone beeped. "I wouldn't take this call, but it's Alethea. I need to make sure it's not about the baby."

"Go take your call."

"Think about what I said, Dominic."

Dominic didn't say he would, but not going over and over their conversation proved impossible. From the moment his wife, Abby, had come into his life, it had been like he'd been given a second chance. She hadn't known who he was, what he'd done, or how many people feared him. Her faith in him had reignited his conscience, and although that hadn't been a good feeling in the beginning, it had made him a better man.

He'd made a lot of mistakes.

Hurt more people than he cared to remember.

Never Abby or their child. He'd made sure the rage within him stayed far outside his marriage and his home. His daughter, Judy, saw him as a big softy. For her, he was.

With Abby at his side, Dominic had changed his business practices. He'd poured billions each year into community development, both in the US and abroad. He funded research, especially anything to aid the poor. If good deeds could cleanse a man of his sins, Dominic had at least brought balance to his tally sheet.

Marc didn't need to tell him Abby was worried. The problem with acting less like the man he knew she deserved was that he couldn't look her in the eye while doing it. So he'd withdrawn from her, found a hundred reasons to be with her and Judy less over the last few months.

If it was possible, he hated himself even more for it.

He hated everyone who'd played a part in making him into someone he didn't want to be. If he could win over the fury within him, lock it back into whatever corner he'd kept it in for so long, he would. So far, that hadn't been possible. The closest he'd come to feeling anything since he'd been turned away from seeing his grandmother was a mild satisfaction each time he bought another lot of land out from beneath the people who excused their behavior by calling him the lord of hell.

If I am the devil, then my wrath will surely burn Montalcino to the ground.

A creak from a door opening drew Dominic's attention away from the window. He turned in time to see a man he instantly recognized from photos as Christof Romano. *How pathetic that they sent one of their youngest to stop me.*

Hands in the air, Christof stood in the middle of the room and said, "I'm unarmed, relatively harmless. Sure, I took karate one semester in school, but mostly I got my ass kicked. I'm just here to talk."

"What the fuck are you doing here, Romano?"

"You can call me Christof." When Dominic didn't, Christof continued, "Or Romano. Whatever you feel most comfortable with."

"Don't make me ask you twice."

Christof walked farther into the room, oddly bold for someone who had come alone. "Like I said, I'm here to talk."

Dominic frowned. "How the hell did you get past my security?"

Christof shook his head as if he was embarrassed. "That's not important." He walked over to the chairs in front of Dominic's desk and said, "Mind if I take a seat?" He sat without waiting for permission.

Dominic strode across the room and stood there, towering over him. "I'll save us both time. There's nothing you could say that will stop me. In fact, the first person who denies me access to my grandmother will hold the honor of being the reason I wipe Montalcino off the map."

"Wow," Christof said in a tone only someone of his generation would use. They really were cocky bastards. "That's a hefty threat."

"More like a promise."

"I admire your commitment to this near-villain role, but—"

"Fuck with me, and I won't stop there. Think your family's business is safe? Get in my way, and I'll crush you."

Christof sat back, placed his hands on his thighs, and expelled an audible breath. "Don't take this the wrong way, but short of killing me—which I'm confident you won't because you're not your father—you can't hurt me. Or my family. Strip away our company, our money, my car—and I really like Mack—but strip all that away, and we still have everything that matters. I'd still have my fiancée, my family, my friends, and on most days my dignity. My father always says he was just as happy with one store, all of us, and some wine."

Dominic folded his arms across his chest. "That's not what you'll be saying when you're living on the streets."

Christof's eyebrows rose, but his expression remained calm. "You do realize we're cousins."

"You're not family to me. There's no one here I care about."

Christof rose to his feet and went toe to toe with Dominic. "Then why are you here? From what I've heard, you have a wife, a child, and more money than God. Why are you so angry, and what is it you think anyone in Montalcino owes you?"

"Answers," Dominic growled in a tortured tone that he hated had come from him. It was the truth, though. All he wanted was for someone to look him in the eye and tell him why they'd let him suffer, thinking his mother was dead, and why he still wasn't worth their time.

Christof's expression changed. For a moment he looked—sympathetic? "And you deserve answers. I don't know everything, but I believe I have the ones you're looking for."

"Do you?" Dominic asked in a disgusted tone.

"I do, and I'll tell you everything I know. On one condition."

Oh, this should be good. How much does he think I'm willing to pay for what probably isn't even the truth? Okay, I'll play. "What's the condition?"

"That after you listen to the whole story, which I'm hoping will change your mind about the fate of Montalcino, you consider coming to meet your grandmother tomorrow."

Dominic's hands fisted. "Is this some kind of a fucking joke? She doesn't want to see me."

Christof took a seat again as if he'd been invited to stay. "You want answers? All I'm asking is that you listen with an open mind."

"You're a cocky little shit, aren't you? What are you hoping to get out of this?"

"Honestly? I have three brothers. Two older. One younger."

"And this matters to me why?"

"Because my youngest brother is actually *your* brother. His biological mother's name is Rosella. He's never been to Montalcino because our mother is afraid what people will say to him. He just learned about you, but he's always known he was adopted. He was left by your mother too. He's flying in tonight. If we do this right, he could forever say he has four brothers."

Dominic sat in the chair beside Christof. "And a sister—Nicole."

"And a sister." Christof looked Dominic right in the eye and said, "I have a pretty good idea why you're here. I don't blame you. You feel like the family turned their back on you when you needed them the most. What you don't know is that when you came looking for your mother, your father came as well. He threatened to kill her if he found her. They had to lie to you. It was the only way to keep her safe."

Dominic's whole body tightened painfully. "And later? I never stopped looking for her."

"She'd started a new life under a new name. Her second husband died shortly after Gian was born. She thought your father was responsible. He might have been. That's how Gian came to our family, and your mother went deeper into hiding."

"She doesn't talk about that time in her life." His head started to pound. "I didn't know she had another child. No one thought that was something I might want to know? I could have protected him."

"Telling you would have been too much of a risk. Your father took out his anger on everyone he thought was helping your mother. Stripped them of everything. I can't blame any of them for cringing when they hear the name Corisi. Things don't have to remain that way, though. Gian is on his way. You could meet him tomorrow morning also if—"

"If?" *Here it comes.*

"I know what you've survived, and I can only guess what that has done to your head, but the people you're considering ripping everything away from—they're innocents. Your father ruined their businesses, stole their land, brought them to their knees—but he didn't break them.

206

They are good people with strong family values. I won't let you near any of them if I feel you're here to hurt them. *Our* brother Gian is coming to meet *family*. Family doesn't keep grudges. We make mistakes. We disagree. We yell. Then we apologize, forgive, and move on. You're welcome tomorrow morning, but only if you come as family."

Dominic rubbed a hand over his face. Christof was painting a nice picture, but it wasn't a realistic one. With no ill intentions and an open mind, Dominic had come to the family just a few months ago, and they'd shut him out as coldly as they had all those years ago. One smooth-talking cousin wouldn't change that. "They don't want me there."

"Because they don't know you." A small smile stretched Christof's lips. "I should warn you: Nona might not understand who you are. Don't be offended—she thinks I'm Mauricio half the time."

Negotiations were as much a part of Dominic's life as getting up each morning and putting on pants. They were a part of business, and he'd participated in all kinds. The key to winning any negotiation was to understand what the other side wanted and use it as leverage. *Christof knows what I want; what is he hoping to leave with?* It couldn't be as straightforward as what he was claiming. Dominic shook his head. "What do you really want?"

"To put an end to the fighting. It's time to. Nothing matters more than family."

"You think inviting the man who is buying up everyone's land to breakfast has any chance of not ending badly? They call me the devil." It was what they'd called him when they'd blocked him from seeing his grandmother. Something ugly had risen in him, something that was only now beginning to subside.

"I didn't come here without finding out as much as I could about you. You've done a lot of good over the past decade. Unless that was all an act, you're not as badass as you think you are. You're in a position to right something your father did. Give them their land back, their businesses. Help rebuild what your father tore down." Christof stood. "That's what I would do if I were you." With that, Christof walked to the bathroom door and opened it. "I'll let myself out the way I came in. If you want to meet Nona, come at nine a.m., and come hungry. We'll make extra for you."

Dominic rose to his feet. "I'll be there."

Christof nodded. "I'll make sure everything on my side is good. I'd leave the security squad behind. They'll only make people nervous."

Dominic stood there staring at the once-again-closed door to the bathroom. Not much about the meeting had felt real. He wouldn't have been shocked if Christof's last words had been, *You'll be visited by three spirits . . .*

He opened the door to the bathroom and saw a discreetly disguised door on the other side. Christof had come in through a fucking hidden door in the bathroom. How would he have even known it was there?

Alethea.

It had to be.

Dominic took out his phone and called his head of security. "Marc, your wife is here in Italy. Tell her to come see me."

"Oh no, what did she do?"

Still weighing everything he'd just learned, Dominic said, "Nothing unforgivable. In fact, I might have to thank her."

CHAPTER THIRTY-ONE

MᴄKᴇɴɴᴀ

Finally, after what felt like a lifetime, Christof said, "Still alive and in one piece. Stepping out the back of the building."

In a scramble, I pocketed my phone and let myself out of the car. I remembered this feeling of relief and pride. Every time my father had won a race and I'd seen him standing safely outside his car again, my heart would soar. I hadn't let myself be afraid for my father when he raced, and I'd held my fear in check the whole time Christof had spoken to Dominic. He was safe, though, and I could finally let my emotions out. I half ran, half flew, I thought, down the block to the alley he'd disappeared into earlier.

As soon as I spotted him, I launched myself at him, wrapped my legs around his waist, dug my hands into his hair, and kissed him with all the emotion welling inside me. It was a long, deep expression of gratitude with a dash of never-put-me-through-that-again passion.

When we came up for air, we were both breathing raggedly and half laughing. "So," he joked, "tell me how you really feel."

"I'm hating you a little right now," I said even as I squeezed my thighs around him tighter.

He chuckled. "I like the way you hate."

I kissed his smug mouth, then nipped his bottom lip. "That was pure torture."

"I'll make it up to you." The look he gave me was a mixture of desire and pride. "Did you hear everything?"

"I did."

"I wasn't sure I could sway him."

"I was." It wasn't a lie. Christof was a man I imagined most people found easy to believe in.

"If my family wasn't due to arrive at Nona's soon, I'd take you right back to the guesthouse."

Oh yes. I easily imagined all the ways we could release some of the nervous tension in me, but the look in his eyes told me he was also pulled by responsibility. I respected that about him. Slowly, I released him and slid down the length of him until I was back on my own feet. *We're here for a reason. Focus, McKenna.* "Gian handled talking to Nona for the first time better than I would have expected."

"I'm sure my brother and his wife played a large part in that. Seeing her in person will be more of a challenge. I'll ask Luigi to gather some of the family for tonight. Gian would like that. When Dominic comes, I think having Gian, Nona, Mauricio, and Wren there will be enough."

Holding hands, we started back toward the car. "Would it be best if I make myself scarce?"

He stopped and turned me toward him. "Hey, we're doing this together, right?"

"Right." It was difficult to breathe when he looked at me like we were so much more to each other than we were. "Do your brothers know we're engaged?"

"Shit, I didn't mention it. I'm not sure. They know you're here, though."

That stung a bit. It shouldn't have, but it did. I didn't want to make this about me, but I also didn't like feeling like an afterthought. "Will you tell them the truth?"

He didn't answer at first, and we started toward the car again. "I can't lie to my brothers. They know me too well. Wren would figure it out also. The two of you have a lot in common; she also likes to know how things work. Did I tell you she's an engineer? She and Mauricio are developing prosthetic limbs that incorporate AI. It's fascinating stuff."

"Really?" I didn't tell him that he had shared some of that with me already because I was beginning to think he was speaking to fill the silence. When he'd spoken to the woman in the alley, he'd said he was nervous. He hadn't sounded it, but maybe he had been.

"She's a brilliant woman." He opened my car door for me and, in a deceptively sweet tone, added, "Had no problem changing her last name when they married."

My head snapped up, and whatever rush of irritation I'd felt dissolved when I saw the laughter in his eyes. "You really want to go there?"

"Just saying. McKenna Romano has a ring to it."

He was just giving me shit. I decided to give it right back. After I slid into my seat, I said, "Almost as good as Christof Decker. Now that's a name that would open doors."

Ironically he closed mine after I said it. In the time it took him to walk around the car and get in on his side, I had time to wonder if this was a topic we should have reopened.

Before he started the engine, he paused. "What do *you* want me to tell my brothers?" His question was so simply stated some might have missed the enormity of it, but I didn't. He cared how I felt—even in the chaos. That was the Christof I'd come to Italy to help, the one I was helplessly falling for.

"The truth, I guess. I can handle it. I'm a big girl."

"If I threaten his life, Mauricio should be able to keep our secret." He searched my face, then started the car. "I told myself I'd take things slowly with you. How am I doing so far?"

"I enjoyed the guesthouse." The tension ebbed out of me. The more I thought about it, the more sense it made that Christof hadn't told his brothers everything already. The most successful strategies were often the least complicated ones. He was adapting to the situation as it evolved . . . just as I was. "My crew doesn't know about our fake engagement, either, because I didn't want them to think I'd lost my mind."

He pulled out into traffic. "It is a little crazy."

"A little."

He offered me his free hand. I took it. "I don't regret it. I've never brought a woman to meet Nona. Now I can't imagine bringing anyone else."

I closed my eyes and savored his words. One day soon we'd be heading home. Would he say the same then, or were we both caught up in the magic of our Italian adventure? I joked, "Is your mother as quick with a wooden spoon?"

"She used to be. She's mellowing with age. Don't tell her I said that."

I promised not to, even though I had no idea if I'd ever actually meet her.

The ride back was mostly uneventful. Christof made a few calls and arranged for Luigi to pick up his car later that evening when he visited with Gian.

While stopped at a crossroad, Christof met my gaze. "Mauricio should be able to take a call even if they're still up in the air. If I'm going to tell him, I should do it before they're at Nona's."

"I agree."

He dialed his brother, put it on speakerphone, and gave it to me to hold. As soon as it connected, he said, "Mauricio, how far off are you?"

"We land in about a half hour," a male voice responded.

"Is everyone awake?"

A woman chimed in, "And having coffee."

"Everything still good there, Christof?" a younger-sounding male voice asked. Gian?

"It's good." I half expected him to share how his meeting with Dominic had gone, but when he didn't, I could see the sense in that as well. There were only so many bombs you could drop on a person at a time. "There's something I forgot to mention earlier."

"Okay," the voice that likely belonged to Mauricio said.

Christof met my gaze one last time, as if confirming that I was still okay with them knowing the truth. I nodded. "Coming here was Mom and Dad's idea. They were hoping things would go as they have, and funny thing, it was also their idea to not only bring McKenna but . . ."

"But?" Mauricio asked.

I held my breath.

"To tell everyone we're engaged," Christof said. "They thought it would set a festive tone that would put everyone in a better mood, and it has."

"You're engaged?" his sister-in-law asked in a squeal of delight.

"That's not what he's saying," Mauricio cut in.

"So it's all a pretense," his younger brother clarified.

"It's a bit of a mess," Christof said, then met my gaze again. "McKenna means a lot to me. We're full-on pretending to be engaged for now. We'll figure out the rest when we get home. For now, we need all of you to play along. No one here knows it's not real."

I had asked him to be honest. There it was, the truth about how he saw this going. What would I have done had he proclaimed he loved me already? I doubted I would have believed it.

Something he'd said echoed in my head. "No one here knows it's not real." *No one besides us,* I amended silently. All I had to do was not get distracted by the lure of the lie.

"Is she there with you?" the female voice asked.

"She is," Christof answered. "And you're all on speaker."

"We should at least introduce ourselves, then. Hi, McKenna. I'm Wren. I can't wait to meet you. This is my husband, Mauricio. Mauricio, say something."

"Welcome to the family?" Mauricio said in an amused tone.

"You must be a good sport to have agreed to this. I'm Gian. Ignore most of what Mauricio says. The rest of us do." A second later, Gian said, "Ouch. I would punch you back if seeing you cry wouldn't upset your wife."

Mauricio laughed. "Have you ever seen Gian so feisty? I think he's nervous."

"Shut the fuck up, Mauricio."

Christof intervened. "There's nothing to worry about, Gian. What you need to remember, though, is that Nona gets confused easily. If she calls you someone else's name or says something that doesn't fit what we're discussing, just go with it. If you correct her too much, she gets upset."

"What's the cause? Has she been diagnosed with Alzheimer's? Lewy body disorder? There are many possible causes for confusion in the elderly. She might have vitamin deficiencies or a UTI. People think confusion is a natural byproduct of aging, so often it goes untreated."

Christof looked uncomfortable as he admitted he didn't know what steps the family had taken with her doctors.

"I'll look into it while I'm there," Gian said with the same confidence I'd seen in Christof. He might have been young and walking into an emotional and possibly explosive situation, but his pedal was to the floor. I respected that.

Mauricio said, "The pilot just announced we're beginning our descent. I hired a car to take us to Nona's. My thought was to give Gian a little time alone with Nona before we open the floodgate of family."

"I agree," Christof said. "We'll meet you at the house." The call ended, and Christof looked deep in thought.

When a significant amount of time had passed without him speaking, I asked, "What are you thinking?"

"A thousand different things, not many of them good."

I took his hand in mine again and said, "Tell me one."

He sighed. "How do I not know if Nona is being treated for dementia or not? Seems like something I should have inquired about."

"Hey, hey. You're not studying to be a doctor. Gian is, right?"

"Yes."

"Since I met you, you've been saying that your family pulls together when there's a problem and that you raise each other up. When I heard Gian's questions, I saw that in action. If you all had the same skills, the same personality, you wouldn't be able to help each other the way you do. Everyone in the pit crew has their own part they play. Don't undervalue what you bring to the table."

He smiled. "You?"

"Damn right." I decided to go with his joke to lighten the mood. "There is no better fake fiancée in all of Italy . . . nay, I'd say in all of Europe."

"The world."

"The fucking universe."

He laughed, then sobered. "I'm glad we told them the truth."

"Me too."

Even if I didn't want it, I needed a reality check on a regular basis.

The ride back to Nona's felt a thousand times shorter. We parked Luigi's car where he had the day before. Funny how much could change in a day. As I walked back into the house, it didn't feel foreign.

Nona met us at the door, apron on, hands on hips. She said something in Italian, then greeted me and asked if I was hungry.

"Starving," I said. I was. In all the excitement of the day, we'd forgotten to eat. "Haven't had anything since breakfast."

Nona wagged a finger at Christof, said something in a sarcastic tone, then turned and headed toward the kitchen. I couldn't contain my curiosity. "What did she say?"

"She said in her day when a man gave his fiancée a 'tour of the town,' he at least fed her. She said she thought my mother had raised me better."

I laughed into my hand. "I love her."

He gave me a hug and a kiss on the forehead. "I'm not surprised. The two of you have a lot in common—well, outside of the dementia."

I tipped my head to one side. Nothing against Nona, but we didn't seem to have much, if anything, in common. "Thanks?"

"I'm serious. Nona survived World War II, Mussolini—although she would tell you some things were better when he was in charge, at least before the war. She has real grit. The loss of her husband couldn't have been easy. Then an all-out battle with a vindictive billionaire? Imagine—no matter what he did, she never bowed to Antonio Corisi, never told him where Aunt Rosella was. He took their land, their jobs, their very homes . . . but she made sure he didn't break their spirits. The family is still here, still close. Life threw some tough challenges her way, but she faced them . . . and won. Her dream might have been a different one than yours, but you faced your own challenges and came out on top. You're both incredibly strong women."

I loved the version of me I saw reflected in his eyes—the connection he'd drawn between me and his grandmother. Could I have held it together through everything Nona had? "Today you reminded me of my father."

"I did? When?"

"When you were talking to Dominic, I could tell you had left all the second-guessing and nerves at the door. It reminded me of the zone my father would go into as soon as he got behind the wheel of a stock car. He'd practiced, strategized, done everything ahead of time. When he hit the racetrack, he trusted his instincts and just floored it."

Christof smiled. "That's kind of how it felt. Once I was in there, I kept my focus on what I wanted him to hear, and thankfully it was what he needed as well."

"McKenna!" Nona called from the kitchen. "Christof. The food does not have legs."

"She knows my name," I said with a huge grin.

"We'd better get in there." Christof looked as if there was more he wanted to say, but Nona's appearance at the kitchen door brought an end to our conversation.

We made our way hastily toward the amazing smells.

On the way to the table, I stopped in front of Christof's grandmother and said, "Thank you, Nona, for everything."

She waved off my gratitude, but a huge smile spread across her face. "You can thank me with babies. Name one of them after me."

"We will," I promised before I caught myself. It was too easy to forget none of this was real.

Christof made a face while he held out a chair for me. "Her name is Edna."

I sat and took a whiff of the beef braciola. "A beautiful name."

"Eddie."

I rolled my eyes. "Stop."

Christof sat across from me. "Eddie Romano. Eh. I guess it's not so bad."

"Nona," I said in the sweetest tone I could muster, "where's your wooden spoon?"

Christof barked out a laugh.

Nona came to sit with us, laughing along and rambling away to herself in Italian.

I took a huge bite of spinach, which was cooked so perfectly that I'd never tasted anything better.

CHAPTER THIRTY-TWO

McKenna

Christof and I had just finished washing the dishes when he received a text announcing that Gian, Mauricio, and Wren had just pulled into the drive. Nona had excused herself a few minutes earlier, saying she wanted to lie down.

Christof wiped his hands one last time on a towel. "Here we go. Say a quick prayer with me." He took both of my hands in his.

"I don't—" I stopped there. His eyes were closed, and I, too, wanted Gian's visit to go well. *Okay, sure. I'll try. If anyone is up there, it's me, which I'm sure you know if you're all-knowing. Sorry about the whole not believing in you and stuff. Let's not focus on the negative. If you're there and can hear me, this is a really nice family. I'm sure there are a lot of really nice people going through worse, so I hate to bother you like this, but anyway, anything you could do for them would be welcome. End transmission now? I don't know how to hang up.*

Christof opened his eyes. "Thank you."

"You're welcome."

"I'll go get Nona. Could you let everyone in?"

"Sure."

I opened the door to a tired but friendly-looking trio. "Hi, I'm McKenna. Christof is getting Nona. Come on in."

They entered, each carrying a bag of luggage that they placed off to the side of the door. Wren greeted me with a hug. Mauricio and Gian shook my hand. I wondered if that was the same way they would have greeted a real fiancée, then gave myself a mental shake. That question served no purpose beyond tormenting myself.

Nona came into the room on Christof's arm. She smiled. "Mauricio. Wren."

They were both enveloped in long hugs from her and a long string of fast Italian. Even as he hugged her, Mauricio said, "Half the time I have no idea what she's saying. I've forgotten a lot."

In a quiet tone, Gian said, "She said you are as handsome as she remembered and warned Wren to keep you on a short leash because you've always been trouble."

"She told me I've gotten fat," Christof said with humor, slipping an arm around my waist.

"You're not," I said softly enough for him alone to hear.

When she released Mauricio, the smile left her face. She stepped closer to Gian and stood before him for a long moment. When she started speaking, I cursed myself for not knowing Italian. As if he could read my thoughts, Christof lowered his head and translated softly into my ear. "She says he looks like her brother Vincenzo did when he was his age. She says his face makes her sad for so many reasons."

Gian's expression tightened. He stood there, immobile. My heart went out to him. I wanted to stop Nona right there and tell her to hug him.

In my ear, Christof continued as Nona began to speak again. "She said there are pictures of his mother in the closet in the hall. He can have them, but she doesn't want to see them. She said they bring her too much pain to look at."

Gian nodded and blinked a few times, then began to also speak in Italian.

Christof said, "He said he understands, and he is grateful she agreed to see him." Christof sniffed.

I looked up at him. "Are you—?"

He shook his head.

Nona touched a hand to Gian's cheek. "You traveled a long way. You must be hungry. I'll make you a big bowl of tortellini. Come."

When Gian didn't immediately move, Nona looked at me and winked. "Just don't eat too much, Gian, or you'll end up fat like Christof."

Nona understood a lot more than people gave her credit for. I wiped a tear from the corner of my eye and leaned into Christof's hug.

His chest rumbled with protest. "Best shape of my life."

I smiled up at him. "She knows. You're right—she and I do have a lot in common. We both like to bust on you."

He sighed, but he was smiling as he watched Gian follow Nona into the kitchen. "Relationships take time."

For a second I thought he was referring to ours, but then I realized his focus was still on Gian. Rightfully so. "They seem off to a good start."

Mauricio said, "I imagined worse, so I'm relieved."

Christof released me to give his brother and his wife a hug. "Should we go in or give them a few minutes alone?"

"I'd say we let them talk for a bit; then Wren and I are heading in." He shrugged when his wife gave him a quizzical look. "I'm starving. My wife barely feeds me."

Christof laughed. "Wren, how do you deal with him?"

She hugged Mauricio. "He has his moments."

"Moments?" He wiggled his eyebrows. "You mean hours."

Christof groaned. "I've heard *seconds*."

I burst out laughing.

Mauricio waved a fist at Christof, but they were both smiling.

So different, yet obviously close. Mauricio was a magazine-cover kind of good looking, but I couldn't see myself with a man who spent more time grooming than I did. Christof was more grounded. More humble. Definitely more my type.

We headed into the kitchen to find Nona sitting across from Gian, having a conversation in Italian. They already seemed more comfortable with each other.

When Nona noticed us, she went to stand, but Christof told her he knew where everything was and would feed Mauricio and Wren. In that moment it was easy to picture raising a family with Christof. I had a flash of him coming down to the garage with one of our children on his hip, another holding his hand, and asking me if he should cook or if I wanted to order out.

Next I saw us in my kitchen. Me in just an apron. Him standing behind me, buck naked, teaching me one of his family's recipes. The image was so clear it felt like a memory rather than a fantasy. My cheeks warmed as I imagined how his hands would caress me as we cooked, how he'd kiss my neck between whispered instructions.

"You okay?" Christof asked after setting full plates in front of his family.

"Yeah. Just thinking," I said quickly. "Should I pour some wine?"

"Always," he answered before sneaking a quick kiss.

The sound of the door opening was followed by the sound of multiple voices. The kitchen quickly filled with everyone who had greeted me the day before as well as some faces I didn't recognize. They each greeted me with a kiss, then moved around the room. English and Italian flowed as easy as the laughter did. I had a hundred wonderful conversations with more people than I'd probably ever spoken to in one evening.

Babies cried.

Children whined and were scolded.

Hurt knees were kissed.

Voices rose and fell. It was loud. Crazy and absolutely wonderful. Christof moved from my side to sit beside his brothers, and for a long time I was satisfied to watch.

The long day hit me all at once. I decided no one would miss me if I slipped away for a moment to the quiet of my room.

I lay down with the intention of resting my eyes briefly and then returning to the kitchen, but I dozed off.

221

CHAPTER THIRTY-THREE

CHRISTOF

As soon as I noticed McKenna had slipped away, I went to check on her. I found her, still dressed, lying across the top of her blankets. Snoring.

So adorable I wanted to roll onto that bed with her. Instead, I slipped her shoes off and wrapped a blanket around her.

Gian appeared at the door. "Everyone is heading out. Nona says you and I are on couches in the living room. Mauricio and Wren will be in your room."

I nodded. "Sounds about right."

"I can't begin to express how much today meant to me, Christof." He leaned against the doorjamb.

"I know. Me too. You belong here, Gian. You always have."

"She only called me your name once."

I smiled. "That's good for her."

"Luigi gave me the name of her doctor. It sounds like he's done all the right testing, but I'll talk to him tomorrow."

"Oh, and don't forget we have a radio to find."

"Right. From some repairman who is older than she is. Do we know his name?"

"It's a small town. Finding him won't be the difficult part. Getting out of his shop without talking to him half the day might be."

Gian smiled, then said, "I didn't tell Mom and Dad we were coming. I wasn't ready to explain it."

"This is for you, Gian. Do it the way that makes it okay."

He looked down at McKenna. "Nothing seemed fake about the two of you tonight."

"It's complicated." I cleared my throat. "Speaking of complicated, I met Dominic Corisi today."

Gian straightened off the wall. "And?"

"We talked. Like you, he's never met Nona. There's a lot of ugly history between him and the family."

"Luigi said the devil is in town and circling our family again. Was he referring to Dominic?"

"That's what they call him."

"Does he know about me?"

"I told him."

"And?"

"He was sad this was the first he's heard of you. He'll be here tomorrow morning."

Some of the color left Gian's face. "Tomorrow morning."

"Yes. Before you meet him, there's some things you need to know about him." I gave Gian an abridged version of Dominic's clashes with the family, but I didn't gloss over the sins of his father.

"Do you think his father killed mine?"

I raised and lowered a shoulder. "I don't know. He doesn't know. Maybe it's better none of us do. Dominic carries enough guilt for things he didn't do."

"He really purchased half of Montalcino?"

"And the farmland surrounding it."

"Why?"

"Because we weren't here to show him there was a better way. He has a lot more money than we ever will, but we're rich in a way he was deprived of. We've always had each other to depend on. I was intimidated to go see him, but once I was in the room with him, I felt mostly sympathy. I wouldn't be who I am if Mom and Dad had not been the parents they were. I don't want to even imagine my life without you, Sebastian, and Mauricio in it. You're the glue that holds me together when I start to unravel. Dominic didn't have that. He came looking for it and was turned away."

"So he's coming to meet Nona."

"And you. He needs you, Gian. It won't be easy when he first meets the family. Also, he may need tutoring on how to be a good brother, but you've always excelled in that department."

The hug Gian gave me nearly knocked me off my feet, but I righted myself before we both tumbled down onto the sleeping McKenna. When he stepped back, he said, "I was so angry with you, Christof. It wasn't until I talked to Mauricio and Wren that I started to see how lucky I am. Everything I've learned about my biological mother points to an emotionally unstable person. I could hate her for leaving me or be thankful to her for giving me a stable family, with parents who have supported me every step of the way and brothers like you."

"That's a mature way of looking at it." I yawned at the wrong moment but couldn't help myself. "Sorry. It's been a long day. We should probably get some sleep, because tomorrow will be another one."

"Thanks, Christof."

"Stop thanking me. This is what brothers do."

Nona called down the hallway, "Gian, did you find Christof? Make sure he is not in McKenna's room."

Gian called back, "He's not, Nona."

We both laughed as we had when we were younger and getting in trouble. "We'd better grab some blankets and get to the living room before she comes for us."

CHAPTER THIRTY-FOUR

McKenna

I woke early, showered, changed, texted a message to Ty because it was still night back home, then headed out to see if anyone else was awake. No one appeared to be. I made myself a cup of coffee and sat outside with the intention of soaking in the peace of the early morning, but I found I was too restless.

I poked my head into the living room. In a T-shirt and lounge pants, Christof was sprawled across one couch. Gian was on the other couch, appearing to still be just as deeply asleep.

I decided to head back to my bedroom for a bit, possibly to be productive and read some emails on my phone, but I paused in front of a closet door. Nona had said there were photos for Gian. I told myself whatever was in that closet was none of my business, but I couldn't force myself beyond the door.

Peeking at old photos that would soon be brought out couldn't hurt anything, could it? I tested the door. If it was locked, that would be the sign that I should forget about the photos.

It wasn't.

I looked over my shoulder. Not a single sound from anyone stirring.

Would they care if they found me looking at photos? Would anyone be upset? I already knew the whole story.

Piles of old albums met me as I cracked open the door, as well as loose papers and other items. I sat down, slipped an album out from beneath the mess, and opened it on my lap. The stories Christof had told me came to life as I flipped through the pages. A young Nona laughing on her wedding day with a handsome groom.

You go, Nona. I would have overlooked the smell of cow for him too.

There were photos of their home on a small farm. I couldn't read the notes written off to the side, but from what I could determine, she and her husband had owned a small vineyard as well. There were photos of them purchasing machinery, then holding up bottles with pride.

I smiled right through that album and didn't hesitate before reaching for the next. They had dates on the front page of each. Once I noticed that, I reshuffled them.

The history of Christof's family unfolded before me. Nona pregnant. Rosella as a baby. Rosella's christening. Pages and pages of photos of Rosella awake, Rosella asleep, Rosella's first step. Nona pregnant again. Aw, Camilla, Christof's mother, had been a cherub. Two beautiful daughters. One happy family.

As soon as I finished the second album, I went on to the third. Rosella and Camilla as children. Both simply beautiful. Rosella and Camilla as teenagers. Rosella blossomed. Yowza, she could have been a pinup model. Camilla looked a little rounder, a little meeker. They seemed close, though. Always smiling in the photos.

So many celebrations for both daughters.

Then several empty pages, as well as spots where photos appeared to have been torn out. Could this have been when the daughters had had their falling-out? When Rosella stole Camilla's boyfriend?

The next album started with Camilla with a handsome young man. His name was written next to a few. Basil. Wedding photos of Camilla and Basil posing with a cow. One with Christof's grandfather laughing with his arm around the cow while Camilla made a funny face at Basil. Two pages of photos of that cow. Weird. Then photos of Camilla and Basil's first son, Sebastian. Mauricio was not far behind. Then Christof. Oh, those three boys looked like trouble for sure. There were many shots of them running across fields or playing with their cousins. Lots of smiles, lots of happy faces. No Rosella.

The next album was full of loose photos that were labeled in another person's handwriting. Camilla's? There were pictures of her and Basil in front of a small house in Connecticut, in front of a neighborhood store with a sign that read **ROMANO CONVENIENCE STORE.**

Four smiling boys—three older and one toddler, Gian. All looking like a handful, but Camilla and Basil didn't seem bothered by their antics.

I sifted through piles of loose photos until I'd pieced together a logical order to them. After a span of time when not many photos had been taken, they started up again with younger versions of the cousins I'd met. No more farm. Simpler clothing.

Photos of Christof's grandfather ended abruptly. I hugged the last one I found to my chest. He'd left when his family had needed him the most. Nona must have felt so alone. I knew that feeling well. She'd survived, though. Just as I had.

We did have a lot in common.

Nona had envelopes overflowing with photos of Christof and his siblings. I became lost in them as well. When I came across a photo of Christof around the same age as when we'd first met, I put it aside. I didn't have my phone with me, but I wanted to snap a photo of it before we left. No matter what happened between Christof and me, he was part of my story and belonged in my own, if solely digital, albums.

I put the albums back in a nice pile, with the ordered loose photos off to one side. When Christof woke up, I'd tell him I'd looked through them and what I'd seen in them. I'd kept that one photo out and was preparing to pocket it when I noticed light from behind me illuminating an envelope tucked up against the back wall of the closet.

I went back onto my knees, leaned deep into the closet, and picked up the stiff yellowed piece of mail. It was unopened. Addressed to

Christof's mother. Absolutely none of my business. I was about to put it back.

"Hey, you."

I startled at the sound of Christof's voice behind me and sat back onto my heels. The closet door was still open, and I was sure there was enough guilt in my expression that he guessed what I'd been up to before I said, "I hope you don't mind that I wanted to see the photos Nona mentioned last night."

He slid down the wall and sat beside me. "Not at all. It was on my list to do this morning. I want Gian to have photos of Rosella, but I wanted to make sure there was nothing in there he'd be hurt about if he saw."

"I don't think there is." Christof had easily accepted what I probably would have chewed his head off for. "You're not upset?"

"That I dragged you into so much of my family's drama that you wanted to see photos of everyone we've been talking about? Why would I be?"

I kissed him then.

Being with someone should be as easy as he made it.

"Look what I found." I held up the photo of him in college. "I remember this man."

Christof took the photo from my hand and groaned. "I forgot I used to make my hair stick up in the front like that. You kissed this douche? Where were your standards?"

I took the photo back. "I thought he was adorable." I shot a side glance at Christof. "I still think he's kind of hot."

"Kind of?" He laughed. "I'm spending more time in the gym and less in my garage when I get home."

"Stop," I said with a laugh.

"What else did you find?" He nodded toward the envelope I'd forgotten in my other hand.

"This. I don't know. It just kind of jumped out at me. The light was hitting it just right." I looked into the fully dark closet over my shoulder for what might have been the source of its illumination, then shrugged. Weird. "Anyway, it's a letter to your mother. Doesn't look as if it's ever been opened." I handed it to Christof.

He frowned as he turned it over. "Not my father's handwriting."

"I don't think it's Nona's either. She labeled a lot of the photos in the album."

He waved it between us. "I should take it back with me and give it to her. Unless it's from an old boyfriend." He wrinkled his nose. "My parents are happily married. No need to rock that boat."

"You think a letter could do that?"

He shrugged. "Depends what's in it, I guess. I've had about all the surprises I can handle for one week."

I nodded. "I don't blame you. So maybe we should stash it back where I found it."

He turned the envelope in his hand again. "For Gian to find? He doesn't need another surprise either."

"So what will you do with it?"

"What could be in here that my mother would want to read?"

"It could be a note from her childhood best friend telling her where she hid a treasure."

The look he gave me said, *Please take this seriously.*

I put a hand on his knee and ignored how that small act sent my heart racing and my body revving. "There's only one way to know."

"It's probably nothing."

"Most likely."

"It might be a family recipe one of our aunts didn't want her to forget," he said in a more upbeat tone.

"See, then she'd be grateful you found it."

"I'm just going to open it." He did. "It's in Italian." He translated as he read:

Camilla, I know you don't understand why I did what I did. I'm okay if you never forgive me for it, because if I had the chance to do it all over again, I would do the same.

Our eyes met before he flipped the letter over to check the end for a signature. "It's from Aunt Rosella."

I scooted closer to look at it with him, even though I wasn't able to translate what it said. "So far it doesn't sound like much of an apology."

"No, it doesn't." He pressed his lips together, then turned the letter back over. "I wonder if this is about Antonio. My mother said she had a crush on him before Rosella married him."

I gripped Christof's thigh. "What does Rosella say? Keep reading."

He gave me an odd look, then shook his head and read the beginning part again.

If I had the chance to do it all over again, I would do the same. You think Antonio is a nice man, but he isn't. It's all lies. I've talked to people from his town. People fear him. He's a violent man who made his money by selling his soul to the devil. That's what anyone who knows him well calls him—the devil. When you told me you were pregnant, I knew it was his.

Christof stopped. "What the fuck?"

"Camilla was pregnant from Antonio? Do you think your oldest brother . . ."

Christof started reading again.

I couldn't let you marry him. I couldn't let you tell him about the baby. You would never have been able to escape him. I did have sex with him. Hate me if you must, but it was the only way to save you. I thought he would leave when I told everyone. I didn't think he and Papa would fight. I didn't know Papa would threaten him if he didn't marry me. He's so angry. He says he'll kill Papa. I have to get him away from Montalcino. You belong with Basil. He loves you.

Christof stopped. "Sebastian is Antonio's son. Oh my God, it all makes sense now. How did I not see how much they look alike? Of course my mother didn't want Sebastian here. She wasn't afraid he'd explode; she was afraid Dominic would discover he had two brothers no one had told him about. One from Aunt Rosella. One from my mother." He stuffed the letter back into its envelope, folded it, jammed it into his pajama pocket, then kicked the door closed with the side of his foot. My heart ached for him when he rubbed his hands over his eyes and said, "The last thing I need is another family secret."

When he lowered his hands, I took one between mine. "I over-stepped. I was curious. I shouldn't have—"

He growled, "It's not your fault my aunt and mother fucked the same man."

My eyes rounded, and I took a deep breath. He wasn't angry with me, but he was angry. I couldn't blame him. Each time he sewed the fabric of his family back together, it seemed to unravel in another corner. I said the only thing I could think of. "I'm so sorry." Then I wrapped my arms around him and simply hugged him.

He let out a long breath. With me still tucked beneath his chin, he asked, "Do I pretend I didn't find the letter? Do I tell Sebastian?"

"I don't know," I mumbled into his chest. I wished I did.

"God, I hate secrets."

Me too. I wasn't very happy with myself, either, for laying another one on him. "It's okay if you're upset with me. I'm upset with me."

His arms wrapped around me tighter. His heart was beating loudly beneath my ear, but not nearly as wildly as before. "How is it that you're not racing for the nearest airport?"

"Leaving hasn't crossed my mind once." As I uttered the words, I realized how true they were. I tipped my head back, and his kiss was everything I needed in that moment.

Everything else slid away as soon as his lips touched mine. His hands went to my hair. I shifted my position to straddle him. Beneath me, his cock sprang to life. I ground my still-clothed sex against it.

For a moment, in my mind at least, we were back in the guesthouse as if no time had passed. His kiss was as hungry and impatient as mine.

The sound of Nona's bedroom door opening and closing brought the kiss to a hasty end. I slid off his lap, nodded toward the impressive tenting of his bottoms, and did my best not to smile. "You can't greet her like that."

"You think she'd notice?" he joked as he stood before helping me to my feet.

"Do you think she saw us?" I asked. I felt naughty and so much younger than I was.

Nona's bedroom door opened and shut again. Then again. Each time a little louder. Christof laughed. "I'd say yes."

"Hey, at least we're not in my room this time. That has to count for something."

"Sure. Try to tell her that, but be quick on your feet if you do." With one last kiss, he said, "I'm going to hit a cold shower."

I grasped one of his hands as he was about to turn away. "Christof?"

"Yes?" The heated look he gave me was so intense I nearly forgot what I wanted to ask him.

But it came back to me. "What will you do about the letter?"

His expression tightened. "I don't know. I guess first we should see how Dominic does at meeting one brother before telling him he has another."

"Your mother thinks her sister stole Antonio from her because she wanted him for herself. Maybe reading that letter would help her forgive her sister."

"Or tear my family apart. My mother is a proud woman. This would be taking everything she's likely been too ashamed to tell anyone and forcing her to face it."

"Do you think your father knows about Sebastian?"

Christof winced. "God, I hope so. I really fucking hope so."

"Want some good news?"

His eyes were riveted to mine. "Would love some."

"Your boner is gone. You're free to walk about the house."

He looked down, then met my gaze again and started to laugh. "Is that good news?"

"It is when Nona is heading down the hall toward us like she is." I waved to his grandmother. "Morning, Nona."

Christof greeted her as well.

She didn't stop, just nodded at us, then walked right past in a long cotton housedress, mumbling in Italian.

Christof and I shared a guilty look. We knew we shouldn't, but we couldn't hold it back; we laughed like little kids caught breaking the rules.

"What did she say?" I asked.

"She said we should ask Salvatore about borrowing his guesthouse."

CHAPTER THIRTY-FIVE

CHRISTOF

About fifteen minutes before the expected arrival of Dominic Corisi, Mauricio, Wren, Gian, McKenna, and I were seated in the living room waiting. Each of us appeared to be shooting for the same not-worried-about-this expression. I didn't know how they were faring, but I was silently freaking the fuck out.

Nona had thrown us out of her kitchen—said all our hovering was driving her crazy. It probably was. It didn't take a genius to figure out that something was up with us. Nona's house was normally overrun with family dropping in, but that morning Luigi must have done as I'd asked, because it was just us.

The letter from my aunt to my mother was stuffed into the back pocket of my jeans. I wanted to share it with my brothers. I debated whether or not I should call Sebastian and tell him to come on over so we could get this family reunion done in one wild day.

In the end I decided the secret wasn't mine to reveal. The letter wasn't addressed to me. It needed to be delivered to who it was meant for. Perhaps if my mother had been a horrible person, I would have felt justified in outing her secret. Or if my father hadn't been such a good role model of how humble and steady love should be. I'd had a wonderful childhood. All four of us—me, Sebastian, Mauricio, and Gian—credited the quality of our childhood as well as the fraternal bond we shared to our parents.

When we'd fought, and we had, our punishments had been a list of team chores. We'd been forced to work together when we were unhappy with each other, and it had taught us how to keep moving in the same direction even through bumpy times. My mother deserved a chance to tell her truth—or maybe keep her secret.

I didn't know.

Gian had spent so much of his life wondering, worrying that we would leave him, too, because something inside him whispered it was his fault his mother had left him. As if somehow he hadn't been good enough. Meeting Dominic, building a connection with another person who had been left behind by the same mother—Gian could benefit from that.

Dominic could as well.

What good was there in telling Sebastian his biological father wasn't the good man who'd raised him but an evil bastard our mother had slept with and then lost to her sister? Would Dominic find any comfort in another half sibling?

Did my father know about Sebastian, or had my mother lied to him too?

As someone who had a foot in two cultures, someone who had heard stories of what life had been like in Italy when my mother was young . . . I couldn't blame her if she had lied. An unwed mother in this small town? All those years ago? The family, wonderful as they were, would not have handled that well.

McKenna squeezed my hand. "Just a few more minutes. How are you holding up?"

"I'm fine," I said automatically.

"You don't have to be." She lowered her voice. "Everything you've done, you've done out of love. This will work out."

I leaned over and kissed her temple. "Is this how you imagined your first trip to Italy?"

"No. It's better."

I was about to call bullshit, but then she gave me this look . . . one so full of . . . love? I found it difficult to breathe.

"He said he'd be here at nine o'clock, right?" Gian asked.

"Five more minutes," I said.

Mauricio tapped his fingers on his knees. "I wonder if he is as nervous as we are."

"I'm sure he is," his wife said.

Jumping into the conversation, McKenna added, "Don't expect him to look it, even if he is. People who are always in the public eye learn quickly how to hide how they feel. Some of the best drivers I've ever met sound like assholes right before a race. It's all nerves. If you talk to them later, you realize that's just how they deal."

"This can't be easy for him," I said. "None of the memories he has of coming here are good. Let's do our best to change that today."

Nona stepped into the living room and announced that breakfast was ready. None of us moved. She took a moment to study each of our faces and then asked, "Did someone die and you think I can't handle the news? At my age, death is no longer a stranger. He is someone who comes whether or not you invite him. You can either live your life fearing him or embrace your relationship with him and change how you live because of him. So spit it out. Has death come to my door one more time?"

A loud knock on the outside door of Nona's house made all of us jump. "No one died, Nona," I said. *Death isn't here. Just the devil.*

I cursed my inner voice for making a joke I would have skewered my brothers for making, but I gave myself credit for not saying it aloud. I stood and made my way to open the door.

Although dressed in a casual pair of dark slacks and a light button-down shirt, Dominic didn't look a bit more relaxed than he had in his office.

"Dominic." I held out a hand in greeting. "Welcome." He didn't shake my hand, and I was pretty sure I heard a sound akin to a growl, but I lowered my hand and forced a smile and reminded myself what McKenna had said about drivers before a race. This couldn't have been easy for him. He was likely mentally prepared for an ambush. "Quick tip? Everyone here is on your side. We all want you and Nona to have a good visit. Gian is excited but nervous to meet you. They'll all like you a lot more if you attempt a smile." He flashed his teeth at me. Not a smile, but in my mind, almost a joke . . . which I saw as progress.

Nona came to the door. "Sebastian! Where is Heather? Don't step foot in my house without my sweet Heather."

To give Nona credit, Dominic and Sebastian did look a lot alike. *Here we go.* I put a hand on Dominic's shoulder and ignored the way he tried to shrug my touch off. "Nona, this is Dominic." I left off his last name. It was a trigger the situation didn't require. "Rosella's oldest boy."

Nona froze.

Mauricio and Wren moved to flank her. I nodded in approval. Mauricio said, "Dominic, it is always a pleasure to meet more family."

Wren said something similar.

My attention went to Gian, who stepped out from behind them. He looked from Nona's angry expression to Dominic's unsmiling one. "Maybe this isn't such a good idea."

I closed the door behind Dominic. "It'll be fine," I said, even though my own gut was undecided on the direction this was about to go. "Nona, we'd like to have breakfast with Dominic, but it's your house. Will you invite him in?"

Head held high, Nona walked until she was right in front of Dominic. Nothing about her stance was welcoming.

She's going to throw him out.

This is her house. That's her right. Please don't, Nona.

Papa, if you're here, we have never needed you more.

Nona looked Dominic over slowly. "Your mother is dead to me. She is no welcome in my house."

Dominic dipped his head. "I'm here alone."

"Your father hurt this family. Hurt us many times." She went from English into Italian as she described Antonio as the devil.

In crisp Italian, Dominic said, "He was the devil. He hurt his wife and children as well. Thankfully he's dead."

Nona raised a hand near his face. "Is there any of him in you?"

Dominic didn't answer at first, but when he did, it was in a guttural tone. "Yes, but it's a demon I give a very short leash."

She lowered her hand. "You look just like Sebastian. He fights his dark side too."

Oh no.

Does she know?

Has she always known?

Not now, Nona.

Continuing in English, I quickly interjected, "My brother lost his wife and unborn child seven years ago. It was a tough time for our family."

"I'm sorry to hear that," Dominic said.

"He's doing better now. He's remarried, with an adorable little girl and a second child on the way." I touched Nona's arm to bring her attention to me. "We'd lost Sebastian for a while, remember, Nona? He was so sad and so angry. But we stuck by him because he's family and we all have our demons to fight. Dominic is my cousin. Gian's brother. Your grandchild. Papa's grandchild. He will always be welcome in my home. Will you make him welcome in yours?"

Gian came to stand beside me. He addressed his comment to both Nona and Dominic. "He'll always be welcome in mine."

Mauricio put his arm around Wren. "Ours as well."

Nona took a moment to answer. No one moved as we all hung on her next words. "Are you hungry?"

Dominic blinked quickly a few times, the only sign that she might have surprised him. "Always."

"Then why are we standing in the hallway? You want all the food to get cold so you can say I'm not the best cook in Montalcino?" Nona mumbled something more in Italian and turned to make her way back to the kitchen.

I let out a relieved breath and gave Dominic a pat on the back. He didn't seem to like it, but if he was going to stick around, he'd have to loosen up a little. "Dom, you haven't met my fiancée yet. McKenna, this is my cousin Dominic."

She stepped forward with a huge smile. I didn't know how to interpret the look in her eyes until she gave him a huge hug, one he didn't look as if he had any idea what to do about. He just kind of held his hands out to the sides and stood there like a mannequin. When she released him, she winked at me, then said, "Welcome to the family. Now calm the fuck down, and don't forget to compliment Nona on her cooking. She's very proud of her frittata."

Dominic nodded slowly, then smiled, then actually—holy shit— laughed. "Thanks."

We were heading toward the kitchen when the outside door flew open and Luigi came rushing in. "Is he here?"

"If you're referring to me, then yes, he is here," Dominic said in a similar tone to what he'd used in his office with me the day before.

Luigi switched to Italian. "Christof, don't hate me, but remember when you told me not to tell anyone? I might have told one person."

In Italian, Dominic added, "*He* also speaks Italian."

I exchanged a quick look with McKenna. *You're right: I shouldn't have told him.* I turned back to Luigi. "Who knows?"

"Everyone?" Luigi answered weakly.

I groaned. "You did tell them to stay away this morning, right?"

"They're on their way."

Mauricio went to stand beside Dominic. "You won't want to meet them at the door. Let's go have breakfast. Christof is good at handling things like this."

Gian moved closer to Dominic as well. "You have every right to be here, Dominic. Nona is the only one who can ask you to leave, and she offered to feed you."

I started going over all the possible ways this could work out as well as blow up. "McKenna, do you think you can keep Nona occupied long enough for me to calm everyone down?"

"No problem," she said confidently. *God, I love that woman.*

Luigi added in Italian, "You might want to have this reunion somewhere else. I tried to say we should wait and see what comes from the visit but was met with a bit of a mob mentality. Not that I can blame them. I don't like the devil in this house any more than they do."

"There is no devil here." I went to stand with my brothers beside Dominic. "Dominic, this is your cousin Luigi. My best friend as a child, good man, faithful husband, great father, very, very bad secret keeper. Luigi, this is Dominic Corisi. Your cousin. Good guy, great husband and father, was not expecting to meet the whole family today. We all want the same thing—for today to go well. Dominic, it might help if you told Luigi what your plans are for the land you bought up."

"Yes, I would be very interested in your plans," Luigi said in a harsh tone. I was used to seeing the lighter side of my cousin, but the wounds here were deep.

In the silence that followed, I had time to worry that Dominic was going to ruin this for himself. There was only so much you could do for another person, though. I'd gotten him there, shown my support, and suggested a way he could move forward as part of the family. The rest was his choice.

Dominic looked from Mauricio, to Gian, to me . . . as if realizing then that we stood with him in support. He swallowed visibly, pocketed his hands, and said, "I've hired an attorney to assist in ensuring each parcel of land is deeded back to its rightful owners. I cannot undo all the damage my father did to this town, but I can right many things."

"You bought the land to return it?" Luigi asked with skepticism.

Dominic looked about to confess the truth, but I put a hand on his shoulder and spoke instead. "Until a person gives me a reason not to, I believe them. We can dredge up the past, waste all our time on things we cannot change, or we can move forward—together—as family."

Luigi didn't soften.

So I added, "Luigi, I know that look, but you need to hear me. No one was innocent in this. When Dominic was in need of the family, you all turned your backs on him. Although you had reason to, it still wasn't right. Imagine what he has endured. You have the power to right that wrong. Stand with him, with us, and greet the family when they arrive, Luigi. If you accept Dominic, they will." Dominic opened his mouth to say something, but I raised my hand. "Let me handle this one, Dominic. Just trust me."

Luigi remained quiet for a moment, then said, "I was one of the ones who thought it would be better for Nona if she never met you. My father lost his vineyard to your father. The Corisi name has been a curse on our house. But Christof is right: those crimes were your father's—not yours. He wanted to break us, but he only made us stronger. It's time to move forward."

I said what had become obvious to me. "He wanted to break Dominic as well, but here he is—stronger, very much like us. What tries to tear us apart only brings us closer."

In a tight tone, Dominic said, "All I ever wanted was to move forward with the family."

Eh, that was mostly true, so I let it slide.

Appearing in the doorway were Salvatore and his wife.

Luigi gave me one look as if to ask, *Are you sure?*

I nodded.

He turned to greet the couple. "You're here just in time to welcome Dominic. Wait until you hear what his plans are for the land he bought. You might be able to finally start that wine label you've been talking about."

"We don't need his charity," Salvatore said in a cold tone.

Dominic stepped forward. "There is no charity in returning something that was stolen from you."

I added, "Looks like we not only have many reasons to celebrate today, but we'll also need more food. Could you swing by the bakery and pick up some pastries?"

Nona called out from the other room, "Did I cook another plate for no one? Someone tell Dominic in my house food doesn't have legs and at my age I don't wait to eat."

Salvatore asked, "She's okay with him being here?"

I answered, "You just heard her. Not only okay but impatient for him to get his ass in her kitchen."

Dominic smiled. "Then I'd better head in."

After he headed in and Salvatore left to get pastries, McKenna returned from the kitchen and slid under my arm. "How is it going out here?"

I kissed her briefly. "Luigi and I only have to explain to about seventy-five more family members that Dominic is welcome. Right, Luigi?"

Luigi smiled. "I'll call Pia. You think I have a big mouth? Tell her, and even those on their way will know before they arrive."

"Luigi, you're a genius."

Looking pleased with himself, Luigi stepped away to make the call.

McKenna looked up at me. "You're pretty amazing, you know that?"

"That's what she said," I joked.

McKenna pinned me with one of her long looks. "I'm serious."

Turning her in my arms, I kissed her with all the gratitude welling inside me. When I raised my head, I said, "I don't know how to begin to thank you. You've been the best fake fiancée a man could ask for."

I expected her to smile, but she didn't.

She shuddered against me, then stepped back. "I should head back into the kitchen."

Luigi was back, smiling, saying there was no reason to worry; everything was going to work out.

I wasn't so sure, but my concern wasn't related to Dominic's visit. I couldn't shake the look that had been in McKenna's eyes just before she'd walked away. She'd looked—hurt? I hadn't meant my words to express anything more than how glad I was she was there with me.

Family began to arrive before I had a chance to act on my concern. Having Luigi not only at my side but also adamant about Dominic's right to visit Nona brought a calm to a situation that otherwise might have quickly gotten out of hand.

Soon the kitchen was overflowing with cousins of all ages. Children were once again running between adults; parents were laughing, scolding, arguing about everything and nothing. When Luigi's wife arrived, he brought her to meet Dominic in the kitchen as well.

Dominic stepped out of the kitchen. "Christof."

I met him halfway. "A bit overwhelming en masse? Many of them took the day off from work to meet you."

One nod said it all. "Thank you."

"You're welcome." In that moment I saw real potential for him to be a good brother to Gian and a good cousin to me and Mauricio. And Sebastian? It wasn't the time to add to that relationship. If there was one thing Sebastian didn't handle well, it was surprises. I was torn between his right to know and my mother's right to her secret. Love was complicated.

"How long are you in Montalcino?" he asked.

I doubted he was curious about only me. "Gian should go back tomorrow or the next day. He is missing classes to be here. He'll probably fly back with Mauricio and Wren. I might hang back a few more days so I can show McKenna some of Italy—Venice, Florence, definitely a little of Rome."

"I have an extra jet if you'd like to borrow it."

"An extra? Like, one just hanging around?" I joked. My family had become successful through Romano Superstores, but Dominic's level of wealth was so far above ours I couldn't fully imagine it.

He wasn't an easy man to make smile. "The offer is on the table. I assume your family will be using your plane. If you'd prefer the use of my yacht, it's currently off the Amalfi Coast."

"Do you know what I would like more than that?"

His eyes narrowed as he waited.

I said, "I'd like you to come to Sunday dinner next week at Gian's place. My mother usually makes a big dinner there. Bring your wife, your little girl, your sister too. Sebastian and Heather will be there with Ava, who is almost six."

"I'd like that."

"Also your mother, if she's willing to come."

"My mother?" He didn't seem keen on the idea.

I wasn't sure I was, either, but this wasn't about how I felt. "I'll talk to Gian, but I believe he wants to meet her. My mother might not be happy with it at first, but we need to stop letting the past have such a stranglehold on us. It's time to move on—together, if that's at all possible."

"I can see why Alethea thought you were worth sneaking in to meet me."

"I didn't sneak—" I stopped. *Ballbuster.* It was a good sign. "I'll make you a deal. When I tell my future children about you, I'll forget the devil part, if you leave off that I popped out of your bathroom. In my mind, I'm much more of a strut-through-the-front-door kind of man."

Dominic laughed at that, his face transforming as he smiled. "I can do that." A twinge of sadness filled his eyes again. "I never wanted to be the devil." He shook his head. "When I think about how close I came—"

"But you didn't," I cut in. "We all have something we regret. We all make mistakes. I don't trust anyone who says they don't. The world can be a very unforgiving place, but that's not how family should be."

Dominic offered me his hand.

I shook it.

We stood there afterward in prolonged silence. He spoke first. "There have been a handful of people who have come into my life and changed the course of it. My wife and daughter. A few close friends. And a man who has become like a father to me, Alessandro Andrade. You sound a lot like him. Do you know him?"

"No, should I?"

Dominic shook his head. "I suppose not. I can't shake the feeling, though, that this has all worked out too well. Almost as if it were orchestrated. Was it your idea to come to Montalcino to meet me?"

I could have lied, if for no other reason than how lame the truth would sound, but I was intrigued. "No, it was my parents'. My mother's mostly."

"Did she have any unexpected meetings? Was she invited to something she found unusual?"

"She did attend a fundraiser hosted by the queen of Vandorra."

The smile returned to Dominic's face. "Queen Delinda of Vandorra, until recently Delinda Westerly, a.k.a. one of Alessandro's closest friends. Looks like they are still up to their old antics. Not that I'm not grateful for the intervention."

"I don't understand."

"How long have you and McKenna been engaged? Don't tell me—it was very recent."

My expression must have given the truth away, because he added, "Is the engagement real or staged for this visit?"

I frowned.

Dominic continued. "Classic Alessandro and Delinda. You poor man. Don't worry, their success rate is nearly perfect."

"Success rate?" Perhaps it was because there was so much running through my head that day, but I had no idea what he was talking about.

"Forget I said anything, but invite me to the wedding."

The wedding. Words that would have once made me feel trapped had the opposite effect on me then. I wanted the engagement to be real.

I love McKenna.

Oh my God.

I love McKenna.

She chose that moment to appear in the doorway of the kitchen. Her expression seemed concerned at first; then she smiled as she noted who I was with.

My heart started thudding in my chest. I didn't care about what we'd found or how my mother would respond to Dominic as well as his wife, child, and mother coming to Sunday dinner. All I wanted was to get McKenna alone and show her how much she meant to me.

"Dominic," I said. "About that extra jet—"

CHAPTER THIRTY-SIX

McKenna

I stood off to one side of a kitchen full of people speaking a language I didn't understand. Whenever I spoke, the conversation around me reverted to English, but I was taking a moment to breathe.

I looked around the room, soaking in the laughter and excited chatter, and was filled with a sense of wonder. Christof's wins weren't gaining him a trophy, prize money, fame, or sponsors. He didn't care about anything like that. Everything he'd achieved on this trip he'd done out of love.

Dominic had won the lottery when it came to cousins. I could still hear Christof telling him that short of killing him, there was no way to hurt him, because even if someone stripped all his family's money away, he'd still have the things he needed to be happy: his family, his friends . . . his fiancée.

Me?

Had he said it because he meant it or simply to keep up the charade of our engagement? I struggled with how I felt about either possibility. I had what some might call a jaded view of people as well as relationships. Yet there I was in Italy, falling in love with a man who had just called me the best fake fiancée a man could wish for. I hugged my arms around myself and admitted to myself how deeply those words had stung.

They were true, but hurtful because they no longer matched how I felt. Pia motioned to me from across the room as if to ask if I was okay. I nodded in reassurance because I was, and that was also unsettling.

I should have felt alone, the way I'd felt so often in my life, but Christof's family had welcomed me as one of their own. They believed our lie, and because of it they'd made room in their hearts for me. The only place I felt this comfortable was at Decker Park with my crew.

I was invested in these people. When Gian bent to hear something Nona was saying, then straightened and laughed . . . I felt his joy. When Mauricio's cousins teased him about finally finding a woman who was too smart for his bullshit and his only response was to hug Wren closer and say, "Thank God." I was happy they'd found each other. Christof's family had experienced some dark times, but their unshakable ability to love was their strength.

My kind of people.

I wanted to be part of this world almost as much as I'd ever wanted Decker Park. It was a scary revelation. I didn't want to give up one for the other, but could I have both?

Christof entered the room a short time later with Dominic. A hush fell over the room; then someone made a joke in Italian, Dominic smiled, and conversation resumed. Could love be that easy? I wanted to believe so.

Christof spotted me, and for a moment it felt as if I was the most important person in the room to him. He walked toward me, never looking away, then put his arms around me and nuzzled my neck. "How are you holding up?"

I rested my head on his shoulder. "You did it. You brought them all together."

"We did it. I couldn't have done it without you."

I nodded but knew it wasn't true. Christof would have found a way, but I was grateful to have been part of the journey.

"About tomorrow," Christof said. "Would you like to come with me, Gian, and Dominic to find Nona's radio? We could stay with the two of them long enough to retrieve the radio, make sure it works, then slip off somewhere we can be alone."

I smiled up at him. "Like a guesthouse?"

"Are you a mind reader?"

That or the feel of his cock hardening against my stomach was a clear hint of where his mind had gone. "You're an easy read."

"Am I?" he murmured, nuzzling my neck again. "Is that a good thing?"

I thought about all the men who'd danced around how they felt and relaxed back against Christof. "Oh yes." Neither of us spoke for the next few minutes as we simply enjoyed the closeness. "I'd love to go with you tomorrow."

We exchanged a heated look that left us both breathless. No matter where this took us, I was glad I'd agreed to go to Italy with him. This experience was something I'd remember for the rest of my days. As I thought how the next day would start, I said, "Do you think the radio guy will be afraid when we show up with Dominic?"

Christof took a moment to think about it. "We'll bring wine."

"That's all it takes?"

"I'm hoping it'll say, 'We come in peace.'"

Truthfully, I could see it working. "Nona's stock?"

"Absolutely. The family label used to be a big thing in the area. In the past we've offered to help bring it back, but she always said it would never feel like her wine until the grapes were grown on her soil. For the first time I can see that happening again. By returning the land, Dominic will breathe life back into the local economy. No one wants a handout, but Pia told me many cried when she told them land that was theirs for nearly a century will be returned to the family. I wouldn't be surprised if by next year you'll see the family label on the shelves in Romano stores."

"I'm so happy for all of them."

Christof smiled again. "I'm happy it all worked out." He hugged me tighter. "And that we shared this."

I tensed. Was the trip over? "Me too."

"You don't have to rush back yet, do you?" he asked.

I expelled an audible breath of relief. "No."

"Would you like to play tourist with me?"

Does he really need to ask? "Sure."

He chuckled. "I still have that surprise I promised you."

I lowered my voice. "Don't even bring it up if you're not going to tell me what it is."

His smile was shameless. "You're going to love it."

"You know I'm not good at surprises."

He lowered his head so he could murmur into my ear. "How about I give you a chance to tempt the details out of me tonight?"

Desire shot through me, and I writhed against him as I imagined all the ways I could. "You're on."

The evidence of just how easy that would be pulsed against me. I shifted ever so slightly back and forth against it.

"You're going to get me smacked again," he growled into my ear.

Feeling young and free, I laughed. "I'm okay with that."

Our brief kiss went unnoticed in the happy chaos, and I wanted that moment to last forever. I couldn't imagine life ever being better.

Christof and I sneaked out to the guesthouse that night, and I realized it could. What we shared went beyond the sex I'd had with others. It went beyond even what we'd shared together. For the first time in my life, I understood what it meant to make love to someone.

Yes, there was passion, but there was also laughter and tenderness. The connection I felt with Christof was so intimate, so moving, I almost burst into tears afterward. I didn't, though, because I didn't want to do a single thing that would bring any of this to an end.

The next morning we woke in each other's arms, showered together, then spent half the day with Dominic, Gian, and Alberto, who turned out to be distantly related to Christof's family. A bottle of Nona's wine was all it took for him to cautiously welcome them into his home. Even Dominic, though it took half the bottle for Alberto to stop frowning at him.

After another night in the guesthouse, during which I did everything I could imagine to pry the details out of Christof, I grew suspicious that he liked my efforts too much to cave and tell me anything substantial. When I confronted him about it, he shrugged and gave me that adorable, shameless smile of his.

I laughed because, although I wouldn't admit it, I would have been disappointed if he'd told me. I loved that I'd found a man who was strong without being cold. I couldn't push him; seeing him able to stand his ground with me turned me on like I had never been before.

It was becoming difficult to imagine not having him in my life.

The next day Christof flew me to southern Italy. Turned out his surprise was a VIP tour of one of the country's most prestigious racing facilities and box seats for a race. So thoughtful. So Christof. Anyone who didn't know me well might have thought the magic of the day would be in watching the race or in meeting the drivers. Christof took the day to a whole new level when he arranged for us to share a meal with one of the pit crews. That was when I knew Christof understood me, and I was overwhelmed by how it made me feel to have a man who was not just a lover but also a friend.

The next few days flew by in a blur of lovemaking and touring. Via the private jet Dominic lent us, we had breakfast in Sicily one day, lunch in Rome overlooking the Colosseum the next, followed by dinner the next day on the Grand Canal in Venice.

I imagined this was how a honeymoon felt.

They were magical days, so perfect they didn't feel real. I'd stepped into a Matrix-like dream where nothing was wrong and our engagement wasn't fake. We didn't talk about his family or mine. Neither of us addressed the future or where our relationship was headed. We kept our enjoyment of each other in the present, like two people who knew anything that good had to be savored because it couldn't last.

Late that Saturday morning I woke to Christof kissing my neck. "Wake up, sleepyhead. We fly home today."

I recognized the feeling that swept over me just then. It was the same a person had when they were having the most amazing dream and their alarm clock called to them to wake. We couldn't stay as we were, but I wasn't ready for this time together to end.

Naked, I rolled onto my back and traced the strong line of his jaw. "What time do we have to leave?"

His kiss was tender and full of promise. "There's no rush, but I have a few things I should do tonight if I don't want our family dinner to be a complete disaster."

Welcome back, reality. "Did you decide what you'll do?"

He lay back against the pillows but kept an arm around me. "I want to talk to my mother before I speak to Sebastian. She needs to know that I know. If that goes well, I'll go see Sebastian. Gian has been texting me. He flew back to meet Dominic's wife and child as well as his sister, Nicole, and her husband and child. It sounds like they've welcomed him into their family."

"And his biological mother?"

"They didn't mention her, so I didn't ask."

"Do your parents know any of this?"

"He told them where he was."

"How did they handle it?"

"Dad's . . . Dad. He takes most things in stride. Mom worries that we'll lose Gian to them, but Sebastian went to see her and reminded her that family is about so much more than blood."

"So he knows as well."

"About Gian, anyway. Dad told him. There was no way not to once I told my parents I invited Dominic and his family to Sunday dinner. They know he's bringing his sister, both spouses, and their children, but I didn't say Rosella will likely also be there."

"That's a lot to spring on your mother."

He sighed. "I'll tell her tonight when I give her the letter. My mother might be upset at first, but I've never seen her not do the right thing. I have to believe she'll be able to put the past to rest for Gian's sake as well as her own."

I waited.

He made no mention of how his parents would feel about meeting me for the first time. Of course he didn't—our engagement wasn't real. During our time together he'd shared his secrets with me, been better to me than any man had ever been, and given me memories that would remain with me forever—but he hadn't said he loved me.

Okay, one time as part of an expression, but never the way I yearned to hear it.

I told myself it made sense for him not to invite me to that dinner. His parents and siblings knew our engagement wasn't real. The pretense was only useful in Montalcino, not back home. I slid the ring off my left hand and held it out to him. "You should give this back to your mother at the same time."

He took the ring and for a moment looked as if he wasn't sure what to say. My imagination ran wild with possibilities. What would I say if he slid it back on my finger and proposed for real? Did he have another ring handy? Would he thank me for being mature enough to understand that sex, even when indulged in as part of a fake engagement, didn't necessarily mean anything?

"I will." He sat up and placed the ring on the bed stand behind him. At times I felt I could almost read his thoughts—this was not one of those times. He looked conflicted. Nausea rushed through my body.

"I'm not looking forward to tonight or tomorrow. You've been so good about riding out the drama here. I can't imagine you'd want to—"

Oh God, I didn't want to be the person who was so afraid of being left they left first, but it was as if I had stepped outside myself and was watching the scene unfold. I sat up and quickly cut in, "I completely understand. I'm actually anxious to get back to the garage. Ty is good, but I don't like not knowing what's in the works."

"McKenna, I—"

I placed a hand over his mouth. He'd been honest with me every step of the way, nothing but extremely good to me. It wasn't his fault I was a coward. Worse than a man who wanted to change me—Christof was someone I wanted so badly I feared I'd lose myself if I gave in to my desperation to hold on to him. So I let him go. "We had a great week together. That's it. Don't make things awkward." I turned away and stood.

He didn't look happy, but I told myself one day he'd see that I'd actually done him a favor. "Come here," he said in quiet command.

"No." I couldn't do it.

Naked and with his cock at full mast, he stood and came to me. My body quivered with excitement at his approach even as my thoughts darkened. "What's going through that head of yours?" he asked.

I didn't want to want him. I wanted to feel nothing. I wasn't a crier, but I wanted to throw myself in his arms and sob my heart out. Or punch him.

He pulled me against him and lifted me and slid his hard cock along my already-wet sex. I was angry with him, angrier with myself. I couldn't find the words to express how I felt, so I pulled his head down and kissed him.

I ground against him, claimed his tongue with mine. His hold on me started gentle, but as I went wild against him, his touch became rougher. He backed up to the bed and sat. I took full advantage of our new position and the control it gave me.

Without breaking off our kiss, I thrust my hips downward, thrusting him inside me, and began pumping furiously. Harder and faster. I took him deeper and deeper.

There was no patience in me, no attempt to ensure he or I found full pleasure in the act. I wanted him to be no different than any man I'd ever fucked.

It was wild, angry sex that brought me an orgasm I resented. He came soon after me, then held me tenderly because he didn't understand that it meant goodbye.

CHAPTER THIRTY-SEVEN

CHRISTOF

On the flight home, McKenna pretended to sleep, but I knew she was awake and listening to music on her headphones. She was scared—I'd seen it in her eyes that morning, when I'd mentioned that we were going home that day. She saw it as an ending rather than the beginning it would be for us.

We'd started off all wrong.

I didn't want her wearing an antique ring she'd put on as part of a ruse. Together, we'd choose something simple she could safely wear even while working on cars.

I couldn't wait to introduce her to my parents, but the conversation I needed to have with my mother wasn't one that would benefit from an audience. And Dominic's visit on Sunday—especially if he brought his mother—was not the way I wanted McKenna to meet my parents.

She deserved to be welcomed as Heather and Wren had been—joyfully, with my parents standing in the doorway anxious to meet her, my brothers hovering in the windows. There was so much that could go wrong the next day that I wanted to shield her from.

I'd almost told her that I loved her. Just before she'd jumped me, I'd been all about talking it out. Okay, maybe talking it out quickly and then fucking, but I couldn't imagine ever waking with a naked McKenna in my arms without getting a boner.

Still, the point was, I was ready to tell her how I felt—she'd made it clear, though, that she wasn't ready to hear it yet. I understood why. McKenna was used to people leaving her. Her mother on purpose, her father to death. She was certain I'd leave her too.

Just as certain as I was that I wouldn't.

And she loved me.

Otherwise, why the anger?

Side note: If that was how she fucked when she was angry, I was willing to commit to a lifetime of arguing with her. I could only imagine how good our makeup sex would be.

And we would make up.

More than McKenna needed a hasty proclamation of love she wouldn't believe, she needed to see me at her garage on Monday, Tuesday, Wednesday . . . however many days it would take for her to believe I wasn't going anywhere.

Like my father, I was a patient man. I'd found the woman I intended to spend the rest of my life with. There was no doubt in me that we would work out. A Romano didn't imagine having children with a woman unless they were meant to be.

I tucked a loose lock of hair behind McKenna's ear. Mauricio, Wren, and Gian already adored her. She didn't know it yet, but her future would be full of loud, crazy Italians. My parents would spoil her as well as our children.

Wren and Heather could commiserate with her on the days when being married to a Romano man wasn't easy. We'd have our ups and downs, I was sure. All marriages did. But I couldn't imagine my life without her in it. She'd become my best friend, my lover, and, God willing, one day the mother of my children.

If she didn't believe it possible at first, I'd woo her with my lasagna. Our family's secret recipe. My mother used to cook it for neighbors or family whenever they were going through hard times. She joked that my father had fallen in love with her the day she'd delivered a pan of it to his family. He never denied that claim.

McKenna opened her eyes and sat up, smoothing her hair as she did. "Are we almost there?"

"Almost, although I anticipate a little turbulence before things smooth out."

She looked out the window. "Did the pilot announce something?"

"No." *I just know you.*

CHAPTER THIRTY-EIGHT

CHRISTOF

That evening I paced the living room of my parents' home while waiting for my mother to return from an errand. "Dad, you did tell her I was coming tonight, right?"

"I told her." My father lowered his Kindle. "She said she'd be back soon. She just wants tomorrow to be perfect." When I didn't say anything, my father raised his Kindle again and resumed reading.

That wasn't unlike my mother. She was a pleaser. Sometimes to the extent that I worried she put so much thought into others that she forgot to think of herself. None of the next day would be easy for her. If I could have spared her the stress of it, I would have. "Gian is flying up?"

My father sighed and lowered his Kindle again. "Yes, we thought it would be easier since Heather is so close to her due date."

"Did Mauricio say anything?"

"About?"

"Anything?"

"Christof, you've never been good with secrets; why don't you just tell me whatever is on your mind?"

I'd wanted to tell my parents together, but I couldn't keep it in any longer. "Dad, I invited Dominic Corisi and his sister to Sunday dinner. They're bringing their spouses and children."

"I know. Mauricio told us."

"What do you mean, Mauricio told you? He wasn't supposed to say anything."

My father placed his Kindle off to the side and stood. "In that case, we have no idea that Dominic might bring Rosella. Your mother is not out shopping because she was too jittery to stay home."

So Mom knew everything. "How is she?"

"Better than I would have expected, but she has had time to prepare herself. Opening the door to Dominic has naturally opened one to Rosella." He sighed. "We all knew it would happen one day. It'll work out."

"Will it?" I stopped and spun on my heel toward him. He was so calm it was impossible to believe he knew about Sebastian. If he had, wouldn't he have been worried that Rosella would spill that secret as well? "How are you not worried?"

"To meet Dominic? Or to see Rosella again?"

"Either. Both."

My father walked over and put a hand on my shoulder. "Christof, I love my wife. I love the family we have made together. No one and nothing could ever change that. I'm proud of you. You went to Montalcino and gave Gian a brother."

"One he always had. If you knew all along, why didn't you tell him sooner?"

My father stepped back and dropped his hand. "That's not easy to answer. I've asked myself many times when the truth is best told and when it is best withheld."

I was still asking myself that exact question in regard to what I'd learned about Sebastian. "And what did you decide?"

"That there is no right time, no day when something can be revealed without a cost. The best you can do is try to choose a time when you think a person is ready to hear the truth. For Gian, I believe the timing was good. He's a man now."

The pit of my stomach twisted. "Dad, when I was at Nona's, I found a letter from Rosella to Mom."

"And you read it."

"I did."

"And?"

"And I'm sorry I did. I should have given it to Mom without reading it. Now I don't know what to do."

"Give the letter to your mother." He returned to the chair where he'd been sitting.

He had to know. "And not tell Sebastian?"

His eyes darkened, but he looked neither shocked nor disapproving. So he did know. I wanted to shake him and demand he tell me what to do; then a thought occurred to me. Maybe being a father didn't mean he had all the answers. Maybe he was just a man, like me, doing the best he could and hoping to hell it all worked out.

The sound of the front door of the house opening and closing broke my train of thought. "Christof?" my mother called out. My father stood.

I rushed to the hallway to meet her. I would have offered to carry a bag in for her, but her hands were empty. We stood there for a long moment simply looking at each other. "You know," she said in a voice thick with emotion.

"Yes."

"How?"

I dug the letter out of my pocket and held it out to her.

As she took it from me, my father joined her, putting an arm around her waist in support. She held it in her hand without reading it at first. "It's from Rosella," my father said.

My mother closed her eyes and swayed against him. "I have spent so much of my life making myself okay with her actions. I can't stomach it anymore. She does as she pleases, treats people like they are nothing, then leaves me to clean up the mess and make things right. There was nothing right about what she did to me, nothing right about how she left her children with that monster or how she left Gian. I don't want to read her excuses. Why must I always be the one who forgives?"

"Because you're the strong one." I took one of my mother's hands in mine. "Let the past fall away, Mom. You have the kind of marriage I hope to one day have, four sons who adore you, two daughters-in-law who do as well, and grandbabies. Everything that happened brought us here."

"For my own sanity I had to stop trying to save her from herself," my mother said, but her eyes misted up. "I—I hate that I didn't do more for her." She gave my hand a squeeze and swallowed hard. "You don't have to remind me how much I have to be grateful for. I count my blessings every night and pray I do enough to deserve them."

Few decisions in life were simple. They were complicated, messy, and sometimes downright painful. Why had McKenna found the letter if it wasn't meant for good?

I looked to my father for guidance. My mother's anguish was mirrored in his eyes, but he wasn't attempting to stop me. He trusted me to do the right thing.

The loving thing.

Did I know what that was? I prayed so.

"I'm not a doctor, or studying to be one like Gian, but your sister sounds like she did the best she could with what she was given. I feel sorry for her. Even when she tried to do good things, she did them in self-destructive ways that reveal a paranoid and extreme personality. I do think she believed every bad decision she made was the only path available to her. Read her letter, Mom. It won't change anything that happened, but it might help you understand that when she hurt you, it wasn't out of a desire to beat you but from what I think was an early sign of her mental illness. When you see the world through her eyes, it's a terrifying place. That doesn't excuse any of her behavior, but it does explain it."

My mother nodded, released my hand, and opened the letter. She read it aloud for the benefit of my father. There were tears in her eyes by the time she read the line about how she belonged with Basil.

My father turned her so she could bury her face in his chest. I had seen my mother cry only a handful of times in my life—usually at the news of a relative dying—but she cried then. My father rocked her against him, murmuring to her in Italian.

With an audible deep breath my mother collected herself, raised her head, and wiped the tears from her cheeks. She read the letter one more time silently to herself, then stuffed it in her pocket and exchanged a look with my father. "Christof, thank you for this. I've been angry with her for so many years, but she couldn't help it, could she? I always thought she slept with Antonio to be vindictive, but it wasn't that. When I look back, even when we were children, she would see evil where I didn't. We could have a conversation with the same person, have been together the whole time, and later recount the event very differently. With her, there was always something to fear."

My father said, "Then you met a man who warranted that reaction."

My mother shuddered. "And she saved me from him. If he had found out about Sebastian—"

"I would have gone to prison," my father said.

My eyes widened, and my mother's mouth rounded.

Without humor my father continued, "We would still be together, Camilla, because you and I were meant to be . . . but I would have killed him had he laid a hand on you."

I didn't doubt for a second that my father would have.

Turning toward me, with tears still welling in her eyes, my mother said, "Where did you find the letter?"

"It was with photos of the two of you together in Nona's closet. Unopened."

"I wish—" my mother started to say, then stopped. "Once I heard of his abuse, I begged her to leave him. Looking back, I should have done more. I was so scared, though. He was insanely rich, so power-ful and vindictive. We had babies on the way. Yes, we helped hide her, but . . . maybe a part of me thought she deserved what he did to her?" Tears poured down my mother's cheeks, and I had to blink quickly, or I would have cried right along with her.

My father hugged her to his chest again. "None of us did all we should have. I—" When a tear slid down my father's cheek, too, I almost lost it.

I struggled to get the next words out. "No. I'm sorry, but I don't agree. From what I've heard, Antonio Corisi had people killed, here in the US and back in Italy, and was never punished for it because he was that powerful. Dad, we needed you with us—not in prison. Mom, you did save your sister. You and the family kept her safe from him until he died. You kept her secrets, and you paid a hefty price for that loyalty. She chose to go with him. She stayed and had two children with him. You can't save someone until they want to be saved."

Above my mother's head, my father nodded slowly. "The past is a story that has already been told. There's no changing it, not even the parts we might want to. But tomorrow we have a chance to make things easier for Gian . . . by welcoming his birth mother."

I put a hand on my mother's back. "Nothing he feels for her will take away from how he feels for you, Mom. It's your voice he'll hear in his head telling him to sit up straight, help clear the table, call his brothers when he hasn't heard from them."

She lifted her head and smiled. "You make me sound like a nag."

"Every good mother is," I joked, the tightness of my chest begin-ning to lighten.

Her swat at me never connected. After taking in an audible breath, she straightened and stepped back from my father. "Does Sebastian know?"

"I don't think so. No one knows about the letter. Well, no one besides McKenna. She found it."

As she wiped the last of her tears from her cheeks, my mother's expression began to return to normal. She studied my face. "You really like her, don't you?"

"I do." I remembered the ring and took it out. "But I need to return this to you."

My mother tucked it into the same pocket she'd stashed the letter in. "I'm sorry it didn't work out, Christof."

"It's not over, Mom; only the fake part is."

"Oh," my mother said.

"Oh, indeed," my father added, then smiled. "Will she be joining us tomorrow?"

I shook my head. "When I bring McKenna home, and I will, I want it to be as happy an event as when we first met Heather and Wren. She's already seen so much of our family drama; I'd like her to see another side of the Romanos."

My father said, "Don't buy her a cow. Sure, at the time it feels like a good idea, but you'll spend the rest of your life trying to explain it."

I barked out a laugh.

My mother smiled.

It was a relief to see the two of them on the other side of the secret and still standing strong. That was the future I saw for myself with McKenna.

My mother's expression sobered. "I kept Sebastian a secret at first because I was ashamed, then because I was afraid. He deserves to know the truth, but is tomorrow the right day to tell him?"

Her question hung in the air.

I would have answered her, but I honestly didn't know.

CHAPTER THIRTY-NINE

McKenna

I threw down a torque wrench, the sound of it bouncing along the floor drowned out by the music I had at full volume. I banged my hand as I spun and swore. The garage had always been my happy place, but even it wasn't enough to drown out thoughts of Christof.

Had he given the letter to his mother?

Was Rosella going to show?

How would Gian feel about meeting his biological mother? Worse, what if she ran away again? I wanted her to want him so badly.

I hadn't heard from Christof, and the silence was slowly killing me. The kiss he'd given me when he'd dropped me off had been accompanied by a promise to call me. Six hours and thirteen minutes later, each time my phone beeped with a message that wasn't from him, I ached.

I removed my gloves, threw them to the floor as well, and covered my face with my hands. I was close to tears and hating myself for it. Had I finally succeeded in pushing him away? Would he have invited me to the talk with his mother if I hadn't given him the ring back?

Was there any way he could be missing me the way I was missing him?

The music cut off suddenly. I lowered my hands, half hoping—then fought back disappointment when the man walking toward me was Ty.

God, I wanted to smack the shit out of myself for mooning over a man to the point where nothing else seemed to matter. I swore I'd never again care about anyone enough that their leaving could break me.

Ty replaced the wrench on the board where it normally hung. "I'd ask how you're doing, but this nearly took out my knee, so I have a general idea."

"Sorry, it slipped." I squared my shoulders. "I didn't realize you were in here."

One of his eyebrows arched. "Wayne said you and Christof seemed fine when he dropped you off."

"We were."

After coming to stand in front of me, Ty folded his arms across his chest. "I don't believe you."

I couldn't look him in the eye because I was embarrassed by my weakness. "That's your choice."

"If he hurt you—"

"He didn't." I rubbed my chin with the back of one of my hands and blinked a few times quickly. "I'm the one who fucked it all up."

"You had sex with his nona?"

I laughed at that and wiped a stray tear from the corner of my eye. "Worse. I fell in love with him."

"With Cal?"

I rolled my eyes, but Ty's jokes were pulling me back from the edge of bawling. "Yes, I'm completely, utterly in love with Cal. Don't tell Wayne."

"Too late," Wayne said as he and Cal appeared next to me. "I'm totally jealous. All this time I thought you had a thing for me."

A smile pulled at the corners of my mouth, but I didn't give in to it. "This isn't helping."

Cal put an arm around my shoulders. "You'll have to get over me, darling. I'm already taken. Have you considered opening your heart to that straight Italian you're engaged to?"

I waved my bare hand at the three of them. "Already over."

"It didn't look over when I saw you together earlier," Wayne said.

I sighed. "We had sex. Good sex. That doesn't mean anything. Right, Ty?"

Ty looked me in the eye before answering. "Did he ask for the ring back?"

My gaze fell to the floor, and I frowned. "I saved him the trouble."

"That boy is in love with you, McKenna," Wayne said.

I shot him a glare. "You didn't see how relieved he looked to take the ring back. And before you say something else in his defense, I'm glad it's over. He's an all-or-nothing kind of man. Geese are like that. Well, I'm not a goose. I'm not changing my name or my life. I have everything exactly the way I want it. What do I need a man for?"

"I'm confused," Wayne said. "Is she upset that he doesn't want to be with her or afraid he does?"

Cal's arm tightened around my shoulders. "Love is confusing, baby, but don't fight it. You might not be ready for it, but when it hits, there's nothing that matters more. And that's okay."

I shrugged his arm off. "No, it's not. I can't lose my garage."

"What are you so afraid of?" Ty asked in a gruff tone.

Wayne shared a look with Cal. "She's afraid to lose us."

I froze. It was true, even though I hadn't been able to see it until Wayne said it. My fears went deeper than simply whether Christof loved me back. A part of me was convinced I'd be forced to choose between two lives I wanted—just as I'd once had to choose between my parents. How had I not seen that before? Decker Park was my dream, but Ty, Cal, and Wayne were my family. The thought of doing anything that might risk losing them was downright terrifying.

Cal nodded, then said, "McKenna, we were all grateful when you offered us a chance to work together again, but this garage isn't what keeps us together. When you came back from school, with or without this place, your ass would have been part of our lives. Hell, Ty had talked about moving closer to you if you settled somewhere else. We're a family, Mack."

"Yes, we are." My eyes welled with tears when he used the same name for me that Christof did. I looked around the garage and thought once again of what Christof had said to Dominic. In my case, Decker Park was a piece of land with a building. If I ever lost it, I would still have what mattered most—my crew. Decker Park was an achievement, but it wasn't who we were.

Even my father—he wasn't in the car he'd given me. His love for me was right there, shining through the eyes of the men who had helped raise me.

I was grateful, scared, sad. "God, I'm a fucking mess."

"No, you're in love," Wayne said.

"With a man we approve of," Cal added.

"I broke it off with him."

"In your head?" Cal asked.

They knew me too well. "Maybe. I don't know."

Wayne smiled. "I have a feeling the two of you are very much not over."

"He hasn't called or texted."

Cal joked, "In weeks? Days? Oh, hang on, it's only been hours, right?"

I groaned. I sounded pathetic. "Okay. Okay. I get it. I need to be patient."

"Or text him yourself," Ty said.

My eyebrows flew up. Really? Relationship advice from someone who barely learned the names of the women he was with? I remembered the one woman he'd looked for after breaking up with her. If I let my fears stop me now, would that be me one day? "He's busy with his family."

His eyes darkened with memories. "It's natural to be afraid, but never let it keep you from the race. If you hold back when that flag goes down, you'll spend the rest of your life regretting it."

Yes, I see that now. I hugged Ty then, hugged him so tight. "I love you, Ty."

He hugged me back.

Wayne joked, "Hey, I thought you loved *me*."

I looked over my shoulder at him. "I do. And you too, Cal."

Cal laughed. "Damn right, and me too. So now that we're over the hump of this, you go call Lover Boy."

I stepped back from Ty. "A quick text. I'll just ask him how he's doing."

Wayne looked on with approval. "Tell him we say hello."

I hugged him and Cal one more time, then stepped away with my phone. Ty's words echoed in my head. My father had never let fear stop him. I wanted to be remembered the same way, even if it wasn't on the racetrack.

I closed the door to my office but looked through the glass portion out at the row of cars in the garage. Take it all away, and I would still have everything that mattered. If I did this right, though, I could have Christof and Decker Park. The Christof I'd fallen in love with wouldn't want me to choose.

I sent a text to Christof: Thinking of you.

His answer was immediate. Missing you.

My heart leaped in my chest, and I smiled. Did everything go as expected with your mother?

Yes and no. Better in some ways.

How do you feel about tomorrow?

I'm not looking forward to it, but hopefully it will surprise me as well.

I put aside my insecurities about not being invited and focused on simply being there for him.

I'll be thinking about you and your family all day. Possibly praying, although I'm not good at that.

You don't know how much that means to me.

I did, and I found comfort in that. There were so many unknowns, but Christof was a good man doing something important for his family. He was putting his worries in the passenger seat and doing what needed to be done. No wonder I loved him. I'm glad. Good luck tomorrow.

I'll call you afterward. I don't know what time dinner will wrap up.

I took a deep breath and then a leap of faith and typed:

I'll be here.

And just like that we were no longer over.

CHAPTER FORTY

CHRISTOF

Sebastian entered the kitchen at my mother's house with Ava and Sara, my parents' dog, on his heels. "Mom said you're making tonight's dinner. I need to see this to believe it."

I hugged him, then lifted Ava into my arms. "Just because your daddy doesn't know how to cook doesn't mean I haven't been secretly learning all the family recipes."

"I love secrets!" Ava exclaimed. "Can I help you, Uncle Christof?"

"Sure," I said easily but then met Sebastian's eyes above her head. He looked tired. "How's Heather? Mom said she was at the doctor's yesterday with labor pains."

"False alarm, but we have a bag in the back of the car just in case. I haven't slept in days."

My father's words came back to me. *There is no right time, no day when something can be revealed without a cost. The best you can do is try to choose a time when you think a person is ready to hear the truth.*

Sebastian was not ready.

One day he would be, and that was when I would tell him, unless my mother told him first. She wouldn't today. Without asking her, I knew my mother would see that Sebastian's full attention was where it belonged. The rest could wait.

Sebastian frowned. "You really know how to cook?"

I smiled and wondered why I'd ever felt less than proud to. "I really do. I'm here every Saturday morning learning from the best."

"Can I?" Ava looked from me to her father. "Daddy, can I learn with Christof?"

"You'd have to ask him," Sebastian said, but he knew what my answer would be.

"Absolutely." I spun around, making her laugh, then added, "And the lessons always end with dessert."

She gave my stomach a pat. "That's why you're fluffy."

"I'm not—" Okay, so compared to my brothers I might have had a few extra pounds, but I was mostly muscle. "Yes, but that only means there's more of me to love."

Ava hugged me tight, like one would a teddy bear, and I laughed. Life was good. Confusing as all hell, but somehow equally a miracle. And once this day was over, I could see it only getting better.

Sebastian lifted Ava from my arms. "We'd offer to help you, but I'm sure we'd only get in the way." His smile was warm. "This is good, though. I'm proud of you, Christof. Now I know why Mom always sounds so happy when I talk to her Saturday evenings. This is great."

I adjusted the apron I'd donned to protect my shirt. "It is." It felt great. I'd offered because my mother had still looked unsettled when I'd arrived, but I was surprised when she'd agreed. My mother never gave up her kitchen to another cook. "Mom didn't need this on top of everything else."

"Ava, could you go see if Mommy needs anything?" Sebastian put his daughter down.

Ava was off like a shot.

He turned back to me. "Mauricio brought me up to speed. You didn't need to handle it alone. I could have—"

"I know, but Heather needs you right now, and I handled it."

He nodded. "You did. You always do. This week let's sit down and discuss your role in Romano Superstores. Mauricio and I were talking about it, and we realized we never asked you what you wanted. It's time we do."

I smiled. This was what kept me going. Right here. Yes, we argued. No, things weren't perfect, but we had each other's backs—always. Without my parents—without these brothers—perhaps I would have been as lost as Dominic seemed. "Sebastian. There's something I need to tell you."

"What?"

I hesitated and chose my next words carefully. "Dominic is a tough read at first, but he wants to be part of our family. Once I understood that, inviting him here was the right thing to do. Not everything is as it appears at first. Give him a chance."

"I will."

The doorbell rang, ending our conversation. I turned the stove down to let the sauce simmer and headed out of the kitchen with Sebastian.

I'd like to say the first meeting wasn't awkward, but it was. It started good, with Dominic introducing his wife, Abby, as well as his eleven-year-old daughter, Judy. Ava was excited to meet another child and began chatting with her straight off. Abby had a warm presence that made her easy to like. Dominic remained guarded, but not anywhere near as much as in Italy. Nicole came in with her husband, Stephan, and their children.

Where things took a bit of a dive was when Rosella entered with her newest husband, Thomas Brogos. She and my mother exchanged strained greetings before my father ushered everyone into the living room.

Gian looked torn between standing beside Dominic or my mother. As I left to check on the food, I caught him having what looked like a painful and stilted conversation with Rosella. We were all on our best behavior, but the tension stayed high.

The quiet of the kitchen was a bit of a relief. I had just placed a pan back in the oven when I heard someone clear their throat from the doorway. I turned, wiping my hands on my apron as I did.

Dominic was standing just inside the kitchen. "Sebastian could be my fucking twin."

Oh, shit. "Family resemblance is something, isn't it?"

He pocketed his hands and nodded. "You have an incredible family."

"So do you." After a moment, I added, "I'm glad you came, Dominic. This is where you belong, even if it doesn't yet feel like it."

His face tightened with emotion. "I want this to work."

When I looked at him, I saw the side of Sebastian I'd always worried about. I needed to reach a common ground with him. "Help me serve the food."

He frowned as if I'd suggested he leap from the roof. "What?"

"Everyone wants to be head of the family. We don't have one here. We're all equal. We become whatever the others need us to be. Sometimes there's glory in that; sometimes there's humility. We don't talk about it; we just do it. If you want to be one of us—*be* one of us. Today I'm the cook because my mother was worried about meeting yours. What are you?"

He didn't say anything for a long moment; then his eyes lit with a look I'd seen in Nona's many times. "Head waiter?"

"It won't be as bad as you think. The moment you walk out of the kitchen with a plate of food, everyone will probably rush in to bring out the rest. It'll change things, though. Trust me."

He walked over and began to place warm rolls on a serving tray. "I do. Must be the fucking apron."

I laughed.

He smiled.

I grabbed a bowl of salad and walked out of the kitchen with Dominic, who carried the tray of bread. As I expected, seeing Dominic pitching in was all it took to ease the tension. It was also the only plate he carried from the kitchen, because as I'd predicted, everyone else jumped up to do their fair share.

Tension was slowly replaced with banter, which led to more relaxed conversations.

The wine helped.

It wasn't perfect, but it wasn't a disaster either.

A good start. Between courses we passed around the photo albums from Nona's, and stories flowed.

A bittersweet win. I should have been happy, but it felt incomplete. When I asked myself why, the answer came easily enough. McKenna wasn't there. I had thought I was sparing her, but I wished I could have shared the experience with her.

After dinner, while everyone was having coffee, I slipped away to the kitchen to check dessert. I told myself there would be plenty more meals like this one. Wanting McKenna there was selfish of me. Hadn't I rushed her enough?

Dominic appeared at the door again.

"It's only one plate. I've got it," I said.

He just stood there, then asked, "Where's your fiancée?"

The strength of my family came from how real we were with each other, so I told him why I hadn't invited her. She'd supported me through enough. I wanted the first time she met my parents to be special.

He cut into my answer and said, "I have a helicopter on call. It could be here in five minutes. Allowing for travel time to Decker Park and a proposal, if you're quick about it, you could be back in a little over an hour. How long does your dessert take to cook?"

"You'd have to take it out in fifteen minutes, or it'll burn."

Ava entered the kitchen. I blurted out, "Ava, go ask Nona for the ring I gave her earlier. I'm going to propose to McKenna."

"Yes!" Ava said, but before she left, she said, "If she doesn't say yes, tell her about the cake. That works with her, remember?"

As soon as we were alone again, Dominic asked, "Does everyone in this family know everything about everyone?"

"Usually," I said. One day I hoped to be able to answer with a simple yes. I got a little giddy as it began to sink in that I was going to propose for real to McKenna.

Ava ran back in with the ring and handed it to me. "Good luck, Christof. And hurry back because I really, really like double chocolate cake."

I looked over in time to see Dominic replacing his phone in his jacket pocket. "All set."

I ruffled Ava's hair, then noticed Judy, Dominic's daughter, in the doorway. "Your dad is lending me his helicopter so I can go propose to McKenna for real this time and get her back in time to celebrate while the family is all here."

Judy walked over and put her hand in her father's. "That's wonderful, Dad. Aren't you happy we came?"

He hugged her to his side. "More than you know."

Over her head he growled, "Don't just stand there, Christof. Go get McKenna. Judy, Ava, and I have this cake thing covered."

Ava clapped her hands together, and I bolted out the side door to the helicopter that was already landing on the lawn.

I didn't stop to explain to anyone where I was going.

Thankfully, it was far from a secret.

CHAPTER FORTY-ONE

McKenna

Helicopters weren't unusual at Decker Park. Lots of wealthy people visited to play with their toys, and some drivers made a show of their arrival. No drivers were scheduled that evening, though, so the sound of someone touching down on the helipad had me heading up toward the garage.

Ty, Cal, and Wayne beat me there and were standing with someone a distance away from the helicopter. They encircled the person at first in a way that blocked my view. When they stepped back, my heart started thudding in my chest.

Christof.

In dark slacks, a light shirt, and . . . an apron?

I forced myself to keep walking even as he broke away from them and started walking toward me. We met in the middle. I put my fears aside, threw my arms around his neck, and kissed him with all the love welling within me.

That passionate, life-changing kiss ended too soon. "Well, this is already going better than I hoped," he joked when he raised his head.

"Is it?" I asked breathlessly. Whatever he'd come to ask me, the answer was yes. "Wait until I get you alone."

He shuddered against me. "I like the way you think, but what I have in mind, at least for the next few hours, involves my family." He looked over my shoulder. "And yours. I want them there as well."

"Where?" Part of me knew. Everything around us faded away, and I knew.

"McKenna Decker, I realized something when Dominic and my family gathered at my parents' house."

"What?" He was killing me. *Just say it.*

"I want to share every batshit-crazy moment of my family with you. Tonight. Tomorrow. Every day for the rest of my life. I thought it was too much to ask. You've been so good to me. I wanted the first time you met my parents to be special, but I realized that every day I'm with you *is* special. I belong with you, and you belong with me. Keep your last name. Keep your garage. I love you just the way you are. I love you, McKenna. Marry me."

"Yes, yes, I love you too, Christof. I'm so sorry I gave you the ring back."

He reached into the pocket of that damn apron and pulled out the ring I'd returned to him. "It had to come back so it could be put on the right way, for the right reasons. I was going to buy you a new one, but I feel like this ring wants to be passed down to our children."

"Our children, huh?"

"Yes, one boy and one girl."

He said it with such confidence; how could I doubt it was true? "McKenna Decker-Romano. I like the sound of it."

"Me too." He kissed me again deeply, then said loudly, "She said yes. Everyone hop in. Sorry about the rush, but they're holding dessert for us, and Romanos get hangry."

Just like that we loaded into the helicopter: me, Christof, Ty, Cal, and Wayne. It was crazy, wonderful, magical. Like all the best moments in life.

As we flew toward his family, I looked into Christof's eyes, and I saw the children he'd mentioned. I saw them as clearly as if he'd shown me a photo.

I'd never been the type to trust anything intangible, but I felt my father smiling down on us and the love of those around me, and there was no question in my mind that I was where I was supposed to be.

I didn't know if anyone above was listening, but I sent up a heartfelt thank-you.

And Christof smiled at me as if he'd heard.

When we landed at his parents' house, the doorways and windows were filled with his family. They spilled out onto the lawn as soon as the helicopter blades had cut off.

After Christof announced that we were engaged—for real this time—it was a hot mess of hugs, kisses, and welcomes. Things were obviously still strained between his mother and her sister, but everyone else seemed at ease.

I felt bad for Rosella. Like my own mother, she'd left her children behind. Had Rosella's choices been justified? She'd left Dominic and Nicole with a man she'd feared so much she thought he was responsible for Gian's father's death. I couldn't imagine any scenario in which I would make the same decision.

Gian didn't appear all that interested in getting to know his biological mother, and I could understand that as well. Although Rosella had left him in a better situation, claiming it was for his safety, she hadn't come back for him after Antonio had died.

Antonio had died the year before Judy was born.

Ten or so years ago? That was a long time to not reach out.

My hope for Gian was the same I had for myself—that acceptance would be the path to easing that pain. Life didn't always work out the way we wanted it to. People didn't automatically become who we needed them to be. As I watched Rosella try to navigate the group, I let more of my anger with my own mother go.

Rosella was doing the best she knew how to. Perhaps my mother was out there somewhere doing the same. Forgiving didn't mean I needed to reach out to my mother again, but it did release a heaviness I'd carried for too long in my heart.

Gian would be okay. His life was full of people who loved him.

Cal paused from a conversation with Mauricio to give me a thumbs-up and a wink. Clearly, he approved of Christof's family. I had a teary, grateful smile on my face when Christof slipped an arm around my waist.

A little girl walked up to me and introduced herself as Ava. She pulled on my hand until I lowered my head near hers. "Do you want to meet Wolfie?"

I shook my head. "Who?"

She held up a well-loved stuffed animal. "You have your dad's car. I have Wolfie."

I petted Wolfie under his chin as if he were real. "He's beautiful."

"Can we have cake now? I think everyone is waiting for you."

Christof joked, "Never get between a young lady and dessert."

Before I had a chance to respond, Mauricio walked by and teased Christof for still having his apron on. Christof tore it off and threw it at Mauricio. Mauricio cracked that he looked better with it on, and a chase ensued that had his mother warning them to be on their best behavior.

Ava grinned. "That is their best."

I was okay with that.

I made my way over to the apron, picked it up, and tossed it to Christof as he ran past. He stopped, kissed me, then twirled it and began to snap it at his brother.

Sebastian scooped his little girl up when Mauricio fell backward, almost on top of her.

"They're crazy," Dominic said from beside me.

I smiled at him. "Don't you fucking love it?"

He nodded and smiled back. "I do."

So do I.

"I'm glad you're here," I said.

Dominic let out an audible breath. "Me too." After a moment, he said, "I'm glad you said yes. I'd hate to have flown over a wedding gift for you two for nothing."

"A what?"

He smiled. "Gianna asked me to have it ready for your wedding."

"The Alfa Romeo?" My mouth dropped open. "Don't you dare change a thing on it. It's perfect the way it is."

"What is?" Christof asked as he joined us.

Our hands naturally linked. "Dominic flew Chris over for us—our gift from Gianna."

The look of joy on Christof's face brought a grin to mine. "We can fix her up together," Christof said.

"Together." Despite what he'd done to Mack's interior, I agreed. Life with Christof wasn't a predictable lap around the track, but I was ready for the adventure. "I'd like that. Best gift ever."

Dominic cleared his throat. "I'm reasonably certain you'll enjoy mine more."

"It's not a competition," I teased, because I liked this side of Christof's cousin. In this moment it was difficult to believe he had another side to him.

Christof laughed. "Don't discourage him. I've seen some of his toys. He might be able to outdo the Romeo."

Dominic arched an eyebrow as if to say, *Challenge accepted.*

I had to admit it would be fun to see what a man like him would come up with.

Later that night, Christof and I stood in the driveway of his parents' home. Dominic had kindly flown Ty, Cal, and Wayne back to the garage.

"Let's go home," Christof said.

"Which one?" I asked.

He pulled me to his chest and said, "That'll never matter as long as I'm with you."

CHAPTER FORTY-TWO

JUDY CORISI, DOMINIC'S DAUGHTER

"Close your eyes, Dad," Judy said from the doorway of her father's home office. "Are they closed?"

"Yes," he promised.

"Mom and I have something to show you." At first, when her mother had offered to help transfer her sketch to a large canvas, Judy hadn't wanted the assistance, but seeing how much family meant to her father had reminded Judy to be grateful for hers.

Yes, her mother almost always had a suggestion for how Judy could do something better, but doing this project together had been good for them. And some of her ideas were actually pretty cool.

Abby Corisi followed her daughter into the office. "There's still time to wrap it if you'd like, Judy."

"No, I want him to see the whole thing all at once," Judy said without hesitation. "Ready, Dad?" She rested the canvas on the front edge of her father's desk, facing it toward him.

"Can I open them yet?"

She adjusted the placement of the canvas on the desk, making sure it was just right, then said, "Yes."

Her father didn't say anything at first; he took a moment to look it over. Then his eyes did something she'd never seen them do before: they got watery. Judy fought back a mild panic as she worried her gift might have upset him.

"It's beautiful," he said in a strained voice.

"She's been working on it for years." Abby put a hand on her daughter's shoulder and gave the side of her head a quick kiss.

"Mom helped," Judy said with pride. "Originally it was a tree with Nicole, Stephan, their children, and Nona Rosella. Well, before that, it had everyone we love on it, but I had to trim it . . . whatever. The important part is everyone we love doesn't fit on one tree anymore, so I made a hedge. See how we're all kind of intertwined even if our roots are different? That's our family. It doesn't matter where we all started; we're together now in one big leafy bush."

"It's perfect." Her father stood, rounded the table, and pulled Judy and her mother to him for a hug. Judy carefully let the canvas drop to his desk.

When he stepped back, Judy said, "I hope it's okay that I put your father's name on there. Without him, I wouldn't have you."

"It's okay. I've made my peace with him." Dominic kept one arm around his wife's waist. "Why is there a blank leaf next to yours on our branch, Judy?"

Abby's eyes rounded, and she smiled. "I was going to tell you, but we decided this is a better way for you to find out."

Dominic swayed on his feet. "Are we—?"

"We are," Judy said with enthusiasm and hugged an arm around both of them. "I'm finally going to have a little sister, a protégée, so to speak. Together we will be unstoppable."

Dominic laughed. "What if it's a boy?"

Judy thought that over. "I guess I could work with that."

Abby smiled up at Dominic. "We're in serious trouble, you know that?"

He didn't look at all worried. "Trouble is my middle name."

After a moment, Abby said she was going downstairs to check on dinner. They were all welcome to join her. Judy said she needed just a moment more.

Alone with her father, Judy asked, "Dad, did you really not know about the Romanos?"

He picked up the canvas and looked at it while he answered. "It's amazing what you can miss when you don't want to see it."

She went to stand beside him. "Are you happy that we found them?"

He ran a hand over the raised names and nodded. "It's more than I ever imagined. Better than I probably deserve."

Judy didn't know what to say to that because to her, her father was everything that was good in the world. One day, she hoped he'd see himself the way she did. "Dad, there is something I need help with."

He replaced the canvas on his desk and turned toward her. "Anything."

"I want to make a family hedge for our cousins in Montalcino. Could we go there so I could have Nona help me with everyone's names?"

Her father let out an audible breath. "I'm sure she'd love that."

"We could ask Gian to come with us."

"He'd like that."

Judy's stomach rumbled, and she said, "What do you think Mom made for dinner?"

Her father smiled again. "Let's go find out."

At the door, Judy paused. "Hey, Dad."

"Yes?"

"Do you think your father had children with any other women?"

CHAPTER FORTY-THREE

CHRISTOF

One year later

The day we opened a new racetrack at Decker Park, the stands were filled with family and friends. The new high-tech track was set on a plot of land McKenna and I had purchased for the expansion. Construction had taken longer than expected because Dominic's team had installed an underground bunker system the size of a small town.

It wasn't the jet I'd thought he'd planned to give us for our wedding, but I had to admit it was the coolest gift we'd received.

Okay, almost the coolest. As I climbed into Mack and revved her engine, I waved to McKenna, who was buckling herself into Chris.

Chris.

Yep, McKenna's favorite car was named after me.

Life was damn near perfect.

I still worked for Romano Superstores, but I was also involved with projects at Decker Park. As I'd always done, I went where I was most needed. My brothers jokingly asked me if I intended to be a stay-at-home dad once the kids came. I very seriously told them I didn't know. When the time came, Mack and I would talk about it, and I was confident we would come up with a plan that would work for us.

Us.

We weren't in competition with each other, not even as we readied ourselves at the starting line of the track. The two of us had sat down before our wedding and talked about what we wanted our life together to look like, and we were living it.

Family.

Friends.

Laughter.

Somewhere in the stands my parents were seated between royalty and men who still had grease under their fingernails—and neither felt out of place. McKenna and I were living our life on our terms, and it was beautiful.

Almost as beautiful as McKenna was as she leaned forward and flexed her hands on the steering wheel of the fully refurbished Alfa Romeo. The playful challenge in her eyes tempted me to send everyone home and forget all about this race.

When we had forever, though, there was no rush.

I gave my car's dashboard a pat.

Don't let me down, Mack. We've got this.

A horn sounded, announcing the beginning of the race. I didn't immediately step on the gas. When McKenna's car didn't pull out in front of mine, I looked over with concern.

She flexed her hands again as if unaware that the race had begun.

My throat tightened when I realized she was waiting for me. However things worked out, we were in this together. I floored my pedal.

She easily kept up.

We took turns taking the lead. Just before the finish line, I slowed and let McKenna fly through first. She was out of her car, helmet off, waiting to greet me with a kiss when I pulled over next to her. She wrapped her arms around my neck, and I nearly forgot we had a rather large audience.

Behind us a loud engine roared to life. We turned in time to see Dominic slide into a Bugatti Veyron Super Sport, another of his gifts to us and arguably the fastest car in the world. We joked that it had actually been a gift for himself, since he came to Decker Park at least once a month to drive it. Either way, all that mattered was that each month a Sunday dinner happened at Decker Park in the enormous dining room we'd added to McKenna's house.

He smiled and waved in our direction. After he flew past us, I said, "He's getting one for Gian. I love to see them together. Dominic is good for Gian."

McKenna watched him go. "You both are. I saw Rosella leave. I understand why she doesn't feel comfortable here, but I'm glad she came."

I sighed and hugged her against me. "You really are a miracle, do you know that? By being so open with Gian about your own mother, you've really helped him accept Rosella the way she is. She'll never be the one who sat up with him when he had a nightmare or patched him back together after a fall, but he's not angry with her anymore."

"Sometimes letting go of the anger is all you can do." She tipped her head back so she could see my face better, and a smile stretched her lips. "You didn't have to let me win."

I brushed my mouth over hers. "I've already won everything that matters."

We kissed then, long enough that the horn sounded again even though there wasn't another race scheduled. We broke off our kiss with a laugh.

"For a fake fiancée," I joked, "you're rocking this real-wife shit."

She went onto her toes and whispered into my ear, "Real enough that you'd be happy if I said I'm pregnant?"

My jaw dropped, and I hugged her closer still. "You are? Seriously? Oh my God, how long have you known?"

"I just took the test this morning. I don't want to say anything yet to anyone because it's so early, but—"

I kissed her then, with all the love and passion in me.

And it didn't matter how many times the horn blew.

My miracle was going to bring another into the world.

ABOUT THE AUTHOR

Ruth Cardello is a *New York Times* bestselling author who loves writing about rich alpha men and the strong women who tame them. She was born the youngest of eleven children in a small city in northern Rhode Island. She lived in Boston, Paris, Orlando, New York, and Rhode Island again before moving to Massachusetts, where she now lives with her husband and three children. Before turning her attention to writing, Ruth was an educator for two decades, including eleven years as a kindergarten teacher. *The Secret One* is the third book in her Corisi Billionaires series. Learn about Ruth's new releases by signing up for her newsletter at www.RuthCardello.com.

Made in the USA
Middletown, DE
16 October 2020